Can her lover be satisfied being her...

HISTRESS

Crystal Lacey Winslow

Praise and Notable Reviews

"There is an authenticity to Crystal's voice and a compelling personal story that readers have come to know," says Patrik Henry Bass, books editor at Essence. "Life, Love, & Loneliness has landed on the magazine's best-seller list twice since April 2003. This is how Terry McMillan emerged. Crystal has huge breakout potential." – **Essence Magazine, Patrik Henry Bass**

"The Brooklyn-bred entrepreneur is on her way to becoming an Oprah-meets-Martha- Stewart mogul." – **New York Daily News**

"Very saucy book (Life, Love, & Loneliness)...this is the kind of book our show loves to read...bitch, bitch, bitch, hustler, singer, actress, model, NBA players, ex-hustlers, drug-dealer hustlers, bitch, sex, Brooklyn...!" – **Wendy Williams, Media mogul**

"The Criss Cross" is an entertaining novel that will take you on a wild motorcycle ride, having you hold your breath in anticipation for the next twist and curve...I highly recommend this novel to those who enjoy a little bit of mystery, sex, lies, drugs, and psychosis, and much more. – **QBR.com**

"Tales of sex, money, and deceit fill Crystal Lacey Winslow's novel (Life, Love, & Loneliness) about four friends who experience great pain in their searches for love." – **Rolling Out magazine**

"Crystal Winslow followed her heart to become an author." – **Black Enterprise magazine**

Melodrama Publishing Makes a Mark – **Publisher's Weekly**

(Crystal Lacey Winslow) is a Drama Queen! – **Upscale Magazine**

Crystal Lacey Winslow is Melodrama's Queen Pen – **Vibe.com**

Self-Publisher of the Year – **Black Issues Book Review**

"Crystal Lacey Winslow does for novels what Quentin Tarantino does for films." – **Michael Presley, National Bestselling Author**

ii

This is a work of fiction. The characters, organizations, and events portrayed in this novel are either the author's imagination or used fictitiously.

DEDICATION

Callie B.
Tyrone M.

PROLOGUE

SUMMER 1987

THE LOUD, BLARING SIRENS WERE INDICATIVE of the trouble he'd gotten himself into. He held onto his new bride tightly to give her the protection and security he had failed to do only moments earlier. The end results were tragic, but there weren't any other options. He was a man. And he was going to stand behind his decision. When her hysteria slowed to a soft whimper, she pushed his strong arms from around her waist and glared at him. She wouldn't speak. His heart broke as he looked at her, his wife, disheveled and battered. Her once vibrant eyes were now swollen and sullen. Her tear-streaked face was puffy and accusatory. His guilt made him look away.

He drew a long breath. "I'm soooo sorry, baby. I should have been here to protect you—"

"Police! Open up!"

"I'll never let anything like this happen ever—"

"I said, open the fucking door!"

"Please don't cry…I love—"

BOOM!

"Baby, look at me—"

BOOM! BOOM! The battering ram pummeled the front door, breaking the locks and ripping it off its hinges.

"POLICE! DON'T NOBODY MOVE!"

Instantly his hands flew up in surrender. A nine-millimeter revolver was pointed directly at the back of his head.

"Get on the ground, asshole. Now! Lie down, face first!"

"Officer, I can explain," he pleaded, still in compliance.

"We have six witnesses that state you murdered a Mr. Emmanuel Morales in cold blood."

They were right. He did murder a man. He chased him out of his apartment and shot Morales once in the back. When Morales dropped to the ground, he unloaded his security-issued .357 Magnum into the back of the dying man's head and neck. He felt no remorse and wouldn't make any apologies. What they didn't know was this:

"He raped my wife!" the man yelled.

"Hmph," the other officer snorted. At the same time, his partner tightened the silver bracelets on the suspect's wrists, digging his knee deep into the suspect's back. "Tell it to the judge."

"He raped my wife!" he screamed again.

"You have the right to remain silent. Anything you say—"

"Baby, please tell them. They're taking me to jail for murder!" He looked at his wife; she looked past him, wide-eyed and frozen.

"Officer, please, just get her some help. She needs to go to the hospital and get treated. Look at her. She's in shock, for God's sake!"

7

CHAPTER

1

ANTHONY CROSS

I KNEW IT WAS OVER THE MOMENT SHE asked to borrow $7,500 because she was behind on her rent. Nothing was more unattractive than a sexy, successful Black woman who could not handle her finances. I watched as she pouted her plump, scarlet, red-colored lips and lowered her naturally sleepy eyes toward the ground.

"I really hate to ask you this, but I'm in a situation, you know," she said.

No, I don't. I wanted to reply dryly. But what would be the point? I knew I wasn't giving her the money. She was using our lack of a sexual relationship as a bargaining chip. Probably thinking that $7,500 wouldn't break the bank for a man in my position. Correct. But where she went wrong was putting too much value on herself. Yes, she was pretty. Gorgeous, to be more exact. But sex was sex. And looks faded. And if anyone knew that—I did. I was one of the few successful Black plastic surgeons in New York. My practice has been open for over a year, and my clientele has steadily increased.

I took another quick look around at *the setup*. She'd invited me over for dinner and drinks. Fresh white lilies decorated her mantel, and large scented candles illuminated her dining and living room areas. All other lights were off. She purposely drank too much during dinner, no doubt, so she could later pretend to be intoxicated while we did unspeakable things in the bedroom. That way, in the morning, she could make believe she was the all-American good girl she'd been portraying these past two weeks. This whole seduction night probably cost two to three hundred, easily. The money she'd spent on tonight should have gone toward her crisis. It made me wonder how many of these setups she pulled each week. Some other schmuck must have shelled out the cash for her to seduce me.

Fuck! The weight of the world was now on my shoulders. During these past two weeks, I thought she could be the one. I may have found something genuine in this woman, some pure qualities other than a money-hungry, gold-digging, scandalous bitch. In my profession, they came out of the woodwork in droves. I couldn't dodge them quickly enough before they tried to get into my deep pockets. She needed to realize that her problems were not my problems. Jeez, I needed to start dating *white* women. Well, let me not get ahead of myself. It wasn't *that* serious.

I decided to either make an excuse and quickly exit or tell her how I felt.

"Is that why you called me over for dinner?" I asked.

"What do you mean?"

"It's like this. Why didn't you ask me for the money over the phone? Did you think it would be harder for me to say no in person?"

"Ant, I didn't know what your response would be."

Straight-faced, I decided to get to the point.

"No."

"No?" she shrieked. "Why?!?"

"I don't need a reason why. It's just no."

"Did you not just hear me say I'm in a situation?" she asked. "I would really, really appreciate it if you could help me out of it."

"Laura, I'm not even going to pretend I'm remotely concerned about your dilemma."

Her eyes stretched open, "Are you serious?"

"This situation's really beneath you."

Her eyes burned with fury. Pursing her lips tightly together, she cleared her throat while straightening her dinner napkin on her lap.

"I understand your reservations. Really, I do. But I never ask you for anything—"

"You're not supposed to!" I exploded. "I hardly know you!"

She shook her head and gesticulated wildly. "You know me enough to want to sleep with me!"

I peered into her eyes. "Are you kidding me?"

"You would sleep with me right here, right now!"

"What kind of stupid-ass statement was that? I could have *slept* with you on our first date. But where I went wrong was trying to *court* you. Treat you like you're more than an object, but" I paused and sighed sympathetically, "Forget it. You're just like everyone else. A waste of my time."

At that point, I had an *a-ha!* moment. As a man, you could always assume women held their secret garden on a pedestal. Still, this chick was holding hers as a seventy-five-hundred-dollar ransom.

"What about my time? And the fact that I was feeling some sort of connection to you and thinking that you felt the same way. Now that money has come into play, you've turned into this different person in a matter of seconds. You would think I asked for a Porsche!" Laura began a roof-shaking temper tantrum.

"Listen, listen, listen, I won't sit here and entertain this a moment longer. I'm so sick of this shit. We, as men, are sick of this shit. Women see a penis and confuse it with an ATM. Do you really think your dry-ass steak dinner will be worth my hard-earned coin?"

"Get out!" she roared as her face distorted into several levels of ugliness.

After a few tense seconds, I got up to leave.

"People always have expensive tastes when it comes to someone else's budget. The Filet Mignon was a nice gesture, but I'd stick to what I could afford if I were you. Chinese takeout, perhaps," I said, getting in the last jab as I exited her place.

I was fortunate enough to live five blocks from my Upper Eastside practice. I owned a modest, two-bedroom apartment in the upper Sixties that cost me a hefty $3.9 million. My mortgage was obscene, but real estate in New York was always a savvy investment. My practice grew since more African Americans and Latinos were getting plastic surgery. To tap into the market, I did a lot of advertising on the radio stations with predominately African American and Latino audiences. At the moment, tummy tucks were most popular with Black women, whereas most non-minority patients opted for breast implants. This morning I had a butt-implant consultation.

Despite the pathetic situation that had unfolded the previous night, I strolled into my office in an upbeat mood. I laughed as I remembered how Laura tried every trick in her book to get that money from me as if I was some sort of trick. One part of me wondered if she needed the money for her crisis. Still, the other part of me—the cynical side—thought she might have used it for a pair of the latest Christian Louboutin stilettos.

The brisk winter air had put a pep in my step, and I'd gotten to the office earlier than planned. My trusty receptionist, Anika, was already there with her signature Starbucks Caramel Macchiato and her cell phone glued to her ear when I walked in.

"That'll kill you," I said, giving her a sly wink.

"I'm shutting off my service tomorrow!" Anika joked.

I noticed Anika had brought me lunch inside my office, neatly packaged in her Glad Tupperware. She cooked for me at least three times a week. Anika would also pick me up what I'd call *care packages* when she was at Duane Reade or CVS. Which would consist of a bag of Mentos candy she knew I liked, a six-pack of Gatorade, or something as random as Condoms. I could smell that she'd prepared my favorite baked macaroni and cheese and turkey chops. The aroma put a smile on my face. That girl was really a sweetheart. I constantly reminded myself that I needed to reciprocate her small yet thoughtful gestures on such occasions. I wanted her to know that I didn't take her for granted. But then I would get so inundated with work—I never followed through. I went into my cell phone wireless phone calendar. I put a reminder to order her a bouquet of *thank-you* flowers, and perhaps I'd take her to see a Broadway play.

I quickly looked at my calendar—three consultations, one breast implant, four patients for BOTOX injections, and one tummy tuck. I had a full schedule and probably wouldn't make it home until after nine o'clock, and my day wouldn't be over. I had to make a follow-up call to each surgical patient to ensure there weren't any complications.

Soon the office was buzzing with my staff, and it wasn't even eight o'clock. I peeked my head out the door, and everyone jumped to attention. No matter how much I tried to lead a staff- and customer-friendly work environment, everyone except Anika was always on pins and needles when I was around. Anika was always too busy flirting with me to be intimidated.

"Doctor Cross, your eight o'clock is already waiting for you inside exam room one," Samantha, my RN, said. Samantha was a stiff-looking, older white woman. She had paper-thin lips, silvery-white hair that was oily and tussled, and a frail, undernourished-looking body.

"Okay, cool," I said while inching over to Anika. "Whew, I have to tell you about last night," I told her.

"Long legs, sleepy eyes, big boobs," Anika said while rolling her eyes. "I bet she was stiff in bed."

"Would you believe that nothing happened?" I asked,

laughing.

"No."

"I'm too sexy, right?" I joked. "How could a woman ever resist me?"

"Pah-leeze, punk! You ain't that fine," she retorted while twirling her fingers dismissively in my face. I leaned in real close.

"You know I'd eat you out until you came in my mouth and then fuck you to sleep," I said softly. "You're waiting for the day I break you off a piece."

Her round eyes got low and seductive as she gave me a throaty whisper.

"You couldn't handle this."

"Don't want to," I said and gave her a soft punch on her shoulder.

"Stupid!"

"Gullible!"

"Womanizer!"

"Cunt!"

With that last remark, Anika's jaw dropped, and I won our little childish battle by default.

Anika was a lovely girl I knew was madly in love with me when she came for an interview. Even though we talked shit, and our conversations, taken in the wrong context, could lead to a sexual harassment lawsuit, I'd only push the envelope with Anika. I trusted her, and I was not that stupid to get that familiar with my other staff. In all honesty, I'd grown to love her in a brotherly-sisterly way. That could be mainly because I wasn't attracted to her. She was a nice-looking girl but too slender for my taste. I liked my women voluptuous, and if they weren't, then BAM! That was what I was there for. My hands could sculpt anybody into a masterpiece, but Anika wasn't having it.

One day I suggested that she consider increasing her As to full Bs, and she almost chewed off my head. She walked around, giving me the cold shoulder for nearly a month before she cooled down. I realized I had hurt her feelings, and her silent treatment taught me a lesson. Out of all my staff, she and I related the most. We liked to laugh and talk shit, maybe because we were close in age. She was twenty-four, and I was thirty-three. Perhaps we weren't that close in age, but the other staff members were well into their late fifties.

That day, my first consultation was with a petite Mexican woman with naturally large breasts and a flat, pancake-looking ass. When she turned around, her ass was saggy with cellulite dimples, and the elasticity was virtually nonexistent. She was looking to get buttock augmentation. I grabbed her chart and leafed through it.

"Mrs. Rodriguez, nice to meet you," I said.

"The pleasure is mine," she replied, gripping my hand. "So strong and handsome."

"Thank you. When we're done, I'll take you to my office and show you sample sizes of the implants. Do you know what size you're looking to get?"

"Sí, sí, yes. I have pictures of Jennifer Lopez. I want to look like J.Lo."

I smiled, but it wasn't toward her. I wished I could personally thank J.Lo for her naturally big ass.

"Mrs. Rodriguez, I want to give you a brief overview of your surgery. I can make an incision where the butt cheek meets the back of the thigh or down the buttock crease." I used my finger to trace her body as she stood looking in the mirror. "I prefer to make the incision in the buttock crease, where scars are not noticeable. But let me warn you: this area does carry a high infection risk."

"Don't worry, doctor, I'm clean," she added, "I don't have any diseases. No HIV, no herpes, no nasty woman tings."

"Okay, great," I replied, and when I looked up, she was staring directly at me, eyes unwavering. Then she smiled as if I'd just read her mind, and we were on the same page. I continued. "I'll create a pocket large enough to insert the butt implants. For a more natural look and feel, I'll place the implants under the *gluteus maximus* muscle, make sure they're symmetrical and look natural, and then you're done. You'll be under general anesthesia; the surgery should take under three hours. Do you have any questions?"

"Why aren't you married?"

I laughed. "Because you're already taken."

CHAPTER

2

GRACIE LANE

I WALKED AROUND MY ULTRA-POSH, 5-bedrooms, 6 ½ bathrooms apartment in the Time Warner Building at Columbus Circle. The former home of celebrity moguls such as Jay-Z and Ricky Martin. I was putting the last finishing touches on the party arrangements for my husband, Ed. We celebrated our tenth wedding anniversary, and I thought it would be a nice gesture to do something unexpected and throw him a surprise dinner.

Ed was a simple man who didn't indulge in the high-end lifestyle that I was afforded. In fact, he still opted to work at Verizon telephone company, although I was worth, thanks to my deceased husband, Phillip, well over one hundred million dollars.

Our marriage worked because I allowed him to be a man. Not a *kept* man. He paid for all the utilities in our apartment, and I always let him pay for dinner when we dined out. Of course, I took care of the bigger tickets, such as the mortgage and condo maintenance fees. When we traveled, we often split the costs at his behest. I always covered the expenses when we dashed off to more exotic locales, such as the South of France, where the menu consisted of foie gras or escargot.

Today's menu was a red velvet cake from the illustrious Cake Man Raven of Brooklyn, soul food from B. Smiths, and top-shelf liquor, including Hennessy Bacardi, Moët, Dom Perignon, Bailey's, and Absolut vodka.

I had decided on a small, quaint setting with a few close friends, family, and Ed's colleagues from work. I didn't let many people know where I lived, allowing even fewer people inside my home. I felt like my house was my personal, private space. And I don't know if my selfish or cautious side protected my whereabouts by any means necessary.

Doing a slight gallop up my winding staircase, I stripped off my clothes in a frenzy, leaving behind a trail of designer garments. I had just under an hour before everyone was due to arrive. At that point, my nerves began to overwhelm me. I desperately wanted everything to be perfect. Careful not to stay too long inside the shower, I timed myself by bathing to track number 14, *Father in You,* on Mary J. Blige's latest CD. The Bryston Surround Sound speakers in the ceiling belted out Mary's soulful voice as I identified with the lyrics. I knew all the words, and the song was roughly four minutes.

The basic black, form-fitting Diane von Furstenberg dress that I was wearing cost $3,000. It was the most expensive dress I owned. Not that I couldn't afford costly garments, but sometimes designers could be insufferable with their prices. If it was worth it, then it was mine, but there weren't many things I felt were worth my money in the fashion industry. Besides, I looked good in anything. I splurged on certain jewelry, coats, shoes, and real estate. If appropriately rocked, those things could make the right *I'm rich-bitch* statement while wearing jeans. It's all in the attitude. I'd purchased the dress four years ago to accompany my husband to a fundraiser held at City Hall. Ed had planned on getting into politics, and I always supported his endeavors.

After I was dressed, I took another look around downstairs and was doing last-minute touchups when the doorbell rang. I told the door attendant there wasn't a need to announce each guest since we were having a party. I instructed that all my guests had to do was give my name and apartment number, and they should be allowed entrance. The first guest to arrive was Ed's sister, Tamara, to my surprise. Taking a deep breath before exhaling all my anticipated stress, I opened the door.

"Hello, gorgeous," Tamara beamed.

She's such a phony bitch, I thought.

I managed a tight smile. "Hey, Tamara, come in. The other guests should arrive any minute," I replied before looking my sister-in-law up and down. "What have you got on?"

"What's wrong with my clothes?" Tamara asked, looking down at her outfit as if she had seen it for the first time.

I took a long look at Tamara's slinky, see-through shirt with exposed breasts, micro-mini skirt, and newly bleached blond hair and wanted to choke the life out of her. Tamara was awkwardly tall like her brother with long limbs, a now bleached-blond short Afro, and dark chocolate skin. She had delicate facial features, a gorgeous smile, and an over-the-top personality that I despised.

"Tamara, you knew this would be a formal dinner, and you waltz through here as if you're going to a nightclub!"

"I don't remember you stating the dress code," she whined.

"Of course, you don't. You have a selective memory. Why should I be shocked?" I sarcastically replied. "You're always doing this to your brother after everything he does to help you."

"Lighten up, Gracie. You're too uptight. I got an extra joint if you want to relax before your guests come."

"Don't you light that up in here!" I bellowed, playing directly into Tamara's hands. She thrived on irking me, knew I didn't indulge in drugs, and would burst a brain cell if she lit up her joint during the party.

Two hours later, the dinner party was bursting with laughter as Ed sat at the head of the table like a king. He was genuinely surprised when he walked in and saw only familiar faces. He barely relaxed his face; his smile seemed permanent.

I beamed in my role as host.

"Would anyone like more champagne?"

"Yes," Tamara replied. The rest of the guests all shook their heads.

"While I'm up, what about more dessert? Anyone?"

"Yeah, bring me more of that cake, too," Tamara blurted out. "I don't turn down anything but my collar. Yes, yes, yes, to any and all your shit."

I glared at Tamara.

As the night began to wind down, the festivities were interrupted by the telephone's incessant ringing. I quickly dashed to the phone and put my index finger into my ear to tune out the jazz music.

"Hello?" I said.

"He's dying," the familiar, husky voice replied. The optimism of the night suddenly became tempered by my bleak reality.

"H-h-how did you find me?" My voice personified my fear.

"Bad move being photographed at that fundraiser last summer. You still look good...you've aged...but you're still recognizable. Again, bad move."

"How did you find me!" My voice personified my anger.

"Calm down. I'm not your enemy. We fam and I'm here to tell you that you should stay out of the papers. Your telephone number was listed under your husband's name. If you're trying to hide from folks, I suggest a non-published number. I reread that newspaper one hundred times. *The wife of hopeful New York council member Edward Lane, Gracie, sat supportively by her husband's side.*"

"Are you kidding me?"

"I'm calling you, right? And I haven't seen you in two decades," Benjamin snickered.

"You won't see me for the next two, either."

"Funny. Your joke...funny," Benjamin replied sarcastically.

My voice was a husky growl, "You think I'm playing games here?"

He ignored my question and said, "I got something to ask you. Your face looks a little different. Did you do something to it? Had it altered? I can't put my finger on it...don't matter...I still recognized your ass."

"This is too much to take right now. Listen, I would really appreciate it if you didn't call—"

"I'm not calling to catch up on old times. I'm calling because the old man's on his deathbed."

"So bury him!"

"Come on, sis, stop being like that. I just said that the old man is dying, and he keeps asking about you. It's time to let go of the past before it's too late."

My brother Benjamin went on to tell me that our father had been diagnosed with a malignant brain tumor. The doctors didn't expect him to live much longer.

"Well, what can I do?" I probed.

"All he wants to do is see you, to make things right before he goes."

My mind couldn't help but drift to the past.

"Daddy, my friend Kim's parents, bought her those new leather sneakers for her birthday. And I thought that since my birthday's next week, and since I made the honor roll again, maybe I could get the same ones. Everyone says we look just alike. She's like the sister I never had. So please, please, please, can you buy me a pair for my fifteenth birthday?" I asked.

"Girl, I don't care what your friend's parents bought for that nappy-headed, ugly gal. If I hear you say one more time that you two look alike, I'ma put my foot so far in your backside, I'll tear you a new asshole. You hear me?"

"Yes, sir. But what about the sneakers?"

"You must be crazy. Those sneakers cost nearly fifty dollars—"

"But you bought Benjamin a pair!" I protested, interrupting my father.

"Benjamin needs a good pair of sneakers to practice in. All those basketball scouts are always looking to draft young kids, and your

brother has a shot. Benjamin needs the best sneakers to do all that dunking, just like Mike," he reasoned.

"What about Andre? You bought him a pair, too!"

"Don't be questioning me, chile. I got good reason to do what I do for my boys. Do you know how hard it is for a Black man in America?"

I rolled my eyes. I'd heard it all before.

"Do you want your brother busting someone upside their head and stealing the money to buy those sneakers? My sons are not gonna be victims of society. They're gonna make me proud one day!"

"What about me? All you care about are your sons! It's not fair!"

"How old are you?"

"Fourteen!" I screamed.

"You about one year too old to be coming in here asking me for expensive shit. All these boys out here, and you asking me? When your mother was with me, I gave her the world . . . ." His words drifted off as he thought about his wife of sixteen years, who'd run off and left him with three kids. He missed her so much that his heart hurt. "Go on and get outta my face! And I better not hear you crying, 'fore I give you something to cry about!"

"Is it safe to come around?" I cautiously asked, snapping back to reality.

"It should be." Benjamin paused and then continued, "No one's been around in a while—years, in fact. But don't take any chances. Come at night and go through the back door. The spare key is still in the same spot."

My forehead scrunched into tight folds. "I can't promise you anything. You know how I feel about George—"

"He's Daddy, not George," Benjamin corrected.

"He's never been, my daddy. He and I only share DNA!"

I felt a little stressed the morning after the party and the disturbing phone call. I contemplated taking the day off from volunteer work at the Adults and Children Community with Learning Disabilities, or ACCLD. I volunteered as a developmental aide for mentally challenged adults in a residential home. It was my way of giving back to society. We took them on trips, helped them develop social skills, cleaned up after them, and dispensed a few medications. The state doctors prescribed so many medicines to mentally handicapped adults that it was a curse and a blessing. Either they walked around like zombies and stayed out of your way all day, or they were violent and had vicious outbursts. In contrast, you had to ultimately fight for your life.

So along with the job came defensive class training. That wasn't too bad because my perk was being around my dysfunctional coworkers. There was always some drama going on, and I loved drama as long as it didn't involve me or my household.

I awoke and stared at my calm-mannered husband. At thirty, Ed was significantly younger than me. I'm thirty-nine.

"Thank you so much for last night," Ed said while kissing me on my neck.

"Are we talking about the party or *last* night," I teased?

"Both." He smiled. "Now, it's time for your present."

"Ed, you didn't have to get me anything."

"Of course, I gotta get you something. It's our tenth wedding anniversary. Are you kidding? Who's luckier than me? I got the most beautiful wife in this world, and I want to give you something you've been considering," Ed exclaimed.

"I can't take the suspense. What did you buy me?"

"Well, I've been listening to you and Anika talk crazy for weeks. And I know you want to see the doctor she works for about a tummy tuck. That's your gift. You can go in and have the procedure done. That's if you still want it."

"Ed don't be silly. You don't have to pay for such an expensive gift. I'm not sure I want the procedure, and if I decide to have it, I can pay for it. No big deal."

"This isn't a debate," he snapped. "I said I can afford to buy my wife a nice gift for our tenth wedding anniversary, and that's what I'm going to do."

"All right. You don't have to get upset."

"Why are you always telling me what you can afford as if I don't know? Don't you think I know what you can or can't afford?"

I knew the question was rhetorical, so I remained silent.

"For once, I'd like to do something nice for you without you feeling sorry for me. I hate hearing the pity in your voice."

"That's not fair at all. Don't be like that…mean and all…I'm sorry," I said, nuzzling Ed's neck, and tightly wrapped my hands around his waist. Instantly, he relaxed. "If you want me to be the gold-digging hoochie I was born and raised to be, just say the word."

"I want you to be my gold-digging hoochie." He kissed my lips.

"Good. You can start by leaving your credit card by the bed on your way out."

"My credit card, huh? I dunno…I wasn't satisfied with your services last night," he joked. I began tickling him, and we wrestled around on the bed until he had to leave for work.

I sat back and thought about how Ed had promised me the world when we first met, and slowly he was making all my dreams come true. I'd come to New York as an escape. I never imagined meeting someone as innocent, gentle, and loving as Ed. Yet he'd always managed to make me feel safe and secure. I was newly widowed and had just inherited a large estate. I met Ed while I was married to a multimillionaire. My husband gave me a monthly allowance, barely enough to get my hair washed and a decent manicure. He was cold, disrespectful, and thrifty. Life with him wasn't a fairytale.

I began long walks in Central Park to escape my husband's smothering ways. That's where I first met Ed. I pretended to be dirt poor, and Ed really was—but we talked about our aspirations and dreams for hours. Ed did most of the talking, and I was a great listener. I told him I had no family, and he accepted my *truth*. I ran into Ed's arms when my husband Phillip died from a fatal asthma attack. We'd had an emotional affair meeting in the park twice weekly for two years. I told him I'd never marry again, and he accepted me. He told me I was too beautiful to marry a guy like him.

Soon we were both riding on a love high when the bad news came. My kidneys weren't functioning, and I was in dire need of a transplant. Of course, I thought that my newfound wealth could buy anything—it couldn't. I had to be put on a donor list like everyone else. I panicked. Surely, I didn't want to die. I was twenty-eight years old and finally ready to live my life fully. At first, I thought it was just a kind gesture to ease my anxieties. Ed said he wanted to get tested to see if his kidney would be compatible. I swatted him away, and he came back even more aggressively. Finally, I allowed him to give me the best gift in the world—life. Ed and I married in my hospital bed. That was ten years ago, and we're still happily married.

Over the years, I contemplated telling him about my past, but my love for him prevented me from getting him involved. I thought that the less he knew, the better off things would be. He'd never be forced to choose sides, nor would he have to live with the burden that was mine to carry.

At first, being older than Ed scared me. Was I too old? Would some younger woman one day come along and take my husband away? But as the years passed and our bond grew, Ed never had so much as looked at another woman lustfully. The night we married, he told me he pledged his eternal love and would never allow another woman to break our bond. I, in return, said nothing.

CHAPTER

3

ANTHONY CROSS

MY WEEK STARTED OFF CRAZY AND HAS now turned mundane. I decided to take off a couple hours between clients to go to the New York Sports Club in Harlem, where all the pretty sistahs worked out. Also, it was great networking. Even though most women were proactive in maintaining great shape or striving to get a great body, no one was perfect. During these sessions, I passed out many business cards and met a lot of potential future wives. I knew I'd never get married before I hit my forty-fifth birthday. But that didn't stop me from dangling the possibility in front of every woman I'd ever dated. Women ate up that shit. Not that I didn't want a life partner, but I didn't have one faithful bone in my well-toned body.

I jogged the three miles up to Harlem, listening to my Apple playlist. I had 10,000 songs programmed, mostly upbeat tunes. I took a shortcut through the park, crossed a thicket of bushes, and then did power walking down a cobblestone path. I made it there in less than 40 minutes.

The instructor for the kickboxing class was no joke. He went hard. Male or female—no one was exempt. He had an in-your-face attitude and loved interacting and pushing everyone to the limit. Sweat poured down my skin as I paced my breathing, taking large gulps of my Smartwater. I could actually hang out here all day. They had many classes I wanted to take, but I had to return to the office for a tummy tuck consultation in less than an hour.

But not before I played into her hands. She'd been eyeing me the whole class, vigorously kicking her long legs, throwing strong left and right jabs. And keeping up with the instructor's two- and three-piece combinations. Her legs were toned, her ass was firm, and her stomach was washboard. Her tiny waist and shapely hips would look better if she had C-cups to complement her assets.

"That was a great workout," I said casually, wiping the sweat from my face.

"Yeah, he's amazing," she said, breathing rapidly.

"Doctor Anthony Cross." I extended my right hand. "Pleasure to meet you."

What could I say? I was shallow.

"Cynthia Rowley," she replied, barely containing her huge grin. "You look so young to be a doctor."

"It's in my genes."

"What type of doctor are you?"

"I'm a board-certified plastic surgeon. I have my own practice on the Upper Eastside, 72nd Street."

"Oh, my gosh, I've heard about you!"

"Is that a fact?" I asked knowingly. This one was going to be easy.

"Well, I mean, I've heard your ads on the radio. This is really cool," she exclaimed.

"Is it really?" I replied. She was savvy enough to detect my sarcasm.

"I must sound foolish. Please forgive me."

"Don't be silly."

My eyes scanned her body one last time and decided she was worth a shot, but I didn't have much time for small talk.

"Listen, Cynthia, here's my business card. Give me a call, and perhaps we could get together."

"I'd like that." She took the card and quickly read it. "I'll give you a call this week."

Cynthia then licked her luscious lips and sauntered away. She didn't realize there wasn't a need to continue flirting. I'd already chosen her within the first sixty seconds of the conversation.

Back at the office, I felt great. The workout had given me momentum, and I was on an adrenaline high.

"Where were you?" Anika asked as I walked through the door.

"Mother, I'm getting too old for a curfew."

"Funny. Your two o'clock has been waiting, and she isn't just any two o'clock. She's my best friend I've been telling you about. It's Gracie. Remember, I told you she wants abdominoplasty."

"Oh, yeah, yeah, I remember. Tell her I'll be there in five minutes. Which examination room is she in?"

"Room Three."

Over the past year, I'd heard so much about Gracie that I felt we were old pals. What Anika didn't mention was that she wasn't bad looking.

As I glanced at her chart, it noted that she had no allergies, was married, had a kidney transplant, and was thirty-nine years old. *That's odd,* I thought. Anika was twenty-four, so why would she be best friends with someone Gracie's age? The better question was, what did a thirty-nine-year-old woman have in common with a twenty-four-year-old? Gracie certainly didn't look anyone's definition of thirty-nine, though. She was definitely well-preserved.

She sat on the exam table with her medical gown opened in the back and her legs dangling like a child. Her hazelnut-colored skin, round, expressive eyes with long eyelashes, and pouty lips were sexy. She looked as if she stayed in sexy mode all year round, as if she walked around with a garter belt, thigh-high stockings, and stilettos all day, every day, for her man. I took another look at this old cougar and got a little turned on. Not much, just a slight tingle. I was jolted back to reality when my RN, Samantha, began speaking.

"Doctor Cross, this is Mrs. Lane. She's interested in a consultation for a tummy tuck."

"Hi, Mrs. Lane. My name's Anthony. How are you doing today?"

"I'm doing well. Thank you."

"Good, good. Well, I like to tell my patients what I'll be doing. That way, there won't be any surprises. I'll lift up your gown just above your belly button, take a marker, and draw lines so that you can see what I'll be removing and sculpting. Are you nervous?"

"Nervous? You're not the first man to see my goodies," she teased. When she smiled, she had two delicious dimples on her honey-colored cheeks. The dimples made her look deceptively innocent. I wondered if she was telling a blatant lie about being thirty-nine.

"Not about that, Mrs. Lane. I'm talking about your tentative surgery."

"Oh, that." She let out a soft chuckle and displayed pearly white teeth. "Not at all."

I noticed a hideous sight as I sat before her and peeled up her gown. Her stomach was splattered with stretchmarks, and she had what I'd describe as a kangaroo pouch belly. I glanced back at her file; she'd put zero for kids. There had to be some mistake.

"Mrs. Lane, it says here that you don't have any children."

"That's correct."

"Okay, good," I replied as I began to make my drawings on her stomach. I didn't probe further, but there wasn't any way she'd get these stretchmarks if not through childbirth.

My silence gave her a reason to explain. "As a child, I was overweight; my stomach's the last remnant of my fatso past. I'm hoping you can remove all traces."

"I'll do my best," I replied. I continued guiding Gracie to the mirror to look at the diagram I drew across her stomach. "I will make a long incision from hipbone to hipbone, just above the pubic area. The second incision's made to free the navel from surrounding tissue. I will then separate the skin from the abdominal wall up to your ribs and lift a large skin flap to reveal the vertical muscles in your abdomen. These muscles are tightened by pulling them close together and stitching them into their new position. This supplies a firmer abdominal wall and narrows the waistline. The skin flap is then stretched down, and the extra skin is removed. A new hole is cut for your navel, then stitched in place. Finally, the incisions will be stitched, dressings will be applied, and a temporary tube may be inserted to drain excess fluid from the surgical site."

"Sounds like it's a bit much, but I'm game," she said, then flashed her warm, seductive smile.

"You don't have to have any reservations," Samantha piped in, "Doctor Cross is one of the best."

"So, I've been told."

"While I'm in there, you may want to consider having liposuction to remove the fat deposits resting around your waist and lower back."

"Liposuction?"

"Yes. I could take a little from here"—I pinched Gracie's excess fat on both sides of her waist— "And sculpt you a new figure. Suck a little out of your back where fat has built up, and you'll look like you're twenty again."

"Why would I want to do that?"

"The liposuction?"

"Go back to being twenty. I dreaded those years," Gracie said, looking aloof. "I'm comfortable in my skin. I say I'm thirty-nine with great pride. In fact, I can't wait to celebrate my fortieth birthday. I didn't come here to run around and pretend to be some little teenybopper."

"That's not what I meant—"

"That's what you said," she snapped.

My mind quickly raced back to see if that was indeed what I'd said. I was used to patients being cuckoo for Coco Puffs, and this one was definitely a candidate.

"Please forgive me, Mrs. Lane, for being presumptuous. You're right. You're perfect as you are. Let's just stick to what you came here for. Shall I have Samantha schedule you for surgery?"

"Do you always fold so easily?"

"Pardon me?"

"Well, as a plastic surgeon, isn't it part of your job to upsell? Isn't that how you stay in business? I'm only asking because I'm inquisitive."

"Now it's you who's being presumptuous. I didn't go to Harvard Medical School to end up being some kind of used-car salesman. I don't force, persuade, or manipulate my patients into getting surgeries they don't need. I suggest all options so they can leave here informed." I tried to keep a level head at her offensive remark. My nonprofessional side wanted to scream on her judgmental ass, but I knew better.

She flopped back down on the examination table and stared me directly in the eyes.

"Anika never said you were self-righteous," she mockingly replied.

"I'm sorry, Mrs. Lane, but is there a problem?" Samantha intervened.

"Only if you want one," she challenged.

I was dead silent as I stared at the woman with a haughty personality. I was about to reconsider taking her on as a patient when she said, "I'm joking...seeing how you hold up under pressure. How much will it cost for the extra surgery? With the lipo, how much will it all cost? Of course, I'll have to talk it over with my Ed. You know, he's paying for this. Isn't that sweet, y'all? He's such an amazing man."

"Mrs. Lane, it's not exactly two separate surgeries. You won't have to pay for the anesthesiologist twice, so you'll only be charged for my services, which will be combined. Anika will fill you in on further details. Talk it over with your husband and let us know."

"Done."

"Without further discussion?"

"I have my ways of persuasion."

"Very well," I said.

After I left the consultation with Mrs. Lane, I was drained. When Anika came into chat, I wasn't in the mood, but I indulged her briefly.

"So, what do you think about Gracie?"

"Oh, her," I remarked dryly. "Is she a friend or family member?"

"She's a friend. Why do you ask?"

"Get rid of her. She's too old for you and too uptight."

"Gracie? Uptight? Never."

"You know, you two look a lot alike. She could pass for your cousin or aunt or something."

"We get that all the time."

"And why is she your friend again?"

"Most of my friends are older than me. That's why I'm so cultured."

"Cultured, my ass! Your ghetto ass has got to be kidding me. And let's not mention your old cougar girlfriend with a nice face and banged-up body. What's wrong with her? I think she's bipolar."

Anika and I burst into gut-twisting laughter that lasted a long moment. Tears streamed down my cheeks as I wondered why I called her a cougar and what Gracie would say if she heard me ripping into her.

"Cougar, huh? You just mad 'cause she wasn't flirting with

your oversexed ass."

"Are you stupid? She was all over me the moment I walked in the door. Oh, doctor, you're so handsome," I said, putting on a show.

"Boy, pah-lezze. Gracie doesn't have eyes for any man other than her husband."

"How long has she been married?"

"She just celebrated her tenth wedding anniversary."

"What does he do?"

"He has a good job. He works for Verizon."

"That's decent."

"Decent? They're making bank over there. I wish I had a piece of that," she said longingly.

"Then go get it," I replied. My tone got serious. Although I would hate to lose Anika, she was a bright girl. She could do much better than being my or anyone else's receptionist.

"Really? I heard the entrance test is almost as hard as brain surgery."

"You're not giving yourself enough credit. All you have to do is study. If you get the book, then I'll help you."

"You'd do that for me?"

"Of course."

"But why?"

"Why?" I was perplexed by her question. Why wouldn't I want to see her better herself?

"Why would you take the time to help me?"

"Jesus, because anything I can do to get you out of my face every day."

"Yeah, right. You love me, and you know it."

"As you would say, 'pah-leeze.'"

"You do the girlie impression a little bit too well," she joked.

"Oh, for real?" I replied in a flamboyant, effeminate voice and began prancing around, doing vogue hand movements made famous by Madonna. Anika laughed so hard, holding her stomach while her eyes slanted shut. I only did this because no one was in the waiting area, and I also got a kick out of acting silly. It relieved my stress. After she calmed down, I went back to my line of questioning.

"What does Gracie do?"

"Huh?" she retorted, trying to catch her breath.

"The woman, your friend, what does she do?"

"Watch soap operas," she replied, dramatically rolling her eyes.

On that note, I decided to call it a day.

CHAPTER

4

GRACIE LANE

HERE SHE GOES AGAIN, I THOUGHT AS VANESSA, a coworker, came strolling into work wearing a full-length mink coat that swept the ground as she walked. The female pelts were at least four inches thick in diameter, representing an expensive cut. Vanessa was a new member of the 40/40 club, which meant she'd just turned forty-years old and was in constant competitive mode with me. Vanessa despised that I was married, and she'd only managed to be another man's mistress. Her string of affairs was just a BAND-AID® to cover what she yearned for, which was the love and stability of a husband. That and my bragging about Ed all day made for a healthy serving of jealousy. But we were too old to ever voice our differences.

"Girl, look at you," I said, realizing that I *had* to make a comment. Vanessa kept her coat on for a full five minutes. "That's a gorgeous mink."

Straightforwardly, Vanessa replied, "This *is* a gorgeous mink, right? You'd have to do a heist to afford it," and sashayed past me, leaving my mouth gaping open. Inwardly, I snickered. No one at my job knew of my wealth or that I was working as a volunteer. That's the way I chose my situation to appear from the onset. I would never walk in all jeweled up, nor did I drive any of my luxury vehicles here. Out front sat my Honda hybrid. My rationalization was to do something good—from my heart—to make up for my past. Not use the opportunity as a platform to upstage anyone. And my common sense superseded any thoughts of retaliation.

I continued, "Who bought you that? Robert?"

"Robert has just about gotten on my last nerve," Vanessa said, finally removing her coat. "This was a blackmail move on my part."

"What? Give me the dirt." I suddenly perked up.

We were inside the living room of the home where we both worked. John and Lisa, two other staff members, were inside the kitchen dispensing medication to mentally handicapped adults. My and Vanessa's job was cleaning up the house after the school bus came to pick up the clients.

John strolled into the living room and flopped on the sofa beside me.

"What's up?" he asked.

I turned up my nose.

"John, do you have any gum?"

He reached in and pulled out a stick.

"No, *you* need it, not me."

"Me?" he asked through lips that were dry and cracked.

"You heard her," Vanessa snapped. "Every day, you come in here smelling like you got a dead body in your throat! Like there's a funeral in that bitch," she exclaimed, and everyone laughed. Everyone was sick of John's tart breath. He refused to get help for what we thought was halitosis.

"Don't start this early in the morning, Vanessa," John said while kicking off his Timberland boots and putting his feet on the coffee table. Our supervisor wasn't in yet. It was just nearing seven o'clock in the morning.

"Well, I'd like to tell my story before Jessica, the Wicked Bitch of the North, comes in," Vanessa said, referring to our supervisor.

"What's up?" John asked.

"Well, as I told Gracie, Robert thinks he's slick. Do you know I caught him almost cheating on me with a girl half my age?"

"Almost? How can you *almost* cheat?" I asked.

"He almost cheated because I busted him before it got any further. The other night I kept calling his cell, which was going to voicemail, so I knew he was up to something. So around two in the morning, I couldn't take it any longer and decided to get in my car and drive to Tiffany's house."

"Who's Tiffany?" I asked.

"My daughter's best friend."

"Why would Robert be at your daughter's friend's house? And why, when he didn't pick up, didn't you just suspect that he was in for the night? I mean, he's a married man," I probed.

"First things first. I'd seen Tiffany eyeing Robert whenever he was over at my house, and second, his fat-ass wife doesn't hold any weight. When I call, he answers!" she exclaimed.

Don't hold any weight? I wondered. *She's his wife.*

"So, get to the point," John commented, already bored with Vanessa's theatrics.

"As I suspected, I drove there, and his car was in the driveway. I went ballistic. I told Tiffany that if she didn't open the door, I would whip her ass old-school style, and she knew I meant what I said. Robert came skulking with his tail between his legs, proclaiming nothing had happened. Two days later, I got this." She smiled as if her reward was the end that justified the means.

"And you believed him?" John asked.

Vanessa gave him a look like, *how dare you even ask such a stupid question.*

"Of course, I do. Did you not hear the part about me getting there in the nick of time?"

"Are you telling me you think they didn't have sex?"

"He said it didn't happen," Vanessa responded with clenched teeth.

"It's like this. If I was on Tyson's jury, he woulda walked. A chick only rolls home with a guy at four in the morning to have sex. The only thing that could convince me otherwise is the videotape. If you're saying you rolled over to her house at two in the morning, and he said nothing happened, that's what he's supposed to say. That doesn't mean you believe him." John shook his head at her dumbness. "I wish my ex-girl was as stupid as you. And your ass is mad old."

I needed to intervene.

"Whether they had sex or not is neither here nor there. Bottom line is that you're sharing, Robert. Whether with one or ten

41

women, it's just arithmetic," I reasoned.

Our female bonding became acrimonious in seconds, and the claws came out.

"Why would you say something like that?!" Vanessa exploded. "You come in here as if you're better than me, each and every day. Ed this, Ed that. I'm so sick of hearing about you and Ed's perfect little house, with the white picket fence, that I wanna throw up each time I hear his—"

Our little powwow was stopped short when our supervisor walked in. Tension was halted as we began picking imaginary lint off the sofa, prodding and plumping pillows, and dusting already clean surfaces.

"Good morning, Jessica," we all sang in unison. Jessica barely acknowledged our greeting before she started in.

"Whose car is blocking the driveway?" she asked. Everyone was speechless. "Vanessa, don't you drive that gas-guzzling BMW X5?"

"Yes, but I know I didn't block the driveway," Vanessa retorted gruffly. Often, she contemplated whipping Jessica's frail, white ass but held back for two reasons—she was too old to be fighting, and the Suffolk County racist police department would lock her up and throw away the key.

"John, come look and tell me what you see." Jessica called her "yes" boy to settle the dispute. John jumped to attention and ran to the window.

"Oh, I see what you're saying. Vanessa, you could have moved back a little. Your front end is partially in the driveway."

Vanessa rolled her eyes and scowled at John.

"Well, I'll move it later. I got work to do," Vanessa sneered, walking upstairs and out of sight.

"I suggest you move it within the hour!" Jessica barked with false bravado.

I was a little pissed that I didn't get a chance to brag about Ed paying for my tummy tuck. I'd have to save that tidbit for tomorrow.

∞

Ed crept upstairs carrying a plate of turkey sausages, egg whites, and apple juice squeezed from a juicer to surprise me early this morning. The aroma from the food made it to me before he did. I got a whiff of breakfast and began to smile.

"Hey, babe," he said, kissing me on the cheek. "Get up."

Slowly turning over, I did a languorous stretch and then yarned.

"What's all of this?" I asked, clearing the phlegm from my throat.

"Just a little something, something I whipped up for you before I headed out to the gym to work on my stubborn belly fat."

"Maybe I should go with you. I want to work on my thighs before I go into surgery."

"Not today," he said. "I don't want to wait for you to get dressed. I'm ready to go. Besides, I need you here."

"Need me here?" I asked as I stuffed the turkey sausage into my mouth. "For what?"

"My sister, Tamara, and her loser boyfriend finally broke up. She'll move in with us for a few weeks to save money. I told her she could have the guest bedroom and wouldn't have a problem with you."

"Ed, please don't do this to me."

"Gracie, don't start. She's my sister, and I can't see her on the street."

"This is the second time she's lived with us in one year. She only drives a wedge between us; I can't allow that. Not this time! Tell that bitch she can't stay."

Ed, who was non-confrontational yet always stern and unwavering in his responses, said, "There's nothing more to discuss. She'll be here in a couple hours."

CHAPTER
5

ANTHONY CROSS

"YOU WANT THIS..." SHE PURRED AND SEDUCTIVELY sauntered toward me. She climbed on me little by little as I admired her nakedness. Her hard nipples dangled provocatively. She began kissing me from the base of my ankles up to my calves, behind my knees, and once she began licking between my thighs, my penis stood at attention. She purposely kissed around my manhood because she didn't give head.

"You like this," she said, jerking me off with her hands.

I dug my hands into her massive hair weave and pulled her up. Dakota allowed me to flip her over, spread her legs wide, and began to taste her sweet nectar. I sucked on her clit until it was swollen, and I heard her moan. Then I started to gently nibble and bite down on her clitoris while finger-fucking her. Dakota began grinding her hips slowly while softly digging into my shoulder blades.

"You taste sweeter than honey," I breathed. "All wet, hot, and sticky."

"Eat it all up, Daddy."

"Mmm, hmm," was my response as I continued to explore her sweet cave until she reached her peak.

"Yeah, babe," she purred. "I want you! Come fuck me...."

"Fuck you!" I said as I pushed my manhood deeper inside her warm, slippery cave. She wrapped her sexy thighs around my waist, and I began to give her solid and steady strokes until we climaxed. I collapsed on top of Dakota until we regained our composure.

I was ready to go again.

"I got something for you."

Groggily, she pulled her tired eyes open but remained silent. She watched me go inside my drawer and pull out a small dildo.

"Anthony, what are you gonna do?"

"Shush, relax, baby," I coaxed. Gently, I turned her over to lie down on her stomach. I parted her legs and rubbed K-Y Jelly on her ass.

"Daddy, nooo," she pleaded. "I don't wanna."

I purposely bought a smaller version of my penis to open her up before entering her. I tried gently to insert the dildo, and she began to squirm and try to wiggle free.

"Babe, relax," I calmly replied, not allowing my voice to reflect my aggravation.

"I don't wanna," she repeated in a baby-like voice, which annoyed me at that moment.

I turned her back around, tossed the dildo on the floor, and rammed my manhood into her resisting flesh. I began to angrily enter her and only got more excited as she responded.

As her legs quivered and she realized she had no control over her movements, she tried to switch positions, but I wouldn't let her. I pushed her back down, missionary, and made her handle it.

"Is this what you want?" I continued to give her angry thrusts, "*Only* this dick!"

Strong waves cascaded down through our bodies, and we moaned in pleasure.

We both came.

Usually, I would have knocked out and gone to sleep, but Dakota decided she wanted to talk. And I wasn't prepared for what she had to say.

"Anthony, do you notice anything different about me?" she asked as she snuggled under my arm and stroked my belly with her manicured hand.

"Dee, please, not tonight. I got a heavy morning ahead of me."

"Ant, I've been holding this back for too long."

"Holding what back?"

"I'm pregnant," she blurted out.

The color drained from my face, and my mouth went dry. I pushed Dakota off me as I bolted straight up in bed. I glared at her as my eyes adjusted to the darkness.

"What happened to your birth control?" I asked in disbelief.

"Remember I told you I had missed a couple of consecutive days, so I had to wait and start over."

"What?" I flipped. "You never said any such thing!"

"Umm, I did. Well, I thought I did." She began biting her bottom lip, which I knew was a sign of lying. We were now facing each other, and it was becoming hostile. "It was a mistake."

"Mistake? I don't make mistakes. You know how I feel about having children without being married. I want my children to live in a stable environment like my parents gave me."

"So why can't we get married?!" She pouted.

"Don't do this."

"Do what?"

"Be a sneaky, conniving bitch! Don't force my hand because you won't like the outcome."

"I would never deceive you," she persisted.

"D-d-don't do that," I stuttered. "Pretend to be all innocent. That act got me, but it won't keep me."

"It's not an act."

"Your *act* has turned me off," I stated, ignoring her. "You can't even fuck me good. When are you going to suck my dick! Get rid of that baby! Now!"

Dakota leaped from the bed, hysterical and in tears, and began dressing frantically. She couldn't get her clothes on fast enough. I sat and watched her—amused, relieved, and angry, all at once.

After she was dressed, she lingered around, wanting attention. "You're not going to take back what you said?" she screamed, throwing a childish tantrum.

"What sense does that make? *'Take back'* what I said! Are you an idiot? Learn how to speak properly. How will you be someone's mother, and you can't even form a proper sentence? I wish your child luck—"

"I HATE YOU!" she screamed like a maniac, folded in half, and fell to the ground. After I ignored her shenanigans, she got up to lunge at me. I blocked her furious blows with my elbows until she got tired, and then I jumped up, grabbed her scrawny little ass by the back of her collar, and tossed her out of my front door!

I lay back on my bed and only hoped to reason with Dakota in the morning. There was no way that I was ready to co-parent, especially with her.

CHAPTER

6

GRACIE LANE

AFTER A LONG DAY OF VOLUNTEER WORK, I walked in to find my house in disarray. Tamara was lying on the sofa, getting her beauty rest. Meanwhile, all the lights were on, including a television that Tamara wasn't watching. And she had cracked each massive window in the living room in the middle of the winter, letting all the heat escape. The house was an icebox.

"Tamara!" I exploded. "Get up."

"What's wrong?" she asked, jumping up in surprise and holding her chest.

Our eyes met solidly.

"What did I tell you about opening the windows and letting

all the heat out?"

"It was baking in here," she replied, wide-eyed and frozen.

"So, turn down the heat. Do you realize our heat bill has tripled since you moved in?" Tamara always took for granted that her brother married wealthy. What she didn't realize was that my money was just that—mine! And I wasn't going to throw it out an open window.

"I'm so sorry, Gracie," she lied as she ran to shut the windows. "It won't happen again."

"That's what you said the last time."

While my hands were full of grocery bags, I walked into the kitchen. I listened intently as Tamara got on her cell to make another appointment to get a facial. This was the second facial she'd had in six weeks. She was surely splurging for someone who was supposed to be on a budget and saving money to move out independently. From weekly colonics, hot stone body massages, manicures, pedicures, facials, body waxes, cocktails at the W Hotel, shopping excursions at Saks, and lobster at Mr. Chow's, she was doing just the opposite of saving. I was tired of complaining to Ed, who couldn't see how his sister was using us. Tamara always put on this syrupy-sweet voice, opened her eyes wide like a cherub, and lied through her straight, big teeth whenever Ed was around.

"You're going to get another facial?" I called out.

"Umm, yeah, you should come," Tamara replied, walking into the kitchen to face me. The granite island was full of groceries, and she didn't even make a weak attempt to help me put them away. "I really don't have the money, but I don't have a choice. Do you see these fine lines appearing on my forehead?" She pointed to imaginary creases. "Can you believe it? I'm only

51

twenty-eight, and already I'm getting wrinkles."

I didn't even bother to look.

"I really wish I could, but I got better things to spend my money on," I sarcastically replied.

"Yeah, I know what you mean. But unlike me, you don't need it. You have great skin. I wish I had skin like yours."

I wouldn't allow myself to fall victim to Tamara and her bullshit game. She thought she was a grade-A con artist, but she was amateur at best. The only person her tactics worked on was Ed. Everyone else saw straight through her, including all of her ex-boyfriends.

Ignoring her fakeness, I prepared to clean the house before my husband got home. What irritated me most was that Tamara was a slob. She was just nasty. She was the type of person that would drop another piece of paper in an already-full wastebasket. Emptying it wasn't an option in her mind. She bathed sporadically. And when she did hop her funky ass in the shower, she wouldn't even contemplate taking a capful of Clorox to disinfect it after she used it.

"What the fuck—" I yelled as my bare feet stepped into a sticky residue plastered on my kitchen floor. One more step backward gave me a small gash into the sole of my right foot as I stepped into a pile of something sharp. "Ouchhhhh!"

"What happened?" Tamara asked. She was back on the sofa watching the 60-inch LCD television.

"I don't know," I responded as I flopped to the floor to get a better look at my foot. While down there, I noticed tiny shards of glass on the kitchen floor and what appeared to be dried-up juice. I followed the trail, looked in the garbage, and saw another broken dish. And, of course, it was expensive China.

"Tamaraaaaa," I said in a long whine. "You broke another dish!"

"Oh, yeah, I'm sorry," she said nonchalantly.

"Sorry?!" I yelled, "Come here."

She took her time walking back into the kitchen.

"When is it going to stop? Every night we come in here, and you've broken something. By next week, we won't have a dish to eat on. And why didn't you mop up this slop on the floor?"

Calmly, Tamara's eyes glanced at the tile.

"I don't see anything," she replied in an even, unfazed voice.

I looked at my cream-colored marble tile with the purplish stain and gave up. I gave a disappointed sigh, then glared at her as I dropped to my knees and began scrubbing the dirt from my floor. Meanwhile, my foot was throbbing, and my nerves were shot. Unaffected, Tamara grabbed the can of cashews I had just bought and excused herself.

"She's got to go, or so help me, I'ma whip her ass in here!" I screamed.

"Lower your voice. Do you want her to hear you?"

"I hope she does hear me! Maybe she'll get out!"

Ed was spent. The constant bickering between the only two women, besides his mother, he loved was wearing upon his sanity. He couldn't understand why we couldn't just get along.

The drive on the New Jersey Turnpike heading south was filled with anxiety. I drove my Honda hybrid to not alert my family about my financial situation. The article that my brother had read was just about a blue-collar worker being active in his community. That's it—nothing on me. In fact, you could barely see my face. It was a side profile shot, which amazes me that Benjamin would be able to recognize me.

I wasn't happy about seeing George or revisiting my past. I was shocked as I drove up to the old, decrepit house, which had seen better days. The white house with burgundy shutters and a white picket fence no longer existed. In front of me, there stood an off-white, dirty exterior, and missing shutters. Flowers that used to decorate the pathway were no more. Vast patches of missing grass were sporadically throughout the yard, while weeds were overgrown in other parts.

I shut off my headlights and pulled around to the backyard. I could barely see as I crept up the chipped concrete, formerly known as stairs. I felt underneath the huge ceramic flower pot and found the spare key. It had been almost two decades since I'd run away from here and vowed to never return.

The screen door creaked as I pulled it open. I peered into the house from the opening of the back door, and my heart palpitated wildly.

Once inside, the pungent smell that permeated the house stopped me in my tracks. Immediately my hand covered my nose, and I held my breath. The smell was so strong; it was literally burning my nostrils. For a split second, I wondered if something or *someone* had died.

"George," I called. "George, are you here? It's me."

I stepped farther into the house, only to notice barely any furniture. George was sleeping in his lazy chair by the window, with a shotgun propped between his legs. Garbage, broken furniture, and flies occupied the once-immaculate residence.

How could this be? I wondered.

"George!" I yelled, startling the old man, who had begun to drool. Without a second thought, he aimed his shotgun directly at my heart.

"It's me, your daughter."

"I know who you are, gal."

"Then why are you still pointing that gun at me?"

"Whatchu doin' here? In my house? Didn't I tell your scandalous ass that I didn't eva wanna see you no more?"

"I had the same sentiments, but Benjamin called and said you asked me to come."

He thought for a moment.

"Oh, I did, didn't I?"

"What do you want from me, George?"

"Those honkies at the bank tryin' to take my house. Damn crackers! I told them I'd shoot up the whole town before letting that happen! That cracker-ass sheriff will be the first to go if he comes around here trying to kick me out!"

Since there wasn't anywhere I could sit, I continued to stand.

"What are you talking about?" I wondered if George was on any medication for his brain tumor and, if so, whether it was making him delusional. "This house has been paid off for years."

Even though my mother had left us when I was young, my parents never divorced. When my mother died in a car accident, her life insurance policy was payable to my father. Back then, $150,000 was a lot of money. George paid off his house and then splurged the rest on his two prized possessions—his sons.

"That was 'fore Andre ran into some trouble and needed to pull the equity out of the house to save his ass. White folk 'round here won't let him keep a job."

"Is that what he told you?" I snapped. "And you fell for his bullshit, as usual."

"You better watch your mouth! I'm still your father. I don't care how old you are. You're never old enough not to feel my foot in ya ass!"

I shrugged off his threats. They meant nothing.

"Again, what is it that you want from me?"

"Is you stupid?" he barked. "I want you to save my house and pay off my mortgage!"

My stomach knotted in disgust. I looked at my DNA donor and got physically sick. His leathery skin had pockmarks from years of bad acne, four rotten teeth remained in his yuck mouth, and his once virile body had shriveled up like an overcooked pea. However, he still had the strength and energy of a bull. He thrived off hate.

"What the hell's wrong—"

My outburst was interrupted by my brother Benjamin. He was a pitiful sight. His body had clear signs that it had been ravaged by drug use. His body was no bigger than a Blow Pop stick, with a big head to match. His clothes hung from his body like a hanger, and he smelled like a mixture of piss and shit.

"Hey, baby girl, you made it," he said, trying to embrace me, but I stepped back and used my hands to put up a barrier.

"Benjamin, how could you let this happen?" I accused.

"What?" he replied, oblivious to their living conditions.

"What do you mean, 'what?' This house is disgusting. We weren't brought up like this!" I retorted.

"Come on, now, it's not that bad."

"Are you crazy? I could, would never live like this."

"You think you so high and mighty like you're better than

somebody," my father said.

"No one's talking to you!" I took his shit as a little girl but refused to take it now as an adult.

"Pops, I got this. Sis, let me speak to you in here." Benjamin led me into the funky kitchen. "Look, we fell on hard times after Andre did his bullshit."

"Yeah, George told me he refinanced the house."

"Did Pops also mention that Andre took all the money and ran?"

"No way," I said as my jaw hung open.

"True story. We must come up with $20,000 before the fifteenth, or we'll get thrown out on the street. And you see, I ain't got that kind of money. A brother is fucked up right now."

"If I had it, I wouldn't give it. But my conscience is clear because I really *don't* have it," I lied with a straight face. "Maybe you can stay with one of our relatives and put the old man in a nursing home. He's dying, anyway."

"Nah, he's not dying. That old dude is gonna outlive all of us. I just said he had a brain tumor to get you to come. No matter how much you say you don't care about him, I knew you'd show up."

I didn't even pretend to be relieved at his admission. "Oh, you're a psychoanalyst now?"

"Something like that," he replied and nudged my arm. "Listen, let me hold something."

"Hold what?" I asked, clueless to his request.

"In layman's terms, that means to give me a couple dollars so I can bounce."

I stared directly into Benjamin's eyes, but he couldn't hold my stare. I knew my brother was strung out on drugs, but I chose not to mention the obvious. I gave him all that I had in my wallet, $110. Before I could say another word, he was gone. I strolled back into the living room to bid a final farewell to my cantankerous father.

"Listen, I'm about to leave."

"You were never invited," he replied, not missing the opportunity to take one last stab.

"Look, I checked your refrigerator, and you don't have any food. I'll order some groceries and toiletries to be delivered online. Make sure you answer the door when they come."

"So that's it, huh?"

"That's all I got to give."

"You're worthless. That cat-trap coochie you got can't save my house," he stated, letting out a hearty cackle.

I realized long ago that my father mistreated me because he never got over my mother breaking his miserable heart. And I looked just like her.

"You're nothing but a bag of noise, old man. A miserable, self-righteous, depressing old devil!"

"Oh, you talking big and bad now! Wait until those people get ya."

"George, they won't *'get me'* because I've made like the gingerbread man and ran. Bye-bye," I sassily replied, and with that, I was gone.

CHAPTER
7

ANTHONY CROSS

MY BOYS AND I WERE ON OUR WAY TO Sue's Rendezvous strip club to celebrate Kevin's first anniversary. After one year of faithfully fucking only his wife, he deserved a little break.

Kevin was meeting us at the club, but Chris came by to get me. He came upstairs instead of calling because he knew I took a long time getting ready. He often joked that I was metrosexual because I liked to look good. I stared in the mirror at my ensemble. I wore dark blue True Religion jeans, which looked feminine, but I was confident with my manhood. My outfit was completed with a black, red, and green Gucci knitted hat, matching sweater, and black Gucci loafers with gold buckle.

My caramel-colored smooth skin, brawny shoulders, broad back, and deep baritone voice combined with my six-foot, one-inch stature—ensured that I looked good in almost anything. My suits were tailored, and I only shopped at high-end stores and boutiques such as Barney's New York and Saks Fifth Avenue. I hate to admit this, but fashion was a passion of mine. Secretly, I TiVo'd Project Runway. I loved that show.

Chris came through, looking more street. He had an oversized, goose-down, cream-colored jacket; baggy Sean John jeans; a matching sweater; and Timberland boots. Chris was always going through an identity crisis. He got beaten up in school because of his lean body, soft voice, and wimpy attitude. Now, as a grown man, he was living the life he thought he should have lived in his youth. His scrawny body had been replaced with muscle and only ten percent body fat. Although he still had a faint voice, his speech had been replaced with street vernacular.

"You still in the mirror?" he joked in his effeminate voice. "Just like a girl."

"Yeah, at least I don't sound like one." Hey, he asked for that one.

"Don't get fucked up in here tonight," he threatened. "I promise you; I don't hit like a girl. I'll bust your whole shit open."

I gave him a stern look.

"Don't get carried away with that tough talk. I'll put you over my knee and spank you like my bitch," I barked back. Chris and I had a love-hate relationship. It was a man thing. We were very competitive, always trying to show who had bigger balls. "Come on, let's go!"

Chris, Kevin, and I rolled into the place shortly after midnight. We sat back in the VIP area, sipping on Armand de Brignac— also known as Ace of Spade champagne. This sexy, petite, African American girl came slinking over. She wore a white and baby blue bra, G-string panties, and white thigh highs with a baby blue garter belt. On her tiny feet was a pair of stilettos. I loved the way her dark chocolate complexion contrasted against the white outfit. I motioned her over.

"Hey, baby," she greeted and smiled. "You want a lap dance?"

"Yes, but not for me. I want you to dance for my man right here. He hasn't been out in a year."

She took a look at Kevin and immediately obliged. I watched as she straddled him and began to grind. As I sat back, drinking in the scene, I didn't notice another person joining us.

"Anthony, this is my man, Gabriel," Chris said.

His name sounded familiar because he was all Chris had spoken about for the past month. He was some sort of investment guru. I looked at his watch—Audemars Piguet; shoes—alligator; fingernails—manicured. Okay, so maybe he was someone I should listen to. I couldn't tell whether Gabriel was Italian or Greek. He had naturally tanned skin; thick, jet-black hair; a sculptured jawbone; and stood around 5' 7" with shoes on. "What's up?" I asked, acknowledging the newcomer while giving him a firm handshake.

"Nothing much. So, I hear you're a hotshot plastic surgeon."

"Yeah, something like that," I replied, sipping my champagne.

Before the night was over, our tab was nearly five grand, and Gabriel picked it up. When we left, he offered to drive us home, and I couldn't help but notice he was pushing a Bentley Phantom. I was impressed. Kevin and I declined the ride and jumped into a yellow taxi, but Chris took Gabriel up on the offer since he was going Gabriel's way.

"Are we still on to watch the game at your house tomorrow?" Chris asked me as Gabriel waited for him in his car.

"Yeah, yeah, no doubt. Listen, bring your man. I may want to pick his brain with this investment situation. He looks as if he's doing well for himself."

Chris and I embraced, gave a quick handshake, and parted ways. Kevin and I went uptown, and Chris and Gabriel headed downtown.

The following day, I prepared for the abdominoplasty on Mrs. Lane. Our first encounter kept going through my head, and I prayed that she didn't start any shit this morning. I decided to go and mess with Anika. She always cheered me up.

"What's up, hussy!" I joked.

"What's your dweeb ass smiling about?"

"Shit. Truthfully, I don't have anything to smile about. My week has been tumultuous. Dakota and I aren't speaking, and it's got me stressed."

"Drop that needy bitch!"

I laughed at her forwardness.

"Speaking of bitches, I hope Mrs. Lane isn't on her period this morning!"

"Why do you care?" she asked suspiciously.

"She better care. Hope I don't skim on the anesthesia. Give her local instead of general; she'll feel every nip and tuck of my big scalpel."

"You freak!"

I stuck my tongue out and flickered it rapidly. "All day!"

Mrs. Lane was unusually cheery as she lay in the hospital bed wearing the cotton hat and gown she was given.

"How are you this morning?" I asked, glancing at her chart.

"I'm doing well. Very well. A little nervous, but excited too."

"You should be. You'll look like an eleven since you're already a ten." I shot some corny-ass game her way, trying to loosen her up. She had me on pins and needles for some reason, and I wasn't sure if my statement would cause her to react crazily. But she just grinned.

"Me? A ten? You think so?"

That was an *a-ha!* moment. A little narcissistic, were we? Loving the praise.

"Of course I do," I replied, then focused on the anesthesiologist who had asked Mrs. Lane to count back from ten. "She's ready," I told him.

"Ten…nine—"

Lights out.

"Let's roll," I said to my staff.

That day had been long and exhausting, and I wasn't in the mood for interruptions while I did a little paperwork. Dakota had called, screaming and sobbing heavily, asking why I was doing this to her? She accused me of ignoring her and playing mind games. Mind games? That was precisely what she was playing with her planned pregnancy. How could I have been such a fool? If she didn't get her pregnancy terminated, I would be looking at at least

63

$5,000 a month, easy. And although I wasn't cheap, that was too much money for child support. Jesus, the thought made me sick to my stomach. I was a new surgeon trying to maintain my practice in a plush neighborhood, a new condo, and an asshole full of student loans. Now wasn't the time to add pampers and baby formula to my long debt list.

The office building I leased my space from had other practitioners as tenants, some of whom I'd grown to like and some I didn't. Arthur was one of those doctors I didn't enjoy speaking with; he always called every second of the day.

"Hey, you busy?" he asked, breathing heavily into the phone receiver. His weight had gotten out of control.

"Yes," I abruptly said.

"Well, this will only take a minute," he replied, oblivious to my annoyance. "I don't know what happened, man, but Eric got fired today."

"Eric, who?"

"The LPN that works with us."

"For what?"

"He didn't say. He said the supervising RN told him he had 20 minutes to leave the building. I feel terrible for him. I mean, what could he have done?"

"He knows what he's done! He could have been downloading kiddy porn or stealing computers. Getting food stamps in phony names, does it matter? They fired his ass, bottom line."

"Poor Eric," he empathized.

"Does he have any kids?"

"No."

"Does he have a wife or sick parent?"

"No."

This guy was dumb, as the day was long. I didn't have the patience to tolerate him much longer.

"Listen, Arthur, I gotta go. Someone just walked into my office."

For at least two seconds, I was lying. That was until my office door flung open and in waltzed Elizabeth. She and her best friend, Gwyneth, were tenants who co-owned and operated a cosmetic podiatry practice.

"I'm so busy," she said while plopping down in the empty chair.

"Then what the hell are you doing in my office?" I asked.

I looked at Elizabeth and realized that she was always exhausted, not from work but from trying to get as many free dinners per week as possible.

"He decided to break it off," she said.

"Who this time?"

"Michael. Remember him? The firefighter."

"Did you sleep with him?"

"Yes."

"Are you surprised that he kicked you to the curb?"

"Of course, I am," she shrilled.

"Come on, you're forty-five competing with twenty-five-year-old women. Even Jordan isn't in the NBA anymore. Don't fool yourself."

"Screw you!"

I was stumped. I looked at Elizabeth and wondered where she had gone wrong? She was a raven-haired, intelligent Jewish woman who owned a lovely apartment on the Upper Eastside, had parents about to die and leave her a boatload of inheritance. She was whoring herself out almost every night to losers. She had a Jones for Black men in uniform, preferably firefighters, who would drop her like a bad habit after the third or fourth date. For some reason, she couldn't keep a man. I kept telling her to stay in her lane. Try dating a nice Jewish man whose age was compatible with hers. But *nooooo*, she wanted men in their twenties who weren't interested in settling down and having babies with an old, white, Jewish woman.

"Okay, I'm sorry for being obnoxious. I'm going out after work with my boys. You're welcome to join us."

"Where are you going?"

"Most likely downtown, either in the Meatpacking District or Soho, to club Chaos."

She took a moment to think.

"Nah, I'll call Wayne and see if he wants to come over."

"Of course." I laughed. "Why pass up definite dick for a maybe?"

"I so hate you!"

"You do not!"

Just as I was about to make up some lame excuse to kick her ass out of my office, my cell vibrated with a text message from Chris, saying that our plans tonight had been canceled. No explanation. Suddenly, I didn't feel like getting rid of Elizabeth.

"Listen, let me ask you a question," I began slowly, "My girlfriend's pregnant, but I'm not ready to have any children. And before you state the obvious, I thought she was using birth control."

"Do you love her?"

"Not at all," I replied truthfully. "Maybe one day I could...but for now, I just like our time together."

"So, it's casual. But let me guess, she thinks differently."

"Precisely."

"You're a pig," she griped.

"I'm not letting you in on my personal life for you to judge me. I need a woman's point of view. If you were in her situation, what could I say to make you have an abortion? I've tried everything in the book! I'm afraid her little girlfriends will get in her head, and the next thing she'll say is, *'I don't need you to help me raise my baby. I can do it all by myself,'* bullshit."

Nodding, she responded. "If she loves you and thinks you love her and the only thing blocking her from running off into the sunset with you is this pregnancy, then she'll have an abortion. If she feels that she doesn't have you, that another woman may have your attention, or there isn't a possibility that you and her have a future, she'll keep the baby. As a keepsake. Something to forever keep you in her life. It's all mental. You hold the key to whether she keeps the baby or not. Unless," she paused. "She's pro-life. And then you're screwed."

My talk with Elizabeth was enlightening. She was cool, after all. I was now prepared for how to move forward with Dakota.

It had been weeks since I'd hit the town, but tonight was a night to celebrate. Dakota had finally terminated the pregnancy, and we were back at it as if we had never stopped. Of course, I bagged up every time now. Sometimes I even doubled up.

Chris, Mike, and I ended up at Butter with the after-work crowd. We rolled downstairs to the bar area to listen to music. There were a few sexy sistahs in four-inch stilettos, tight jeans, and glossy lips with desperation written all over their faces. They were on the prowl, which I liked. As I sat in a corner booth, I had the waiter ask the ladies what they were drinking and told him to put it on my tab. He casually walked up behind the most petite of the trio and whispered in her ear. At first, she looked shocked until what he'd said registered. A huge Colgate grin splattered across her face as she turned to find out who the generous stranger was. We made brief eye contact when I was pointed out, and I decided she was pretty cute. She looked to be around twenty-seven with full lips. Her entourage came over to our table, and we started with the small talk—*names, occupations, have kids, are you married*—stuff like that.

During the night, someone decided we should all start taking shots of Patrón. I should have used better discretion since I had surgery for noon the next day, but I didn't. The full-lipped girl I later found out was named Candy, had attached herself to my hip and already told me she was coming home with me. She now looked on the verge of a coma.

"Let me go and get some bottled water. I think we all need to detox a little," I said. At that point, I was sweating profusely. As I strolled to the bar, I noticed a familiar figure hopping up on a table and beginning a slow grind to "Hit it Shorty" by Lloyd. And, no, it wasn't Paris Hilton. She dropped it like it was hot and did a sexy grind back up. She was cheered on by her friends and bystanders. I walked over and got caught up in the moment. I stared at her as she seductively mesmerized me. I drank in every curve of her now flawless body.

I climbed on the low table and positioned myself behind her. She gave me a private dance as if hundreds of people weren't watching. Her reckless behavior pulled me in.

As we slowly danced to about five fast songs, the alcohol began to get to me, and I realized I was toasted.

I spoke in her ear. "I bet you got the best body in here."

She finally turned to face the stranger and was surprised to see me. "If it isn't Doctor Cross."

"The one and only."

"Out hunting, I suppose?"

"More like perusing."

"Me too, but I think I've found what I want."

I liked her forwardness, but maybe it was the liquor talking.

"I think I need a physical exam Doctor Cross," she said coyly.

I looked into her eyes and realized she was serious.

"Not here," I replied and gave her a sly wink.

CHAPTER

8

GRACIE LANE

ANTHONY'S APARTMENT WAS VERY PLUSH. He had beautiful parquet floors sanded to a pale beige and a vast Sony flat-screen, 50-inch LCD television with Surround Sound hung on his wide wall. A costly, large brown leather sofa with giant suede pillows—embroidered with the initials A.C.—a round marble coffee table and an old-school CD player completed the décor. His dining room set was a masculine maple wood with beautifully decorated place settings. His bedroom door was closed, and his apartment smelled of a combination of warm cinnamon and vanilla.

He had huge candle holders everywhere lamps should have

been. Obviously, the doctor had done very well for himself. His Upper Eastside address and door attendant contributed to my admiration. I was *somewhat* impressed. My apartment was three times as big and cost four times more, but at least he'd earned what he had and earned my respect.

I walked farther into his apartment in my stiletto heels. I purposely took languorous steps, and as I walked, my ass jiggled slightly in my form-fitting skirt and thongs.

"May I?" I asked as I slowly turned the knob to his bedroom door.

"Do you," he replied.

One by one, I stepped out of my shoes and left them by his bed. I was too drunk to think about the consequences and too horny to care. I wanted someone to make me feel good; the doctor was the usual suspect. He grabbed me by my waist, pulled me close, and passionately tongue-kissed me. Our tongues intertwined, and he seemed to enjoy how I playfully bit and sucked his lips. I pulled back to see how badly he really wanted me.

"Come here," he said, reaching out to pull me back in so I could feel him aroused. The lust in his eyes took away any uncertainties I may have had. I inhaled his cologne and began to taste his skin.

Gently he put his hand behind my neck and kissed me passionately. His kisses slowly moved down to my earlobe. Then he began to gently suck my neck—not aggressive enough to leave any marks, but assertive enough to stimulate me. He sucked and then blew, sending a tingly sensation through my body. I pulled up my skirt to speed things up, revealing my bald vagina—no low Caesar, no landing strip, nothing. Just all pussy was staring in his face, just like a porn star. Anthony began to take off his boots.

"You can leave your boots on!" I exclaimed. "I came here for one thing."

"Relaxxxx," he soothed. "We got all night."

"You got all night. I'm married and got less than an hour."

"Mrs. Lane," he joked. "May I call you Gracie?"

"Shut up!" I demanded. "And come to mama."

"As long as you call me Daddy."

"Daddy, what's your pleasure?" I asked.

"Everything."

I stood back, pulled off my blouse, and let it tumble to the floor. My skirt went next. Anthony pulled his shirt over his head and let it hit the ground. Following my lead. We stared at each other in silence. He pulled off his jeans while kicking off his boots. Taking one last look at my now-perfect body, he shoved me onto his bed.

"Do you want me to fuck or make love to you?" he asked.

"If I wanted to make love, I'd be home in bed with my husband," I purred. "I came here to fuck."

He grabbed the K-Y Jelly. I was talking in his language.

"Turn around, and you better not say no!" he commanded.

Eagerly I turned around and assumed the position.

"Be easy now," I whispered.

"I got you."

Anthony began to massage the cool jelly between my cheeks while sucking and licking my lower back.

I began moaning my pleasure and almost pleading for him to enter me. I was so aroused. He quickly grabbed a condom from his nightstand and wrapped it up before steadying himself. He gently began to ease into me, pushing through my resisting flesh.

As he began digging deeper into me anally, the tightness had him ready to explode prematurely. He had to slow it down to regain control. He pulled me into the doggy-style position, and I began throwing it back at him.

"How does it feel?" he asked as he slapped my ass, leaving a pink version of his hand on my honey-brown butt cheek.

"I want you to go hard," I demanded through clenched teeth. "I want you to fuck me like you own this!"

Anthony dug his hands into my hair and pulled back as he continued to pump his ass rapidly into my resisting flesh. "Like this..."

"Oh, yes, baby, like that."

"I see you like it rough," he assessed.

We fucked like minxes—hot and sweaty—but I wasn't done.

Naked, we moved into his bathroom. We continued kissing as we stood on his cold, tiled floor. Deep, sloppy, passionate kisses had us both excited. He put his hands around my tiny waist and hoisted me onto his sink. I slightly parted my legs, took Anthony's bulging penis, and guided it toward my opening. I began working my hips, gyrating them until his manhood penetrated. While working my hips, I grabbed his neck and wrapped my legs around his waist. He gripped me by my rear and slowly lifted me up and down until he hit my G-spot.

"Damnnnn, this is so good," I crooned.

We went at it until we came a second time. When Anthony pulled out of me, I instinctively turned around because I wanted to do it from behind. I bent over, holding the wall for support, and reached between my legs, guiding him into me. To help ease into this position, I lifted my left leg and put it on his toilet. As we fucked, I looked over my shoulder at Anthony and moaned seductively. This drove him crazy, and he began thrusting harder. When Anthony came, he pulled out and released on my back.

I sensed he was now ready for me to leave, but I had other ideas.

"Go back in your bedroom and wait for me," I commanded as I ran into his kitchen and fumbled through his refrigerator. "Ah-ha!"

I waltzed into the room with the energy of a child. Anthony lay face down, his head buried into his pillow, snoring loudly. I smacked him hard on his firm ass, startling the tired and weary doctor.

"What's going on?" he panicked.

"Shh," I said sheepishly, covering his lips with mine and softly kissing him. "Let me wake you up."

Slowly, I poured chocolate syrup on his mushroom tip and watched the gooey liquid slide down his shaft. I looked up to see if he was into it. His smile gave me confirmation. I teased him by licking the chocolate from his pole and nibbling on his now tasty tip. His pickle-shaped penis glided in and out of my mouth, and he moaned his pleasure. I enjoyed pleasuring him and began slobbering all over it and making slurping noises. I arched my neck and opened my jaw wide to deep-throat him. He encouraged me with his moans.

"Umm, yes, baby, that feels soooo good," he murmured. "Damn, it feels good."

I went to his chocolaty jewels. I continued to jerk him off with my right hand while my mouth took in both nuts. My tongue flickered rapidly like an expert while pulling them in and out of my mouth. When Anthony started talking gibberish, I knew he was ready to release. I took him entirely into my mouth and sucked until he exploded. He erupted, and I eagerly swallowed.

"Come here…I want to taste you," Anthony murmured. "I want you to sit on my face and come in my mouth."

I moved up and assumed the position, nether region gaping open. At the same time, Anthony slid his long tongue into me as I rocked my experienced hips. His strong hands gripped my shapely thighs while I sat on his face. He couldn't believe my stamina, which only pushed him to keep up. This time, I was silent as I came.

I slid back up and lay on my back in the missionary position. I was extremely aroused as I remembered how much I enjoyed casual sex. We both lay there for long moments, contemplating our next move. When Anthony began stroking my stomach, I tensed up.

"I've got to go," I exclaimed, pulling away.

"But you just got here," he said, half asleep.

"You'll see me again."

He perked up.

"Really? When?"

"In your dreams," I sassily replied. "Goodnight, Doctor Good Dick."

"Girl, do you have any Neosporin? I got fucked something awful last night. I was pulled, ripped, split, licked…," I stated as I walked through the door of my volunteer workplace. Vanessa was making coffee, unenthused by my remark.

"Since when does Ed put it down like that?" she asked, sipping the hot French vanilla coffee.

"You don't know half of what's been going on," I replied while contemplating whether I should confide in her about me and Anthony's escapade. I didn't have anyone to talk to about how good the doctor was in bed. I couldn't talk to Anika, who would typically be my first choice to share juicy gossip. Because I knew that Anika was secretly in love with Doctor Good Dick and wouldn't understand. She just wouldn't.

"Oh, so please do tell," Vanessa encouraged, hoping to get a little piece of dirt to hold over my head. Something she could occasionally dangle to keep me grounded. Or use the dirt to kick me off my throne when I felt happy and complete with Ed.

The desperation in Vanessa's voice made the decision for me.

"Ed has always put it down. Why else would we have celebrated ten wonderful years of marriage? Did I ever tell you about how he proposed?"

"More times than I can count," Vanessa remarked dryly. And then said, "Here comes this bitch."

"Hi, Jessica," we both sang in unison.

Ignoring our greetings, Jessica randomly picked in each nostril as if she was in deep thought.

"Gracie, Human Resources called yesterday, saying that the social security number you gave is incorrect."

"Incorrect? That's been my number for thirty-nine years. There must be a misunderstanding."

"Yeah, maybe. I'm just telling you what they said."

"Well, what do they want me to do to straighten this out?"

"I'll need to follow up with a telephone call. They just left that message on our machine."

"Okay, thank you."

Before admiring my new figure, I went home that night and soaked in a long, luxurious bath. I did look just as I had when I was twenty. Doctor Good Dick was right. As I began dressing for bed, my phone rang. Hoping it was the doctor, I was slightly disappointed when Anika's name flashed across my screen. I allowed her to go to voicemail and then dialed Anthony.

"Hello?"

"Hi, this is Gracie."

"How are you?" he replied. I felt I detected a slight reservation in his voice. My mind quickly wondered which approach I'd take to ensnare him. There wasn't anyway, I only wanted him for a one-night stand. I felt that I needed to allow him to be the aggressor. Men loved the chase.

"I'm not doing too well after last night."

"Really?" his voice rose with skepticism. He sounded guarded. "I thought we had a good time."

"Well, yes…I mean, I'm so embarrassed. We were both intoxicated, and I should have never crossed the line. I'm married, happily, and I want to apologize and assure you that you don't have to worry about me telling Anika or trying to take this further. It was one time—"

"Hey, wait a minute. Do I have a say in this?"

"What are you talking about?"

"You're calling me to end something that hasn't started."

"I'm calling to apologize for what we both know was a mistake and should never happen again."

"I don't know about you, but I really want to see you again after last night. I haven't felt like that in a long time…the way you made me feel."

"I can't…I'm married—"

"Did I mention how sweet your coochie juices are," he breathed, arousing me as he spoke.

"Did you . . . did we . . . I can't remember everything. I was a bit intoxicated," I lied as my mind replayed every juicy scene.

"I *did* eat you out, and I can still taste and smell you like it was happening right now," Anthony exclaimed.

I blushed.

"Stop it," I purred.

"I can't stop it. I'm already hooked on your wet, tight pussy."

"I mean, we can't continue like this. My husband...I've never done anything like this before in my life."

"I know you're a good woman." He paused and then continued, "And I'd never do anything to jeopardize your marriage. But I can't get you out of my mind. I'll give you my word; your husband will never find out about us. I have to see you again. All you have to do is say yes. Trust me, no one will ever find out. I don't kiss and tell."

CHAPTER
9

ANTHONY CROSS

LIFE WAS FULL OF SURPRISES, BUT NOT LIKE Gracie! In all my conquests, I never would have imagined meeting Mrs. Stuck-Up in a club, taking her home, and having the best sex I've had in years. And she was good, too. Any man's dream. A perfect one-night stand. I sat in my office with my feet on my solid oak desk, contemplating last week's events. *Gracie* . . . the name surreptitiously crept through my mind repeatedly.

I heard trustworthy Anika stroll into the office, and when I came out, she was sitting there, sipping on her coffee and yapping away on her cell. Impatiently, I waited for her to hang up. Finally, she got the hint and ended her nonsense.

"Who was that?" I asked, the nosey side of me winning.

"None-ya," she replied.

"Fuck you. Listen, what's up with your friend?" A level of anticipation had developed. I tried to keep my voice monotone and casual.

"Who? What friend?"

"The married pain in the ass."

"Gracie?"

"Yeah, her."

"What do you mean, what's up with her?" she asked, and I could feel her pressure going up.

"How's she recovering?" I lied, sensing the tension.

"Oh," Anika replied, exhaling. "You can ask her yourself. She's in examination Room Two."

"Right now?" I asked, panicking. "She's not due for her final checkup until next week."

"Well, she's here early."

"I can see that."

Briefly, I wondered how I looked. Was my tie on straight, my haircut clean, did I choose the right shoes? My insecurities had me baffled. I was a don; I shouldn't be behaving this way.

"Okay," I continued, "I'm going to check on her."

"Alone? That's against the rules. I'll go with you—"

"You'll do no such thing," I insisted. "She's a friend of yours. I doubt she'll be accusing me of sexual assault. I'll have her in and out in a few minutes. I need you out front."

I tapped lightly on the door before gently pushing it in. Gracie sat conservatively on the examination table, and her stern face immediately unnerved me.

I stepped in, leaving the door slightly ajar, grabbed the chair, and positioned it right before her.

"Mrs. Lane, how are we doing today?" I formally asked her.

"Very well, doctor," she replied, and to my amazement, she parted her legs to reveal a panty-less pussy. "You've got to apologize to her for the other night."

Nervously, I looked over my shoulder.

"Really?"

"Yes, really."

"What does she want from me?" I asked, enjoying this dangerous game.

"She wants you to kiss it," she purred.

"That can be arranged," I said, immediately positioning myself before her opening invitation.

Roughly I stretched her legs open as far as they could maneuver in her form-fitting skirt. I leaned in close, placed my wet tongue on her clit, and began cunnilingus as if I were eating a peach. She stifled a moan as I licked her nether lips and started fingering her. Just as her hips began grinding, I heard someone coming. Their heavy feet galloped—*click-clack, click-clack*. Quickly I backed away from Gracie, just in time as the door swung.

My RN, Samantha, flung open the door to catch something gratuitous.

"Doctor Cross, am I late?"

"Of course not. We're early. And we're done. Mrs. Lane, you're all done."

"My pleasure."

"Likewise."

When Gracie left, Samantha whispered in a low, annoyed voice, "What's going on?!" Her porcelain complexion turned beet-red with fury.

"Get back to work!" I snapped and pushed past her. I guess

she didn't know who buttered her bread. I made a mental note that if she rechallenged me—ever—in my office—her ass was gone!

She'll be easy, I thought. The girl from the gym—damn, what was her name?—oh, yeah, Cynthia. She was coming over tonight for dinner and a Blockbuster film, or so she thought. Little did she know we'd be making our own movie. My housekeeper had already cleaned the apartment and made my favorite pan-seared salmon marinated in balsamic vinaigrette with a Caesar salad. Nothing too fancy, but it still made a statement.

After showering, I stood naked in front of my full-length mirror in my small walk-in closet. I admired my biceps and triceps and began doing my routine ego-boosting, flexing my muscles in the mirror. Next, I looked at my svelte waistline, masculine thighs, and eight-pack stomach and realized I was every woman's dream. You couldn't get any better than me.

I decided to play it casually, so I put on a pair of dark blue denim jeans, a Polo button-up shirt, and Bond No. 9 cologne. I was ready for the sexy lady.

Moments before she arrived, I added a blank tape to my bedroom's hidden video camera. This expensive, high-tech system wasn't for protection against burglars; I was a voyeur. Call me foolish, a freak, an asshole, or just plain stupid, but I've been videotaping my sexual liaisons since high school. It started out as a way to fit in. I had been going to St. John's Preparatory, a private high school in Astoria, Queens, when I started hanging out with a few students on the other side of town. These guys grew up in Baisley, a housing project where gun shootouts were everyday normalcy, and the streets were littered with drug dealers and users. In any event, it was rumored that they videotaped having sex with girls. Those same videotapes were circulating around our five boroughs. One day I was inside a small, three-bedroom home in Jamaica, Queens, with my newfound friend Mike. At eighteen, Mike was slightly older and had two girls in there from my high school, Tina and Michele. Their faces weren't anything to talk about, but they both had bodies that would rival most women.

Before they'd arrived, Mike took me to the bedroom and showed me the hidden video camera. I was excited and scared at the same time but played it off like I was cool with it. All I kept thinking about was getting busted and what my parents would think. However, we didn't get caught. We all fucked clumsily and fast as we experienced our first orgy. When the two girls left, we watched the tape repeatedly, cracking jokes and pointing out the highlights. The thrill and adrenaline high that secretly videotaping the girls gave me has carried over into my adult life. I still get the same rush that I'd gotten back then. Have I ever considered telling my sexual encounters that I want to tape them? Nope. The pleasure comes from each woman being unaware of what's going down. I didn't need anyone playing up for the camera, only wanting to be filmed on the right side because they felt their left wasn't as attractive. Any nonsense like that would take away from the raw, uncut footage. Even though what I did was wrong, I never have—and won't ever—share my tapes with anyone. They were my personal stash, and I kept them under lock and key.

Just as I slammed the camera shut, the front desk called.

"Doctor Cross, you have a Ms. Cynthia Rowley here to see you."

"Please send her up," I replied.

Cynthia came sauntering in, wearing fuck-me pumps, and her skimpy, cheap dress barely covered her plump ass, not to mention her boobs, which were oozing out. The six-inch stilettos and dress were hardly proper for a dinner date, but who was I to complain? She came here knowing what she wanted. I must admit that I was a little shocked, though. Her nighttime attire was quite different from her daywear.

"Hey, babe," I said as if we'd known each other forever. "You look great."

"Thank you," she replied. "I wanted to look good for you."

"You did all this for me?" I complimented her while grabbing both her hands in mine.

$$\infty$$

Later, after dinner, we sat in the living room to watch the movie. Being presumptuous, I thought we'd only watch the first ten minutes before engaging in sweaty sex. But to my surprise, our small talk turned into a long, stimulating conversation.

"I had no idea you were a lawyer," I said, not allowing my voice to mask my surprise.

"Why do you sound so shocked?" she asked.

"Actually, I really don't know."

"Well, you're not the only one who seems stumped once they ask my occupation. Truthfully, being a lawyer was my destiny. When I was eleven, my brother, Richard, was falsely accused and convicted of rape. He was sentenced to twenty-five years to life in a maximum-security prison. My family had no money, so he had an overworked and underpaid public defender. Most importantly, the attorney believed that my brother was guilty."

"Did you ever question his innocence?" I asked.

"Never!" she replied defiantly.

"What about your parents?"

"We *knew* he was innocent. I still remember sitting in the courtroom when the verdict was read. Three corrections officers huddled around him in anticipation of the guilty verdict. When the judge asked him to stand, and the guilty verdict was read, I still remember the look in his eyes as he turned around and told my mother not to worry about him. Can you imagine being sentenced to spend the rest of your natural life in prison at only twenty years old? And you tell your family not to worry about you?"

She was so passionate as she spoke about her brother. You could sense that it was an intimate matter that still troubled her.

"Anyway, in my first year at law school, I wrote to the Innocence Project about my brother's case. I told the organization that DNA testing wasn't yet developed when my brother was convicted. Not only did the Innocence Project agree to take on my brother's case, but the attorney working on his defense allowed me to help. My brother was freed four years ago and now lives a productive life."

"That's quite a story," I told her as I refilled her wine glass.

"Enough about me. Tell me more about you."

"Well," I said softly, kissing her lips, "I like to party like a rock star." We both laughed, and then I continued. "I basically got a secure career, no kids, no wife—"

"What about a girlfriend?" she asked.

"None of those."

"Are you a womanizer?"

"My girlfriend and I broke up."

"I'm sorry to hear that," she lied. "Was it recently?"

Good lawyering, lawyer, I thought, *making sure you're not a rebound.*

"A little over a year."

"Was it serious?" she probed, and I got turned off. I didn't want a deep conversation, especially about a phantom ex-girlfriend.

"I'm over her. It's all about you now," I said, and she melted. I leaned in, kissed her neck, and led her to my bedroom. I stood behind her and slowly slid her dress over her head. Maybe I did it too slowly because she took this as a sign to unclasp her bra. Her large breasts fell into my hands as I nestled behind her. I pressed my manhood against her lower back, and she began to grind slowly, making my penis grow. She turned around to face me. I bent down and began to lick and suck her pink nipples. I paused for a minute to admire her hot pink areolas.

"You have perfect breasts," I whispered and continued to suck on her nipples.

We went to my bed and playfully fell on it, my body resting on hers. I removed my jeans and boxers, slowly slid off her panties, pushed two fingers inside her wet cave, and twirled. Warm juices seeped onto my fingers, and we both got excited.

"Play with yourself while I watch."

She began masturbating on my king-sized bed. Her fingers penetrated her cave feverishly while simultaneously massaging her ample breasts. She continued moaning sexily and chanting my name.

"Anthony, you feel sooo good," she crooned as she ground her hips into her fingers. "I love your big cock!"

I almost went limp when this Black female said *cock,* but I revived it and decided to get on with the deed.

I stood over her and began to jerk off on her chest. I released myself everywhere, and she wasn't even embarrassed. She started moaning even louder. The kinkiness of the moment was sexually gratifying.

I slid on my Magnum and then slid inside her with ease. It was too easy! And I prided myself on being a big guy with a big package. What was this world coming to? After several deep thrusts, I contemplated changing condoms and taking a chance on her to let me enter her from the back, but I was turned off. I pretended to come, which was a first for me, and collapsed on my bed, burying my face in my pillow from frustration.

Visions of Gracie kept going through my head. Sexy, freaky, uninhibited Gracie.

"That was good, right, baby?" she asked.

"No."

"I said that was good, right?" she repeated, perplexed.

"I heard you, and you heard me."

"Seriously?"

"Have you ever thought about having labiaplasty?"

"What? What are you talking about?"

"It's a cosmetic procedure that tightens your vaginal walls so that there will be more friction for your partner. It's a non-evasive procedu—"

"You're an asshole!" she screamed as she leaped from my bed. She put her hooker clothes back on quickly and was gone in sixty seconds.

Jeez, what a waste of a good meal, I thought as I hopped up and hit rewind on the tape. I needed an instant replay of her facial expression when she called me an asshole.

The following Sunday, Chris and Gabriel came over to watch the game. It was supposed to be just a guy's day in, but I had other plans. Gabriel was tight-lipped about his power moves, and I intended to pry them out of him. Chris came to the party fully loaded with Heineken, pizza, chips, and cocaine. Personally, I didn't do drugs, but Chris occasionally indulged. He was his own man. I gave him my opinion about his drug use one time too many a few years back, and he went berserk. He was coked up, had the energy of a bull, and wanted nothing less than a street brawl. His first punch caught me in my left jaw, and I whipped his ass. But that one lucky punch he landed knocked the sense in me that I needed to mind my own business. Since then, we've had an unspoken understanding.

As we gulped down beer and got hyped from the game, I sporadically took sneak peeks at Chris. He had a platter of uncut, pure cocaine, a razor blade, and determination in his eyes. As early as a year ago, Chris would do three-inch lines. Now, he's superseded his previous limit and has cut four lines at least twelve inches in diameter. He was officially out of control. At first, I thought that Gabriel didn't indulge since Chris had been at it for almost an hour, and Gabriel, like I, had only watched. But soon enough, Chris passed the plate to Gabriel, and he held one nostril closed while inhaling the powdery, white substance with the other.

The game was over, but those two were like glassy-eyed zombies sprawled on my sofa. They looked like two pimps. Both had three-piece suits, but Chris sported a fedora hat, and Gabriel rocked a pair of pink alligator shoes. Ten years ago, the pink alligator shoes would have been on-trend during the Gianni Versace era. Now they just looked gay.

Chris was obviously heavily influenced by Gabriel. I could see that in his new wardrobe and demeanor. He was a one-dimensional, jean-and-boot type of guy, so it surprised me to see him in wing-tip shoes and tailored suits.

I took this opportunity to crack on the information I so desperately wanted. Financially, I knew that I would be well off in five years. My practice will continue to get a steady clientele, and I'm confident I'll have a household name. In fact, I'd hired a publicist and entertainment manager to pitch a reality show to Lifetime, VH-1, and BET, following me and my growing practice. I wanted to be the Black Dr. 90210. But until my big break, I needed to steadily build my practice and make wise investments to support my lifestyle and repay my student loans.

"Gabriel, Chris told me about this top-secret investment deal you're putting together."

Before answering, he sucked on his teeth and dug in his left ear; his eyes rolled back in his head like he was about to orgasm. The scene was annoying. Finally, he answered.

"Yeah, that deals a win-win."

"I thought there wasn't any such thing?"

"You've been socializing with the wrong people."

I laughed a superficial snicker.

"Yeah, I guess you're right. Tell me about what you're working on."

"Anthony, let me find out—" Chris sniffed, "that you're trying to get in on this deal."

"Nah, I'm just asking questions. What's wrong with that?" I asked, pretending the moment was innocent.

"He just wants to be informed, that's all," Gabriel said in my defense. "Chris, if I didn't know any better, I'd think you were trying to keep your man in the dark and make all the money without putting him on."

"Yeah, put me on!" I cosigned.

"Don't you have enough money?" Chris sneered.

I was caught off guard by Chris's demeanor. He was a bail guarantor, owned his own company, and made quite a lot of money. The only thing was he didn't know how to manage it. He splurged on unnecessary things, I guess. What? I don't know. He didn't have a car, didn't have a steady girlfriend, and didn't buy expensive clothing, but again, he just didn't manage his money right.

"C'mon, man, you can never have enough money. I may want in!"

"Well, it's like this: I got this deal I put together where you'll get a 20 percent return on your investment within thirty days. The minimum you'll need to get in is $20,000, and there isn't a max."

Skeptically, I listened.

"United Oil International Liberty is an investment that allows you to buy in at $10,000 per unit. Within the first 30 days of your initial investment, you'll see a 20 percent return. I can have my lawyer forward you copies of our periodic letters and brochures outlining the proceeds from the oil and gas properties. In-depth, he'll explain the prospectus regarding United Oil International Liberty acquiring rights in various oil and gas-producing properties in Missouri, Texas, Louisiana, Oklahoma, Mississippi, and Belize."

As Gabriel explained how I would gain from my investment,

I thought about how much I would invest when he answered that question.

"If you want in, I'll need your cashier's check before next Friday. Also, I don't know how much liquid you have, but you can't come in on more than the $20,000."

"That's it?" I asked.

"Yes."

"But you said that there wasn't a maximum."

"Had you gotten in earlier, there wouldn't be a maximum, but you're the last one, and there's only room for that investment."

Twenty-thousand dollars was hardly a significant investment. I could lose that in one minute in the temperamental stock market. They teach you to invest only what you're prepared to lose. Meaning, don't invest your mortgage money. At the moment, I didn't have "fuck you" funds. I wasn't anywhere near broke, but I was on a budget. I had a lot to take into consideration. My practice employed eleven people who garnered large paychecks, not to mention the building lease and all the amenities it takes to run an office of that size. And what about my lifestyle? I had purchased a 1300 square foot Upper Eastside apartment with a hefty price tag. And my maintenance fee was obscene. Even though I had liquid assets, one false move could bring me under. Truthfully, I did have a small amount of money that I could risk if my investment went sour because the flip side is that it could pay off. I decided to sit this one out and research Gabriel and his company. I didn't quite trust him, his expensive suits and flashy lifestyle.

Yes, I'll sit on the sideline and watch how Chris's situation unfolds.

CHAPTER
10

GRACIE LANE

THAT NIGHT, ANTHONY INVITED ME TO A quaint, romantic restaurant where I wouldn't fear getting caught by one of my husband's colleagues. When I asked him where he was taking me, he was vague. I guess he wanted me to be surprised.

"Gracieeeee," Tamara called out. The mere sound of her voice almost swayed my mood.

"What is it?" I snapped.

"Anika's on the phone!" Tamara obviously detected the annoyance in my voice. Hurriedly, I walked over to my home phone just to make sure everything was all right with Anika.

"Hey, are you all right?"

"Yeah, why you ask that?"

"Because you're calling the house phone. You usually call my cell first."

"I did, but it kept going straight to voicemail."

"Really? That's odd." I was only half-listening. I was checking out my curves in the mirror.

"So, what's up for tonight? What are you doing?"

If you only knew...I thought. *You wouldn't like it...*

"I'm going out with a few women from my job."

"Thank you for not inviting me," she laughed. "Okay, really quickly, and then I'll let you go. What do you think of him?"

"Him?"

"Anthony...my future husband." Her words stung.

"Umm, well, I guess he's all right. A little insufferable, though. I can't see how you can stand to work around him. He seems as if he's in the mirror all day."

"Yup, that's Anthony."

"And he seems chauvinistic, not to mention a womanizer—"

"A womanizer? Why would you say that? Did he make a pass at you?" Her voice had elevated as she panicked.

"Of course, he didn't. He knows we're friends. He just seems as if he has a lot of acquaintances. He's successful, in his early thirties, and not married. That's a combination of a womanizer." I hoped my explanation would suffice.

"Gracie, he's not a womanizer. He's just trying to find the right woman. He's so sweet and funny and cute. I have the biggest crush—"

"Anika, sweetheart, I must run. I have people waiting for me. I'll call you tomorrow."

"Oh, okay. Have a good night."

"You do the same."

I heard Anika talk longingly about Anthony numerous times, but tonight it felt strange. I hadn't met him before, and we hadn't been intimate. I feel so sneaky and low and a little sorry for her being in love with someone who doesn't want her. If I knew one thing, I knew Anika could never find out about me and Anthony's affair.

I slipped on the same Diane von Furstenberg black dress I'd worn to my husband's anniversary dinner. And a pair of sexier high heels with black leather straps. I stood back to see my reflection in the mirror. I looked regal. I applied a little foundation, gold eye shadow, Christian Dior copper lip gloss and was pleased with the result.

I looked alluring in my all-black get-up but felt something was missing. I walked to my dresser, opened my jewelry box, and pulled out a beautiful brooch Ed had given me for our eighth wedding anniversary. It was gold-plated with faux ruby and emerald stones. I adorned my small wrist with an eight-carat diamond tennis bracelet and five-carat, emerald-cut diamond earrings my late husband, Phillip, had bought to compliment the costume brooch. I told Ed I was invited to have dinner with Vanessa to celebrate her 40th birthday. And Tamara felt that she needed an explanation as well.

"Going somewhere…again?" Tamara's voice dripped sarcasm as she watched me put on my finishing touches of makeup.

Ignoring her sarcasm, I decided to be on the offensive. As I puckered my pouty lips and dabbed on another layer of lip gloss, I casually replied, "You're still living here?"

Tamara gave me a once-over. "And she's wearing her *one* good dress…I hope he's worth it."

"Perhaps you should wear your *one* good dress and go out as well…oh, I forgot, you have no friends."

Tamara knew I could buy a million of these dresses if I wanted, but what frustrated her most was that I didn't. She couldn't understand how I chose to spend my money. It annoyed her that I shopped at Target or Wal-Mart and cut coupons on the weekends. She didn't know how I amassed my fortune, and I didn't tell her because it wasn't her business. I didn't need to tell her that before I married rich, I lived off Ramen noodles and pizza, so I knew how it felt to not have any money, and I wasn't ever going back to that lifestyle. Now, I live off the interest of the money I have in the bank. My late husband was a financial guru. But it's not like I had the business savvy to continue to pull in multi-million-dollar mega-deals when he unexpectedly died. I hired a financial advisor, invested a lot of the money into conservative mutual funds, and began volunteering.

I grabbed my Hermés purse and pushed past Tamara, leaving her scowling in the hallway.

The Buddha Bar restaurant was upscale and cozy. I decided to bite my tongue because I'd been here with and without my husband several times. Its earth-tone colors beset the giant, gold-plated Buddha statues. High-back, eloquent chairs with round tables, substantial tropical plants, and brick stucco were on the walls. Anthony led the way through the crowd, and I followed close behind, one leg extending after the other with the grace of a panther. My hips swayed one way, my head the other.

We were led to the V.I.P. area in the far-right wing of the restaurant.

"Take your pick. You can choose any table you'd like," Anthony boasted. He had paid to have the whole area for only us.

I beamed. "Then I choose this one right here."

Our table could easily have seated fifteen people. When I looked down underneath the table, I pretended to be surprised by the aquarium. The clear blue water was bursting with exotic fish. You could literally look down and see fish swimming under your feet.

"Oh my gosh, how spectacular," I squealed.

"Yes, it is. If you want, I could have the owner open it up, and you can dip your feet in the water."

"Really?"

"Yes, really."

I thought for a moment. "Nice gesture, but I think I'll pass."

Anthony couldn't take his eyes off me. "You look absolutely stunning."

"Thank you."

His eyes zeroed in on my jewelry. "That's an impressive bracelet. Let me see it."

His firm, masculine hands quickly grabbed my wrist and began to inspect my trinket.

"And those earrings...wow."

I snatched my wrist back. "Thank you."

"Those are..." his voice trailed off.

"Real?"

"Are they?"

"Of course."

He nodded. "A gift?"

"From my husband."

"Really? I thought he worked for Verizon."

"How would you know that?" I asked, annoyed for two reasons: One, he was prying into my personal life, and two, Anika was running her mouth about my situation, and she should have known better.

"Oh, I think you mentioned it."

"No, I didn't." My voice was stern and unwavering. Anthony looked away, and I sensed he wanted to change the subject. He cleared his throat, hoping to cut the tension that had built up.

Suddenly, I thought I spotted Ed's supervisor, Michael, at a table. He was having a conversation with a woman. It looked as if she had asked him something, and then he leaned in close and kissed her.

My heartbeat accelerated, and my palms began to sweat. This always happened when I was nervous. As I continued to stare intently, I could see that it wasn't my husband's boss after all, and I was immediately relieved.

The candle in the middle of the table flickered playfully and cast a golden, seductive light upon Anthony's face. I thought he looked picture-perfect.

"How was your day?" he asked. He took my hand and snugly placed it in between his.

"It was pleasant enough. Nothing to discuss. And yours?"

"It's always a good day for me when there aren't any complications during my surgeries. Other than that, it was all pretty much humdrum."

"I guess you haven't read the newspaper?" I asked.

"Was I supposed to?"

"Well, when you're in it, you should."

"I was in the papers today?"

"Don't act like you didn't have a clue," I teased.

"I honestly didn't. What did they say? How I'm the number-one, most sought-after bachelor in New York?" he asked cockily.

"Nooo!" I laughed. "There were two sentences on the *Page Six* column of the *New York Post,* saying that you're about to be a father."

His expression turned to stone.

"Are you serious?"

"As a terrorist attack."

"Jeez, where do they get this information?" His annoyed tone complemented the sudden fuchsia tones in his dark complexion.

"Who cares? It's free publicity."

"I guess you're right," he replied. "But it's not true."

"If it were, it wouldn't change anything with our arrangement. Well, at least not for me, it wouldn't."

Changing the subject, Anthony asked, "I'm glad you could get away tonight. I really wanted to see you. How were you able to sneak away?"

"Ed's at a fundraiser tonight, so I told him I was having dinner with the girls."

He looked deep into my eyes and then stuck his index finger into my dimpled smile.

"You have the cutest smile."

"Of course, I do. I'm an eleven, remember?"

He laughed, "Right, right...the day of your surgery...you remembered."

"My memory's long."

"I hate to be the bearer of bad news, but I was lying!"

Playfully, I punched him on his shoulder. "You were not."

"No, I wasn't. You're that and more." He leaned in and gave me a soft kiss on my lips. "Tell me about yourself."

I tensed up.

"Not much to tell."

"What was your childhood like?"

"It was okay." I looked away, detached.

"What about your parents? Do you have any siblings?"

"Really, my life isn't worth your time. How about you tell me about you and your parents? Any siblings? How did you decide to go into cosmetic surgery? I haven't met too many Black plastic surgeons."

"Who you kidding? You haven't met *any*," he joked. "But to answer your questions, my childhood was great. No siblings. My father is an open-heart surgeon, and my mother was a stay-at-home parent. My parents have old-fashioned values, and I really had a wonderful upbringing."

"Really? No skeletons in your family's closet? Daddy didn't get caught fucking the nanny?"

"Of course, he did." Anthony laughed. "But the nanny was my mother."

"You really did have a great childhood."

"Yeah, so being close to my father and admiring him for years, I knew I'd follow in his footsteps, and my parents couldn't be more pleased. The only thing left is getting married and having a family."

"How close are you to that goal? Anyone special in your life?"

"Gracie, I'll answer in a moment. Our *maître's d* is here. May I take the liberty of ordering for you?"

"Please do." I loved his take-charge attitude. It was a turn-on.

"For our appetizers, I'll have steamed oysters, and she'll have sashimi. Our main course will be the Atlantic bluefin tuna for me, and the lady will have the Peking duck smothered in caviar. The lady will have the Madeleine truffle for dessert, and I'll have the Golden Plum Soufflé. Please bring us a bottle of Pinot Noir. That'll be all, thank you." The *maîtres' d* left, and we continued our conversation.

"How did you know I'd like sushi and caviar?" I asked, grinning.

"There's something edgy about you," he commented, giving me a sly wink. "Yeah, so back to kids and family. To answer your question, no, I don't have anyone special. I was involved with a young woman, maybe too young, and it didn't work out."

"How young is too young?" I asked and raised a skeptical eyebrow.

"She was legal." Anthony laughed. "I'm talking about mentally. She's twenty-four, but her antics and childish behavior ruined the relationship. I had to let her go. I had no choice."

"Did you give her a chance? To grow?"

"I did what I could to make it work, but it didn't. Don't get me wrong, she's a beautiful, smart woman, but we grew apart."

"I'm not judging you, but I find that what people don't realize but making a relationship work is just that—work. Things don't just magically fix themselves. You must put as much care, time, and determination into relationships as you put into your practice. If you want a wife and family, perhaps you should reevaluate your relationship with your baby-momma." I giggled, making Anthony giggle, taking the sting off what sounded like a lecture.

"I want you to be my baby momma," he said, pulling me close for a passionate kiss. His soft lips lulled me in, and I didn't want to let go. I pulled back first and glanced around the room.

He continued. "What about you? Staying married forever?"

I wondered how to handle this question or why he was asking it. At this point, I didn't see a need to deceive him. I'd already gotten what I wanted and only wanted more if he was a willing participant in my adulterous affair.

"Till the end," I stated. Anthony shook his head as if he understood, but his next question caught me off guard.

"Don't you think situations such as these—you know, affairs—could jeopardize that?"

See, this is why I can't be straight up with motherfuckers, I thought. *They always have to start judging. My first mistake was allowing the affair to go further than the bedroom.*

"I didn't plan for this . . . you . . . but there's something about you that I couldn't just walk away from. It was like we had this connection. It felt kinetic and pulled me directly to you. As I told you before, I've never done something like this with anyone else, but meeting and sleeping with you doesn't negate that I'm married."

"If anyone understands, I do. Trust me," Anthony replied.

After having a delicious meal, I thought about Ed. My hubby loves the steak here. I called the *maîtres' d* back over and ordered him a full meal.

Anthony huffed, "Who are you ordering the steak for?"

"Me. Since you took the liberty of ordering my dinner, I couldn't get what I wanted. I wanted the steak, and that's what I'm going to have," I replied dismissively.

When the check came, I offered to pay it, and Anthony looked insulted.

"Well, do you want to split the bill?" I asked, further infuriating the doctor.

"Listen, I'm a man, and I asked you out. That means I pick up the tabs. If you haven't noticed, I own a multi-million-dollar practice." He whipped out his platinum American Express Card. "I can afford to drop three hundred on dinner."

I relented and inwardly laughed at the ego-driven doctor who owned his "multi-million-dollar practice."

Anthony walked me to my car, and I kissed him. In my driver's seat, he knelt between my legs and began to let his hand slide between my thighs. He wanted me to follow him home, but then my husband called.

"Hey, babe." My voice was jovial, hiding the underlying deception that was happening. "I'm on my way home now...we had a great time...Yeah, well, you know Vanessa, always wanting to be praised...I'll see you in 30 minutes...love you, too." I hung up. "I've got to go."

"No. Come home with me. Call him back and tell him you're staying with your girlfriends."

"I can't. I have to go."

"Come on, don't go. Please," Anthony begged. "I want you. Let's drive away together."

"I can't. My husband's waiting." I shoved Anthony, abruptly closed my car door, and damn near ran him over to get out of the parking lot. I didn't care if my behavior didn't sit well with him. If I say I must go, it is what it is.

My phone rang.

"Yes."

"What was that all about?" Anthony was pissed.

"Huh?"

"You could have killed me rushing off like that."

"I think you're being a bit melodramatic, don't you think?"

"No, I don't think!" He was still yelling in my ear like a crazy person. "I asked you to stay."

Calmly, I replied, "And I said no."

"Listen, I'm a busy man, and if I take the time to take you out to an expensive restaurant, the night shouldn't end with you running off to be with another man."

"The other man's my husband, who will always come first! This isn't a seduction playing out here. You don't have to woo me to fuck me. I thought that was understood. I couldn't care less about eating at five-star restaurants, nor am I impressed. Didn't I offer to pay the bill? Perhaps that would have taken away a little of your hostility."

He laughed maniacally. "One thing I hate is a wannabe. I know you don't work and sit home watching soap operas all day and that your little hubby maintains the household with his little Verizon job. But you're disillusioned with your fake brooch, fake diamond bracelet, fake earrings, and fake diva personality. My money's long, Mrs. Lane. And I was doing you and your hubby a favor by not embarrassing you at dinner tonight by allowing you to pick up the check. What your husband makes in a year, I make in two weeks!"

I chuckled at the rude, self-centered man with his reckless mouth. He was pissed. Obviously, he wasn't used to women rushing off to leave him. I guess they were always begging to stay. The good thing is that Anika didn't tell him my whole situation. He must have only gotten bits and pieces. From what I could tell, he thought that I was broke. Funny. In fact, hilarious. If he only knew....

While he was screaming, I calmly pressed END on my phone and shut it off. I didn't tolerate such nonsense. Especially from a histress. Didn't he know his place?

CHAPTER

11

ANTHONY CROSS

EIGHT MESSAGES WERE LEFT ON MY HOME answering machine—all from women—but not one from Gracie. Last night when I heard a dial tone, I wanted to give her the benefit of my doubt and thought that maybe my cellular service had dropped my call. When I called back—numerous times—only to go to voicemail, I knew she'd hung up on me. In short, I felt very disrespected. Usually, I have been blessed with the ability to totally erase something or someone from my life. I expected it would be the same with her, but I missed her. I missed the disrespectful, rude, condescending, cheating bitch! And she was all those things. For Christ's sake, she's cheating on her husband. But why? Why did I miss her? Why did I want her so badly?

I couldn't understand how she could be so determined to rush home last night. Didn't she realize I was a man with pride, and I had swallowed it last night and practically begged her to stay with me? And that's something I didn't do. Something I never had to do.

It was nearing 10 a.m. on a frigid Saturday morning, and I was headed to my parent's house a few blocks from my residence. I wore a sweat suit and a NY Mets hat and was off. A nagging feeling that I couldn't shake kept riding me. I didn't want to admit it, but I was annoyed that after I asked Gracie to stay, she'd left anyway. As if to say that her husband was more important. I mean, theoretically, she was only a fuck buddy. That was a given. But I was still Doctor Anthony Cross, and there wasn't a woman walking this earth that I couldn't have. My terms. My time. My rules.

A cold, biting rain started falling, and I still had a few blocks left. Instead of hopping in a taxi, I decided to tough it out. When I got to the building, I was soaked. I ran up the twenty flights of steps, something I always did, and pounded on the door. My father opened it and greeted me with a warm, crooked smile.

"Hey, Pops," I said, giving him a firm handshake. My father didn't believe in a warm hug or tight embrace between men. "Where's Momma?"

"She's in her room with Shelby."

Shelby was my mother's nurse and my father's mistress, something he'd never admit. My mother had Alzheimer's disease and was diagnosed three years ago. I still hadn't gotten up the courage to tell my friends. All they knew was my textbook answers: "My parents are great, my childhood was great, everything was great." I peered in and could tell Shelby was preparing to bathe my mother. I backpedaled and went into my father's study. It was a reasonably large room with an enormous mahogany desk and four flat-screen televisions, all programmed on different channels: MSNBC, CNN, Bloomberg Television, and NY 1 News. He had a custom floor-to-ceiling bookshelf littered with most books he and I read. That's how I would spend quality time with him as a child: I would sit in his office and read his book collection.

When I walked in, my father was pouring himself a stiff drink: gin and tonic, no ice.

"Drink?"

"Pops, it's ten o'clock in the morning."

"Is it really? I had no idea…" he teased.

I smiled. "Sure, why not. You only live once."

As we sat there sipping on our strong drinks, my childhood flashed before me. "How's Mom doing? I mean, really?"

"Well, some days are good; others are not so good. Shelby takes excellent care of her, though."

"About Shelby—"

"What about her?" he asked defensively.

"Do you think having your mistress look after your wife is a good idea? You don't know what she's doing to Mom while you're at work! She could be pinching, slapping, starving, or plotting to kill her!"

As I said the obvious, my voice began to rise.

"Did I ever tell you I was having an affair with Shelby?" My father asked.

"No."

"When you turned eighteen, what did I tell you about marriage?"

"C'mon, Pops, we've been down this road a million times."

"I told you not to do it until you were at least forty years old and had slept through almost everything walking."

"Yes, yes, I know."

"I married your mother when I was twenty years old and inexperienced. We both said we were in it for life, and I meant that. I meant that until I was working late one night and met Rita. Over the years, there would be many Rita's, but I never allowed any of them to cloud my judgment. I've said all of that to say that I would never, ever put your mother in harm's way or disrespect her by having my mistress be her caretaker. Your mother has given me her whole life and has always been the only one for me. And it pains me that she got sick when I realized that my womanizing ways could have destroyed us, and I finally got my cheating out of my system. I think I'm being punished. These are supposed to be our best years, and I have to live them without her. I'm not thinking about any other woman other than your mother. I'm tired. I don't have the energy."

Sitting there listening to my father helped me better understand myself. We both sat around, showing my mother old pictures from our family album, but she remembered nothing. My time at my parents' house was uplifting because I always felt loved. When I returned to my apartment, I realized Gracie still hadn't called. Then I felt silly. Why couldn't I call her? We had a little situation, but it shouldn't be anything that I couldn't get over. We were adults, and I didn't want her to be my wife. She just fulfilled something that, at the moment, was void. Besides, by next week I'll probably already be bored with her.

She picked up on the second ring, "Hey, Gracie...how are you?"

"I'm doing well. What a nice surprise," Gracie replied. She seemed a little distracted, and I heard a lot of noise in the background. I wondered if her husband was close by.

"Is now a good time?"

"Well, yes and no. I'm at work and can talk until my supervisor comes through the door."

"I didn't know you worked."

"Obviously."

"About the other night—"

"Don't mention it."

"Well, I was thinking about getting tickets to a jazz boat ride that docks at Chelsea Pier, and I wanted to know if you wanted to go?"

"Sounds cool. When?"

"Tonight? Around six?"

"Can't. I'm working all evening. I'm helping to throw a party, and I'm so excited about it. Do you want me to see if I could get away tonight and come by your place for an hour or so? How's your stamina...been eating your Wheaties?"

This was truly only a sex thing for her. I changed the subject. "Where do you work?"

"On Long Island."

"Where?"

"Like, the address?"

"Yes."

"Why?"

"Because I asked."

"I'll text it to you. I've got to go."

Five minutes later, I got the text with Gracie's work address and was headed back out the door. I taxied to Bloomingdale's on 59th Street and shopped for my new lady. After perusing a plethora of high-end designers, I finally settled on a fantastic Badgley Mischka backless dress and headed to the shoe department. I wanted to buy a pair of black stiletto Prada shoes that went perfectly with the dress, but the sales associate said they were cut small. She also warned me against buying Chanel for my mystery "friend." She said I would be safe with Gucci or Ferragamo, but I settled on a great pair of Marc Jacob strappy heels, but I couldn't stop there. There was a matching clutch purse.

I didn't purchase anything for myself and felt satisfied leaving with a bag full of things for Gracie. When I got home, I left the package with my doorman to send FedEx overnight priority to arrive on Monday. I left Gracie's work address and a small note: WEAR THIS NEXT SATURDAY...OR WEAR NOTHING. A.C. Next week, I planned to take Gracie on the jazz cruise, and I couldn't wait to see how her curves would fill out in that dress.

CHAPTER
12

MY WORST NIGHTMARE

IN A PITCH-BLACK LIVING ROOM SAT AN IRATE man. His expansive home on the Upper Eastside seemed to swallow him. In a moment, he thought he'd snap and lose it. His once-attentive wife had begun to ignore his needs and came home at odd hours without solid excuses. He realized that these were signs of an affair. The mere thought made him recoil.

Ed sat in the dark in his favorite chair this evening, drinking his favorite wine. He wanted answers. Deep down, he knew he'd believe whatever explanation she'd give, just as long as she looked into his eyes when she spoke. But the mere thought that she wouldn't look into his eyes had him feeling insecure.

One hour after Gracie was due home from work, she walked into the dimly lit living room. She squinted through the darkness and steadied her eyes on the chaos. The once-tidy house was in disarray. Clothes were casually thrown across the sofa. Instead of being ironed, folded, and put away, a basket of clean laundry sat off to the side near the laundry room. Dirty glasses rested on top of the mantle. Even Ed had to admit his sister was a slob. Perhaps he was one as well. But he wouldn't know because Gracie usually kept their home immaculate with the assistance of their housekeeper, Elana, who came twice a week.

As soon as Gracie clicked on the light, she flipped.

"I volunteer my services all day, almost every day, and I have to come home to this?" Gracie yelled.

"Where have you been?" Ed prodded.

"Where is she? Tamara?" Gracie asked, ignoring Ed's question.

"She went to the movies."

"Movies? With what money? Oh, yeah, she has plenty of money because she's mooching off our stupid asses. Or shall I say my stupid ass!" She glared at her husband.

"I don't want to discuss Tamara," he replied in a low, throaty whisper. "Where have you been?"

It was at that moment that Gracie realized something was up. Something was wrong. Her husband's short, two-stranded twists needed a shape-up. His eyes looked withdrawn and puffy, and he was sporting, to her dismay, a five o'clock shadow that needed to be shaved. Ed needed to be groomed because he looked a hot mess like he'd aged ten years.

"I was working, something your sister doesn't know about," she said, challenging Ed to dismiss her again.

"Didn't I just say I didn't want to discuss my sister!" he roared, and Gracie thought the mantle mirror shook.

"Who are you yelling at?!" she barked back. Not waiting for a response, she screamed, "Get the groceries from the lobby! And fuck you while you're at it."

Realizing that he'd just made a fool out of himself, Ed hopped up and quickly dashed downstairs to the front desk, gathered up the groceries, and brought them inside. Gracie immediately began making dinner. He stood back and looked at his beautiful wife. She was gorgeous, could have any man she wanted, kept a clean home, always cooked his dinner and snacks no matter how late or early he asked to be fed, and she always made love to him and made love very well. But most importantly, to his knowledge, she'd been faithful for their entire marriage, as was he. They both seemed to have old-fashioned values. He knew he'd divorce her without any regrets if he ever found out Gracie was cheating on him. He hoped that he hadn't been taking her for granted.

As Gracie diced red, yellow, and green peppers like a professional chef, Ed walked up behind her, embraced her around her now-tiny waistline, and nuzzled her neck.

"I'm sorry, baby, for raising my voice."

"You should be, and it better not happen again." Gracie puckered up her lips and gave him a quick kiss. "Why are you so uptight? Did you have a bad day at work?" As she spoke, she tossed the peppers into the waiting frying pan and began to sauté them in olive oil. She was making stir-fried shrimp and brown rice. It was quick, healthy, and easy to cook.

"No, I didn't. Work is great, but I need to ask you something." Ed waited until his wife turned around to face him. She knew what he was about to say before he'd said it. "Why are you keeping inconsistent hours lately?"

"What are you talking about?" Her face and voice appeared to be clueless about his implication.

"Lately, you've been coming home at dawn from a night of

partying and hours late after work. I've been going to voicemail on your cell more than normal, and you don't want to make love." Ed couldn't disguise his hurt and insecurities.

Gracie ruminated about how she'd answer his line of questioning. "Are you suggesting I'm having an affair?"

"Are you?" he asked blatantly.

"Ed, I love you."

"Are you having an affair, Gracie?" He stood stone still, staring directly into her eyes. She returned his stare.

"No," she said in an unwavering voice. She continued to cook. "I would never—could never—jeopardize our marriage. We took vows…, and I love you more than I love life. How could you think such a thing?"

Ed waited for a long moment before he shut off the stove.

"What are you doing?" she asked.

He didn't reply. He passionately kissed Gracie's lips and walked her to the sofa.

He sat on the couch and positioned Gracie between his legs. Gently he reached up and removed her shirt. It glided down her shoulders and cascaded to the floor. The spaghetti straps on her bra were the next to go. As his strong, masculine hands slid her clothing to the floor. Gracie watched Ed's glistening eyes as he looked past her breasts, then lingered on her flat stomach, and finally on her perfect, pedicured feet. Her flaming red hooker toenail polish was turning him on. He knew he'd married a freak, but until recently, he figured she was *only* his freak.

Ed put both hands on her hips and guided her to lie on the sofa. Neither one of them knew or cared when Tamara would come barging in. Ed had to satisfy his uncertainty that his wife might have been with someone else. Gracie just wanted to be satisfied.

Ed entered her with slow, firm strokes. His manhood assertively opened her up as he applied controlled pressure. Ed sunk deeper, lower, completely into his wife and did a slow grind that drove Gracie crazy. He teased her for a minute. Rocking his tip in and out until she was overcome with mind-blowing waves of pleasure spiraling through her body. Ed's strong pelvis rocked back and forth, keeping a steady rhythm. As he gently made love to her, he whispered sweet words in her ear.

"Is it good?" he asked.

"It's perfect," she said, her voice barely a whisper.

His broad shoulders and firm pecs covered her breasts and flat stomach. Tenderly he pulled out of her, separated her legs, and began kissing and sucking her inner thighs in circular motions, slowly moving toward her nether region. When he took the tips of his fingers and parted her lips, he applied pressure, and his fingers brushed her clitoris in a steady, firm motion. Inadvertently she gripped his shoulders tightly, trying to stop herself from shuddering.

Ed's eyes met Gracie's, and he held her stare momentarily. Careful not to linger for too long, he kissed her arms, fingers, and neck before reaching her breasts. As soon as the intensity was overbearing, he pulled back momentarily. She slid her tongue inside his mouth, and they both began to grope each other passionately.

Still keeping a slow pace, Ed entered her, digging his hands deep inside Gracie's long hair. He sucked and licked her nipples until they looked like two copper nickels. She moaned as his strong hands groped her body. She squealed with delight as he began to nibble passionately on her neck.

As the moment intensified, she wrapped her legs around Ed's waist, and they gripped each other tightly.

"I'm getting ready to come," he murmured. "Ahh, I'm coming."

"Me, too," Gracie crooned.

As Ed came, he whispered in her ear, "I love you, Gracie. Don't ever leave me...I love you...."

Ed and Gracie lay lovingly on their sofa, languishing after making love for hours in the comfort of their home, when they heard Tamara arrive. They both listened to the keys jangling, and Ed called out to his sister.

"Tamara, don't come in yet!"

They both tried to jump up and get dressed. Still, Tamara, who wasn't fond of being told what to do, forged on and encountered a sight she never thought she'd see—her brother's fully engorged penis staring her in her face.

"Oh, my gosh!" she shrieked in horror. "What are you doing?"

"I told you not to come in!" Ed shouted.

"How rude," she continued. "And disgusting! I nap on that couch."

Tamara was appalled. She felt they should have had the common courtesy not to have sex on the sofa, the same couch she lay on to watch her favorite shows or take a quick catnap during the day. Now she'd forever remember Gracie's landing strip and her brother's dangling dick.

Gracie stood stark naked, hands-on-hips—partly because she was angry, but mainly because she wanted to flaunt her new shape—and started in on Tamara.

115

"Don't you dare stand in my motherfucking house, talking about rude and disgusting, when your funky, non-showering, disrespectful, free-loading ass is living on our dime. If my husband wants to make love on the ceiling or television while you watch *Girlfriends*, so be it! And if you judge us again, you're gone!"

Tamara stood with her lips twisted and her eyes tossed in the sky, ignoring Gracie's tantrum. Ed, trying his best to cover his manhood, tried to put his pants on when Gracie snatched them away.

"Let's go and have dinner, honey!" Gracie demanded.

Gracie led Ed into their dining room, sat her husband down butt naked at the table, lit a few candles, and served him like a king. She refused to allow Tamara the satisfaction of ruining their makeup sex.

Sometime after dawn, Gracie heard the phone ring but refused to answer it. She knew it must be earlier than seven because her alarm hadn't gone off. Ed picked up.

"Yes, hello?" Ed asked in a gruff whisper. "Hello?"

When the caller hung up without replying, Ed couldn't go back to sleep.

"Wrong number?" Gracie asked, still half asleep.

"I guess. They didn't say anything. They just listened."

That news woke up both of them. Neither said anything further about the call, but both had different thoughts. Gracie thought the call could have come from her brother. Ed's insecurities resurfaced, making him believe the caller was Gracie's lover.

Finally, Ed had to hop in the shower and prepare for work. It was shortly after six in the morning. As the shower water rained on Ed, Gracie took the opportunity to dial George's house. He picked up on the first ring.

"George, did you just call here?" She grumbled in a deep morning voice.

"Gal, you better take that bass out of your voice. I'm still your father and will go upside your head if necessary."

Gracie could not believe his audacity.

"What do you want?" she snapped. Without waiting for a response, she asked, "What did I tell you about calling here at odd hours? You're only to call after seven when Ed's left for work."

"How are you gettin' along with that fella?"

"How am I getting along with Ed? He's my husband!" Gracie replied, perplexed at her father's odd question.

"You gonna do him like you did the other one?"

"Goodbye—"

"I suggest you not hang up on me if you know what's good for you—" George began a lung-rattling cough trying to catch his breath.

Gracie's mind raced quickly, trying to ingest the not-so-subtle threat.

"What are you saying?"

"I'm saying that you owe me for my years of silence. You out there living in the lap of luxury, just as your mother did, and left us here to rot."

"I didn't leave! I was thrown out! How dare you twist this around!" Gracie's voice was a strained whisper.

"Don't matter. These are my rules. You better listen closely because I won't repeat myself. Too old. Either you get me the $20,000 I need to keep my house in one week, or you'll get a knock at your door, and I promise you won't like who's on the other side."

"Are you crazy!"

The line went dead. Gracie cradled the receiver in her arms and began trembling. If anyone had warned Gracie that her behavior years ago would cost her more than she could ever dream, she would've told that person to kiss her plump ass. Being young and living on the edge had caused a downward spiral, culminating in a path of destruction for her.

Gracie couldn't shake that memory, no matter how hard she tried. All she could do was cry and hope she'd think of a solution to free her from her past. She dialed George back and took his bank's routing and account numbers. She told him she wasn't making any promises but would do her best to get him the money. He, in return, told her to kiss his ass!

CHAPTER

13

ANTHONY CROSS

THE DOORBELL RANG, BUT I WAS HAVING difficulty distinguishing reality from fantasy. I was in a deep sleep. I'd dozed off on the sofa waiting for Gracie to arrive. She was hours late. As I jumped up, I groggily made my way to the door and stubbed my toe against the coffee table.

"Ooowww," I yelped and did a one-legged hop. I flung open the door, and there she stood—gorgeous, sexy, confident. "How did you get up here without being announced?" I asked.

"I have my ways," she replied with her hands placed cockily on her hips.

"*Mu-ah!*" I kissed her on her lips and led her inside. "You look sensational."

Gracie pulled her hair into a neat bun, a two-piece, form-fitting skirt suit, and black heels. I must admit, she certainly dressed her age. Gracie never wore low-rise jeans, coochie-cutting shorts, hooker shoes, or trampy dresses. She always looked and dressed like a lady, but it was a different story in the bedroom.

"Something smells good," she commented.

"Yes, I had my housekeeper prepare us a rack of lamb. You do eat lamb, correct?"

"Yes, I love lamb. That's Ed's favorite dish. He makes a delicious, smothered lamb and won't tell anybody his secret ingredients. Not even me and I'm his wife...can you imagine that?"

Was she serious? So casually talking about her husband...I ignored her comment.

"Good. I'm glad you love lamb. Let me take a quick shower, and then we'll have dinner. Make yourself at home. *Mi casa es su casa*," I joked. "I also took the liberty of renting *The Bourne Identity*. Did you see that?"

"No, no, but I don't know if I'll have time to watch the whole movie."

Immediately I grew annoyed. She was always rushing home. Her thirty-minute to one-hour stays with me was becoming infuriating. Surely, she could think of a way to spend more time with me. I took another glance at Gracie, and suddenly the gorgeous, sexy temptress didn't look so hot.

"I'll be out in ten minutes," I remarked dryly.

In the shower, I contemplated my situation with a married woman. I was used to women being at my beck and call. Vying for quality time with me, praying that I'd invite them to stay for dinner and a movie, and hoping I didn't throw them out after sex. But this lady only came over for sex and wanted nothing more. As I lathered up my tight, fit body, I realized I didn't need the drama. I had had enough of Mrs. Lane. I wasn't sure I even wanted her to stay for dinner.

Still lathered up, I could hear her on her cell.

She loudly said, "Baby, I love you!" My stomach twisted up in disgust. Or was it jealousy?

Sneakily, I stepped out of the shower and allowed the water to continue running so she wouldn't be alerted that I was trying to catch her. I listened intently to their little love call when I heard faint footsteps across my parquet floors, but they weren't walking toward me.

"I've got to go," I heard her call out.

Did I hear her correctly?

"What?" I asked. No answer.

Still lathered up, I grabbed a towel and stepped out into my living room in time to see her bolting out the front door with her cell clasped tightly to her ear. And then *boom*! My front door slapped shut.

With my towel wrapped around my waist and water dripping on my living room floor, I did a slight jog and flung open my front door. I caught a glimpse of her just as she entered the elevator.

"Where are you going?!" I yelled after her. No response. She never bothered to stop.

In a panic, I ran to my room, threw on a jogging suit, and ran down the eleven flights to the front lobby. I was breathing rapidly and had broken out into a sweat. As I pushed through the front door, the cold, winter air froze my body, only I didn't feel it. I was hyped off pure adrenaline. I stood outside in the blistering cold, heart beating, half-dressed, and confused. I looked up and down the block, but I saw nothing. I stood there for a few minutes until I saw her Honda hybrid make a right turn onto my block and then another right at the corner. The last thing I noticed was her brake lights.

"Gracie!" I called out like a maniac, but she didn't hear me. She continued on her mission. I ran back into the building.

"Is everything all right, Mr. Cross?" the overnight security guard asked. I didn't even acknowledge him.

I ran upstairs and began calling Gracie incessantly on her cell. The first twenty or so times, the phone just rang. Then my calls started going straight to voicemail. I panicked. What was going on?

"Gracie, you have me worried. Is everything all right? Why did you leave so abruptly? Please, please call me when you get this." I left that and many other messages on her phone. Then waited. She never called.

Day number three, and I still hadn't heard from Gracie. For some unknown reason, this situation had me stressed. My usual upbeat mood around the office had turned dark. I began almost stalking Anika, waiting for her by the ladies' room, beating her to work, and walking her to the elevator to elicit information about Gracie.

"Where's your old-timer friend?"

"Again?"

"What do you mean?"

"Here you go again. What's this about?" Anika asked perceptively.

"I'm just worried about you, that's all. And I don't think you should hang around someone much older than you."

"Nah, Gracie's cool. She's not like that. Like, she's not a bad influence. In fact, she's positive. Sort of like a mentor."

Just that little bit of information had me open. Gracie was so private that I couldn't get insight into her personal life. I pressed on.

"How so?" I asked.

"Well, I didn't know anyone when I came to New York. I got mixed up with the wrong crowd and began smoking weed and drinking cocktails at all the hotspots. I was underage, but that didn't stop me from getting into all the clubs. I was going nowhere fast. Bluntly, Gracie told me I needed to get my shit together because me—and only me—was responsible for my future. I slowed down my partying, stopped using drugs, enrolled in college, and started interviewing for jobs."

"What about her husband?"

"Ed? What about him?"

I needed to weigh my words carefully and make it seem that my only and main concern for bringing up Gracie was Anika.

"Is he a mentor to you as well?" I asked.

"No. I don't spend much time around him. He's awkward."

"Awkward? How so?"

"I dunno…like he's reticent when I'm around. I usually shut him down when he tries to join our conversation because he's so corny."

"Is that so?" My voice could hardly hold my excitement. It felt good to hear her trash Gracie's husband.

"Yeah, like you and he would never get along. You and me—we're just alike. You got a lot of style, you know how to dress, you're a corporate thug, and that's what's up. Ed, on the other hand, is a straight nerd."

"What does she see in him?"

"What the fuck do you see in her?!" Anika screamed, startling me.

"Huh?"

"Don't think I'm stupid. You won't stop asking about her!"

"She's my patient," I replied calmly.

"I was hoping that the rumors that are circulating around here about you and her having sex inside the examination room weren't true—"

"What? What rumor?"

"Samantha said she smelled sex!"

"Smelled sex?" My mind raced back to Gracie's sweet coochie. How I sucked and licked her juicy clit inside my examination room with the door slightly ajar and my nosey ass RN trying to catch us.

"Ant, please tell me you're not sleeping with my friend." Her eyes pleaded for me to not break her heart. I wanted to confide in Anika to get more information about Gracie. Anika was like my sister, and she was messing everything up. I decided to tell her what I knew she wanted to hear.

"I'm not sleeping with your friend. I wouldn't ever cross that line with any of my patients. I'll speak with Samantha about spreading false rumors. Truthfully, I was asking about her to get to know you better. You don't have any family here, and she and I are the closest you have."

"Really? You care about me?"

Jokingly, I replied, "You know I don't *really* give a shit about you, but I had you going."

Anika grinned, ambled over to her desk, and was ready to hop on her cell phone and begin her morning chatter. It was barely eight o'clock. When she reached for her cell and gave me an *excuse-me* look.

"Who are you calling?"

"My suga-daddy!"

"Don't be on that phone all day because I will fire your ass!"

"Kick rocks!" she replied and gave me the finger.

Inside my office, I did my best to push Gracie to the back of my mind. From how Anika described her situation, she was a happily married woman, and all was good. So why was I stressing over another man's wife? Good question. Answer—I wasn't. I decided to call Dakota.

"Hey, baby girl."

"Hey, I've missed you." She said the obvious. I'd been giving her the cold shoulder for weeks.

"I miss you, too. I've been so busy lately, but I want to see you tonight. Do you want to come over? I'll cook something, and we can stay in."

"That would be nice," she squealed and then continued. "I got a surprise for you."

Was that a sexy, seductive tone I detected?

"Really? I'm usually the one giving out surprises. Give me a hint."

"No. Then it won't be a surprise."

"Just a hint," I said again, this time in a demanding tone.

"Okay. It's something I think you'll enjoy. I want to show my love for you and prove I'm not the prude you think I am. I can be a freak."

Where did *that* come from? Immediately I thought she'd come over and do a striptease, which I was less than enthused about. Why did all women ultimately strive to strip for their man, as if that was the end-all and be-all? I mean, it was nice, but stripping had its place, preferably in a dark, crowded strip club. But if she wanted to do it, I would pretend to enjoy it.

"A freak, huh? I'll be the judge of that," I said, challenging her to back up her statement.

I just wasn't feeling Dakota. No matter how hard I tried to get into her, I couldn't. She was the quintessential good girl, but that didn't do it for me. I couldn't see myself settling down with her and living happily ever after. I knew she was young, ambitious, and intelligent. Had a good family background, great morals, no kids (thanks to me), a college degree, and was pursuing her master's. She also had a nice body and face but was as dull and boring as a calculus book.

As promised, I had my housekeeper prepare a nice dinner, we talked, and then she wanted to make love. I wasn't in the mood, which was a first for me.

"Something's different," she whined.

"What do you mean?"

"You're not acting the same lately."

"What are you talking about?"

"At first, I thought your behavior changed because of my unexpected pregnancy."

"Unexpected? What do you expect to happen when you have sex without contraceptives?"

"Don't blame only me. You had a hand in my pregnancy as well."

"That's up for debate," I dryly remarked, intentionally being cruel.

"Are you saying that you doubt that you were the father?"

"I'm saying that's always a possibility. Mommy's baby, daddy's maybe."

"Anthony, how could you be so cruel?" she yelled, face flushed, lips quivering. "You know it's been only you!"

Why did I even go there? Why take cheap shots when I wasn't interested in arguing or even being around Dakota tonight, for that matter? I was taking my frustrations about Gracie out on her, which wasn't the right thing to do.

"Listen, you're right. I know that the baby was mine. I apologize for insulting you."

She began to calm down.

"I wouldn't cheat on you, ever."

"I know, babe."

"Is it serious?"

"Is what serious?" I asked, perplexed.

"Your new woman."

"You tell me since you seem to know so much."

"Don't do that," she replied, shaking her head from side to side. "Don't play mind games. Just respect me enough to answer the question."

"You're paranoid."

"Answer the question, Anthony! You owe me that much. I've given you four years of my life. I deserve a truthful answer."

"Look, you're crazy! There isn't anybody else."

For the moment, Dakota seemed to let the topic go. We decided to play a game of Spades, and as I was whipping her ass at the card game, she started in again just as I took her Jack of Spades with my Queen.

"Look, we're not married," she started off slowly. "And I

understand that you're only a man and have needs. If you're seeing another woman or other women, we can change the terms of our relationship and keep it open."

The selfish part of me took over.

"I'd kill you before I let you make love to another man!"

"Not me. I could never let someone else touch me. I love you, and having multiple partners is not who I am. But what I'm trying to tell you is that if you trust me, confide in me, I'll understand. It may even bring us closer."

Maybe I'd taken one too many sips of the Patrón. Maybe her soft voice was enough to convince me my next move was the right one. Whatever the motive, I fell for her game.

We stopped playing for a moment.

"You asked for the truth, so that's just what I'll give you. I do have a few lady friends. I'm an unmarried, successful man, and I like to do me. I'm not ready to be married, nor am I ready to settle down and be faithful. But I promise you that if you ride this out with me, let me get all of being a bachelor out of my system. You're the one I'm going to marry. I want you to be Mrs. Cross."

Everything I'd said was true, up until the part about her being Mrs. Cross. I basically told her what she wanted to hear, or did I? I could see her holding back the hurt from her eyes, but she was doing a lousy job.

"Is there one or many?" she asked, but I thought I had already answered. I decided to fall back a little. I didn't want to scare her into thinking I was some player, so I gave a safe answer.

"Really, there's just one other." Big mistake. I should have seen her angle.

"Do you love her?!" she shouted.

"Lower your voice. Did you not hear anything I just said?"

"What is it that you like about her?"

"Truthfully?"

"No, please lie," she sarcastically answered—her spunk turned me on.

"Well, for one thing, she knows how to treat her man."

"Go ahead. Explain yourself."

"She's uninhibited in the bedroom and allows me to explore all crevices of her body."

"So, she lets you have anal sex with her?"

"All open crevices," I repeated. She'd have to decipher my words on her own.

"What else?" she asked. "Hold on for one second."

She reached inside her pocketbook, pulled out a pad and pen, and jotted down notes. I wasn't surprised—the ever-studious, dull Dakota, at her best.

"She doesn't crowd me. I'm not getting a phone call five times a day at work and again late at night to ensure nobody's here with me. She's secure in her skin and doesn't have low self-esteem." I was speaking of Gracie. "She doesn't need me to validate her. I don't have to shower her with compliments every moment, nor hold her hand in public if a hot woman is walking past. If my eyes roam, she doesn't trip."

"If she's so great, why do you want me? Why not marry her?"

"I met you first."

"No, seriously," she probed. Was she getting cocky? "Is she ugly? Is that it? Some ugly, fat bitch!"

"More beautiful than I could describe. Gorgeous face, nice boobs—nice, big, real boobs," I repeated. "A shape like a Coca-Cola bottle and a great personality."

Gushing over Gracie only made me want her more. As I spoke,

I wondered what had made me say those things. Did I really feel that way about her? I barely knew her. And she was another man's wife. I watched, amused that Dakota was really taking notes. Then I began telling her what I didn't like about her. I was selfish, cruel, mean, the whole gamut, but in my defense, she was asking the questions and backing it up with how she could handle what I was dishing out.

After our meaningful conversation, Dakota became sullen and despondent. She sat on the sofa, her lips poked out like a child. I excused myself, went into my room for privacy, and called Gracie for the umpteenth time, again going straight to voicemail. I must have drifted into a peaceful sleep because I woke to Dakota giving me fellatio.

"Whoa, whoa, be easy," I said as her teeth grazed my penis. When she did it again, I pulled her up.

"What's wrong with you? You're going too hard," I scolded.

"I want to do it from behind," she claimed, almost in desperation.

"You do not," I replied in annoyance.

"Yesss, I do," she stammered, and it was at that moment I realized she was crying. She was like a wounded puppy—sad and pitiful. Momentarily, I felt shallow.

I reached for a condom and made love to Dakota, only I was thinking about Gracie. Exhausted and mentally drained, I didn't persist when she crawled under my arm to cuddle. I was too tired to object. Moments later, the phone rang. I looked over at my caller ID, and my heart began to palpitate. It was her, my baby.

Although I wanted to kick Dakota out and beg Gracie to come over, I knew I couldn't. She'd disrespected me, and I refused to jump when she called. I had to play it cool.

"Hello," I said with a less-than-enthusiastic tone.

"Hey, baby," she purred. Her voice was smooth as silk. "I'm sorry—"

"Listen, I can't talk right now."

"Then why did you pick up?" she asked, and I felt my blood pressure go up. How dare she talk slick!

"Look, I gotta go!" I said and slammed down the phone. Dakota pretended not to sense anything. I pushed her off me, turned my back to her, and dozed into a complicated sleep.

The following day started off superbly. After perusing *The New York Times* financial section, confirming that my stock was doing well, I dropped and did one hundred pushups. Feeling rejuvenated, I asked Dakota to make breakfast. She was back to her old self. She made me breakfast, cleaned the kitchen, and then left for work.

I thought about how the consequences of my actions were simply surface wounds. Nothing I'd said or done was enough to jeopardize me or my lifestyle. I was living like a rock star. I had many beautiful women, all vying for my love and affection; even a beautiful, married woman couldn't get enough of me. My heart had never been hurt in all my years of dating. Again, I had gotten away with not only the insinuation that I was cheating but actually telling Dakota I was. She'd just have to sit and bear it. And she would, as long as she thought she would be the last one standing at the altar with me at the bottom of the ninth inning. The routine was maniacal. I still couldn't get over how she sat there taking notes, listening to me pontificate about how good another woman looked and how great she was in bed. I had all the women hooked on Dr. Cross. And even though Gracie was complicated, vague, elusive, and combative—she was supposed to be. She was married, and she'd never had an affair before. I was her first, and that had to be confusing, wanting to be with someone other than your spouse. Even though improper, her call last night let me know she wanted me. And I wanted her. And that's the end of the story.

It didn't surprise me that when I fell back and stopped calling—she'd start. And that's exactly what she did. I was drinking an afternoon energy drink in my office when she called my private line. This line went straight to my office and bypassed Anika. A sly grin appeared when I saw her number on the caller ID.

"Hello," I barked. My voice needed to reflect my anger from the past week without contact. The rude way she bolted from my apartment and her blatant disrespect.

"Hey, baby," she sang.

"Don't 'hey baby' me. Where have you been? Why haven't you called? Better yet, why haven't you answered any of my calls?"

"I did call. Remember? Somebody couldn't talk."

"Don't be audacious. I'm not in the mood."

There was a long pause, and then, "Anthony, I can't keep going through this. I'm getting yelled at by you and then yelled at by Ed. I'm being pulled in two different directions and losing my mind. I want to be with you because I care about you, but I'm only pushing you away. I don't know what to do."

"All you had to do was pick up the phone. That's it. And give me an explanation of why you had to leave so quickly."

"Why? You don't know?"

"My thoughts are pure conjecture. I want you to tell me."

"Are you sure you want to know? Because once I tell you, there's no going back, and I feel you might judge me." Her voice was soft and fragile. I wanted to pull her through the phone and cradle her. I had no idea what she would say, but I wanted her to say something. Tell me about her, who she is, past, present, and future. Her silence, her need to protect her privacy, was like dangling cheese in front of a mouse. It made me chase her.

"Gracie, I'm not sure who you think I am, but I'm just a regular dude. I wouldn't judge you. Obviously, you don't know how I feel about you."

"I know you care about me," she replied and exhaled. "But I won't allow myself to think you could feel anything more. Ed used to feel the same way about me, and then I cooked his dinner for longer than he liked, and he displayed his anger with a closed fist to my right jaw. He showed me what it was to cry."

"He hits you?" I asked incredulously. My Gracie was married to a woman beater. My stomach felt sick. I wanted to rip his head off. Now everything fell into place. Always rushing off in a panic. I thought it was because she loved him, but the underlying truth was that she didn't want to get that ass-whipping he was placing on her. Thinking that she was risking her safety for me only deepened my feelings. I wanted to protect her.

"I've been able to placate him mostly, but we've got to be more discreet. When I say I must go, please let me, or I'll suffer the consequences. And I'd do it...for you...but I'd rather not. Please, Anthony, work with me. I don't want to lose you."

"Then don't! You don't have to stay with him. Divorce him and be with me."

"Anthony, it's complicated. Too complicated to discuss with you now, at this moment."

"Gracie, he has you brainwashed. You're a victim of domestic violence, and your fear keeps you frozen. No man should ever put his hands on a woman. Ever. Under any circumstance. I don't know how long this has been going on, but you've got to get out."

"See, you're judging me. I knew this would happen. I should have never—"

"Okay, I'm sorry, baby. We don't have to discuss this if you don't want to, but I want you to know I'm here for you. Whatever you need, don't hesitate to ask. If you're afraid to leave because of money—I got you."

"No, I don't need money. I have money."

"Oh, well, good, then you've got *me*," I joked, and we laughed. It felt good to break the ice and put a smile on Gracie's face.

The subject shifted.

"I really want to see you," she said coyly.

"I miss you, too. Did I ever tell you about the dream I had with you down on all fours, and I was eating you out from the back?"

"Did I come?"

"Of course, you did. And I ate it all up."

"I can't wait to kiss your luscious lips…" she purred.

"I rather give you kisses on your lower lips."

Gracie and I hung up, and I sat in silence for long moments. Thinking. Something inside me wanted to step in and rescue her, like a childhood fairytale—her knight in shining armor. But I knew life was more complex than that, and it would be up to Gracie to escape her situation. I only hoped it would be sooner than later, but I didn't know how long I could contain my anger, which had risen and settled in my chest. I knew that if I ever saw her with as much as a hair out of place, I'd probably risk my livelihood and freedom to break Ed's woman-beating ass into pieces.

CHAPTER

14

GRACIE LANE

I SAT CURLED UP UNDER ED'S ARM ON OUR couch, listening to our neighbor, Gloria, cry her little heart out. Her husband, Jonathan, was a high-profile actor who'd gotten caught sleeping with their nanny. Their faces were splattered all over the local and national news and newspapers. She was humiliated.

"I can get past the affair," she sniffled. "But how can he say that he's in love with her? She's just a babyyyyyyy." She wailed so loud, a lung-rattling sob that pierced my heart. All I thought about was Ed. What if Ed found out about my affair? How much pain would he be in?

"Gloria, I'm sure he's just confused at the moment. He loves you and his family. I'm sure he doesn't want to lose you. He probably—"

"He asked for a divorce yesterday. He said he wants to marry her." Her lips trembled, and her fragile hands shook as she dabbed the corner of her eyes with her fingers. "What will I do? How can I start over? I'm thirty-six years old. Who'll want me…a divorcee with three small children? What will I do for money?"

She sounded so wounded and desperate. Ed intervened, "If he wants out, you'll have to let him go. You're a beautiful woman; any man will be honored to have you, but you must be strong for your children. I'm sure he'll take good care of you."

"I signed a prenuptial agreement. Jonathan's worth three-hundred million, and I walk away with the clothes on my back. I have nothing."

"Nothing, my ass!" I piped in. "He'll have to give you seventeen percent of his income to care for your children. You're from Minneapolis, but New York Law is clear."

"They're not his…" her voice trailed off. She repeated, "They're not his."

"Does he know?" My treacherous mind was racing.

"Oh, not like that," Gloria clarified. "We've raised them as our own, but they're my sister's children. She and her husband died in a Vermont car accident when the oldest child was only four. My husband never legally adopted them."

The news was unsettling.

"I'm sure he would want the best for the children. Maybe you should sit and talk with him," Ed stated.

"Why do you think I'm here crying my eyes out? We've already discussed this in length. I have two weeks to get out with the kids."

"That's messed up!" I was outraged. "That piece of shit will trade you and his family in for the nanny?"

"Did I mention she's snow white?" Gloria remarked dryly.

"What?" I roared. "Lionel fucking Ritchie! He's traded you in for a cracker-ass bitch!" I jumped to my feet and began walking in place.

"Gracie, calm down," Ed interjected. "Sometimes, I don't know who you are when you have these outbursts."

My head swung around. "This isn't about me! Did you hear her celebrity husband's leaving her destitute with three small children for the white nanny? Did you hear that part?"

"Yes, I did. But screaming and acting wild and obnoxious won't get Jonathan to come back." Ed was calm. His legs were crossed, and he wore his smoking robe and matching slippers with a $300 Cuban cigar dangling from his fingers. He sat there judging while luxuriating in a lifestyle I had afforded him. "She has to let him go while keeping her dignity. She signed the prenup. No one forced her hand."

We tag-teamed him.

"I signed it because I loved him! I didn't think the man I married would ever treat me so harshly!" Gloria voiced loudly.

"And how could you sit there and take his side, Ed!" I bellowed. "She gave him the best years of her life!"

Ed conceded. "Ladies, please, I know I may sound unsympathetic. He's completely wrong. My point was that a woman should never beg a man to stay. Let him go because he's going to go anyway. Don't let him take your pride and dignity from you. Don't stand in his way if he's determined to leave." Ed stood. "Excuse me, I'm going into the study to read."

I watched Ed scamper away, and I rolled my eyes with disdain.

"Easy for him to say," I retorted. "If I left his sorry ass, he'd be begging and pleading like there wasn't any tomorrow."

"I know that's right." Gloria attempted a faint smile.

"Now, back to you. We gotta get girl power going and devise a plan so you don't leave empty-handed."

"As I said, I signed the prenup. I get nothing."

"I got that point at hello," I joked. "Now, let's get past the legal stuff. Do you have any money stashed away for rainy days that Jonathan doesn't know about?"

"He controlled all the money."

"So, I guess it would be foolish for me to think that you two had a joint bank account."

"He gave me a monthly allowance to cover all the household expenses and a little money to keep myself groomed."

"How much was that?"

"Each month, he'd give me $10,000. Some months I had to stretch that."

"Cheap bastard! How much do you have in your checking account?"

"Less than $200. Yesterday, instead of a check, he gave me divorce papers."

I shook my head, remembering when I was that stupid. On the one hand, her husband's a low-life piece of shit. That's granted. But this fool has lived with this asshole for fifteen years; she should be sitting on a nest egg. How could she have lived under his thumb for so long and not outsmart him? Surely, she had to realize there would be rainy days? And she wasn't the mother of any of his children. That alone was screaming divorce. I'd bet anything that Ms. Doris Day was pregnant.

"I've been inside your apartment numerous times. All the

expensive paintings, vases, and antiques. The Certificate of Authority—are any in your name?"

She shook her head. I started to think she was going to be a lost cause.

"Jewelry. Please say he doesn't have the crown jewels under lock and key."

Her eyes lit up.

"Well, yes and no. We both have keys and are signers on the safe deposit boxes. And we also have a small, hidden safe in the apartment. We don't keep our priciest jewelry there, but a couple of his expensive watches would be, and a few pairs of earrings of mine should."

"What about the safe deposit boxes? What's in there?"

"A host of things. Important papers, some cash, not much, and all our jewelry."

"Important papers such as your prenuptial agreement?" I was hopeful.

"No. Jonathan keeps his copy separate. Besides, his lawyer has the original."

"Okay, back to basics. You go right now and clear out any boxes, including the one at the apartment. Can you do it without Jonathan suspecting anything?"

"He's in Belize, supposedly reshooting a scene for a movie. That's why I have two weeks to get out. He said that if I leave quietly and not linger around, he'll give me $50,000 startup money."

I was seething. That wasn't even 1% of the fortune he'd amassed.

"Call that motherfucker and tell him that Black women don't leave any room quietly!"

We both laughed.

"Okay, first things first: Get all that jewelry and whatever else he has in those boxes and bring everything here for safekeeping. I will have my jeweler, Orlando, come over, and hopefully, he'll take all your pieces. How much do you think it's all worth, retail value?"

She tossed her eyes up in the sky as in deep thought. "I have all the appraisal records for everything. I would say close to ten million dollars over the years."

"Technically, you should only lose 20 percent of the initial cost, but you'll take a bigger hit than that unloading everything at once. You can probably get 60 percent of the original purchase. Make sure you bring your appraisal papers."

Her face beamed.

"What a great plan. But couldn't I get a better deal if I go to our jeweler?"

Damn, she was a knucklehead.

"If you went to your jeweler and tried to sell you and Jonathan's jewelry back, what do you think he'd do? He'd call your husband, and your plan would be foiled. You have to do things on the low."

"Right, right…cool. I'm on my way now. I should be back in less than two hours." She reached up and embraced me. "Gracie, I can't thank you enough. You're like the sister I never had."

Her words touched me.

"Are you camera shy?"

"I don't think so. Why?"

"Because I hardly think six million will be enough for you and your three kids. Especially since you've grown accustomed to a certain lifestyle. I think we could milk another million with an on-air interview. Let's start a bidding war for your story. Barbara Walters exclusive or a US Weekly magazine spread. The press will go bananas over your version of *The Nanny Scandal.* Rich housewives everywhere, beware! Not to mention a tell-all book. I'm sure Jonathan has a few skeletons in his closet. Let them out to the highest bidder!"

She left with promises to return shortly. I was about to join Ed in the study but opted to go upstairs, luxuriate in a long bubble bath, and enjoy my alone time. As I soaked, I thought about my life and how I had reinvented myself, but was I really living? Everything I did was on a cautionary level. I was hiding from my past. Hiding from my family. Hiding from my husband. I'd told so many lies over the years and used manipulation that I didn't know who I was. Who am I? Am I George's child? Gracie Lane? A wealthy widow? An adulterer? Or am I all of the above?

I'm a woman who drives a hybrid during the day to keep her coworkers in the dark about the millions I have in the bank. A woman who volunteers to help soothe a guilty conscience. A woman who wears a faux brooch mixed with a million dollars' worth of jewelry. A woman who loves getting fucked by strangers in dirty hallways. At the same time, her attentive husband waits patiently for her to arrive. And most recently, I'm a woman who has just told her histress that her non-violent husband beats her. What's wrong with me?

I loved my husband, I did. And I loved my new life. But I loved having fun as well. I'm selfish, and I want my cake, and yes, I would love to eat it without explaining the who's, what's, and why's. I wanted Anthony—the freak but not at the cost of losing Ed. But where was he going? Would Ed genuinely leave as he said he would if he were in Gloria's shoes? Or was that just tough talk?

It's always easier when you're on the outside looking in to pass judgment.

I realized that life isn't always black and white, and if I wanted all my needs fulfilled, I'd have to play the manipulation game, and I'd have to play well. I was up against two strong-willed men, and the last thing I wanted was to have to let anyone go. Not now. Not when the fun just got started.

CHAPTER
15

ANTHONY CROSS

THE NIGHT WAS CLEAR AND CALM DESPITE the snowstorm two days ago. Gracie and I found ourselves cuddled up in a cozy bar in TriBeCa. We both felt terrific, despite our previous anxieties about where our relationship was going. Or what we were both getting into. Gracie was gracious and charming that night and had a certain glow. I could swear I felt positive energy exuding from her pores. She was radiant as she drove to *Lucas Michelini Restaurant & Bar* in a chauffeur-driven Mercedes Maybach. She stepped out in a full-length mink coat and an expensive alligator purse dangling from her arm. I was shell-shocked.

"D-d-d-did someone hit the Lotto?" I stammered.

She smiled her dimpled smile. "I'll explain later. Let's go inside."

"Yes, you've got some explaining to do." I concurred.

Once seated, she took off her expensive frock. She was laden with huge, water-clear diamonds sparkling and obviously real. My words flooded back, and I felt humiliated and like a fool for assuming she'd previously worn replicas. These were authentic pieces.

"So, what happened to your hybrid?"

"I still have it."

"And the Mercedes?"

"Listen, I know you know my husband works for Verizon. But you were a bit presumptuous, thinking you're the only one with seven or more decimal points in their bank account."

Sexy, thoughtful, *and* wealthy? Christmas was coming early this year. I listened intently, trying not to show any expression on my face. Although, I was completely taken off guard.

"So your husband's wealthy, and Anika lied when she said he works for Verizon?"

"We have money, and that's the bottom line."

"Why is everything always vague? You can't give a direct answer, which is annoying."

"So be annoyed. But get over it quickly. Preferably within the next few minutes to enjoy our evening together."

"Why are you telling me now?"

"Why not?"

She was indirect and combative, like a ten-year-old child. I decided to fall back and see where this would take us. I'll let her play her little word and mind games—for the moment.

"What do you want from me?" I asked. "Why are you here?"

"You're gentle and tough, all wrapped up in one," Gracie commented as we sipped the finest house wine. "You're intelligent and savvy, and I like spending evenings with you. All I want is some of your free time."

I kissed her lips.

"You've been getting a lot of my free time."

"We don't do anything except eat and fuck." She laughed, and I felt intoxicated by her presence. I wanted to give her a bear hug and take her home with me for good. She didn't have to say it, but her husband was the money man, and that's why she allowed him to beat her. She's working some low-end job, and he probably treats her like shit. I didn't have Maybach money, but I was on my way. My five-year plan would afford me all the amenities that Ed had given Gracie.

I ordered the second round.

"Are you trying to get me drunk?"

"Why would I want to do that?" I laughed. "I've already had my way with you."

"You've had *some* ways, not all ways. All in due time," Gracie replied coyly, and I got hard. I pulled her hand to me so she could feel my bulge.

Gracie leaned in, and we began a long, passionate kiss as we groped each other like two school kids. The mere fact that I had my way with another man's wife was an unexpected turn-on. When her cell rang, she gave me a stern look, put her index finger to her lips, signaling me to be quiet, and then picked up.

"Hey, babe." Gracie's voice was upbeat. "Yes, I've left your plate in the microwave...oh, for real? Yes, I totally understand…why would he say something like that…no, I'm glad you didn't…yes, I love you too…bye."

When she closed her phone, she gave me an apologetic look. I hated to admit it, but I felt cheap. How many nights would I have to be quiet while she talked to her husband on the phone? Better yet, how many nights would she still have a husband?

"That was Ed…he's so funny. He said that his boss almost pushed his buttons to the point that he wanted to give him a karate chop." She laughed hysterically.

I was deadpan and silent. I mean, was I supposed to laugh? It wasn't even funny.

After our second round, she let her guard down a little. She was very flirtatious with me, as well as with the waiters. Soon our smooching subsided, and I got serious again.

"Tell me about your husband," I said. "More than what you've already told me. You've told me about his bad side, but I want to know his better qualities. Why did you fall in love with him? Because he doesn't deserve you."

Gracie swallowed hard and then put her drink down on the table. I was looking her directly in the eye, challenging her credibility.

"When I met Ed, I felt lost. My life was spiraling in several different directions, all leading to nowhere. His love and stability were what kept me focused."

At that time, I didn't know that had I looked deeper into Gracie's eyes, I would have seen her love and devotion for her husband.

"And how do you feel now," I asked as I poured her the third drink.

"Well, as I've always told you, he's a good man," she started slowly. "It wasn't always like this...you know...the fights and arguments. We just began to grow apart."

"Did you try to rekindle the past? Maybe go to marriage counseling?"

"Yes, we've tried, and nothing works. Ed just doesn't understand me, and I'm tired of trying. I try to make it work daily, but he doesn't care. Like when I'm with you...it's like you get me. You know when to fall back and give me my space so I don't feel overwhelmed. You know how to touch me until my whole body is numb from orgasms. You do little romantic things that make me smile—"

"He's not romantic? C'mon, I can't believe that."

"Not romantic anymore! Anymore is the operative word here."

"So why not leave? If it's so bad and you're so unhappy, why don't you just go? If I didn't know any better, I'd think you were feeding me lines. And you and hubby are happier than ever, planning your next wedding anniversary."

"If I were so happy, why would I allow you into my life for more than one night? Huh? Why?"

"Again, you can leave. I don't want to sound pushy, but I dig you. And I can see myself getting into you and letting my feelings take control, but I don't because you're married. If you're miserable and plan to get a divorce, I'm here for you. I want you. I want you all to myself. I need a strong woman by my side."

She closed her eyes and shook her head vehemently.

"It's soooo complicated."

"Why? Tell me," I said, raising my voice out of frustration.

"You were right about me, back at your office."

"The office? What did I say?"

"About me having a kid. We do. We have a 9-year-old son."

She looked down into her lap, and everything made sense: a young child, an abusive husband, a fortune at stake.

"Jeez, the plot thickens."

"I'm sorry I didn't tell you sooner, but I didn't know we would go further than the bedroom. That I'd think about you every night and all during the day. Your strong hands and cute little face." She leaned in and kissed my cheek. "I want you so bad, but I don't know what to do. My hands are tied."

"No, they're not! Your husband's a loser, and I'm tired of women thinking that there aren't any great men out here. Shit, I'm one of them. Leave him and find me because I want you. I want you to want me."

"If I didn't want you, I wouldn't be here."

"Not like that, Gracie. Don't you want not a *good* man but a *great* man in you and your son's life?"

"He really is a great person."

"A great person?" I spat. "How did that happen?"

"You know what I meant," she said, clarifying her last remark while pouring yet another glass of the tasty, expensive wine. "Ed used to be a great person. Isn't that a given? Why would I have married him? I told you already about what he puts me through. Lately, we've been going through marital problems, and he keeps pushing me away. I'm sure he'll get it together," she said, again opting for the avenue of disillusionment.

"You're still his little cheerleader after he's beaten your ass and given you the cold shoulder? I don't believe this."

"I'm no one's cheerleader, but he's my husband, and I need to handle my marriage on my terms. That's it. Can we change the subject and enjoy our time together?"

Ignoring her plea, I asked, "Is another woman involved?"

"Of course not! We've been married for ten years, and he's always been faithful," she exclaimed.

"You really believe that, don't you?" I was shocked that Gracie believed she was the only one cheating in her marriage.

"I just don't believe it. I know it!"

"Okay, okay, don't bite off my head. Tell me how he keeps pushing you away."

"Throughout our marriage, I always support him in all his endeavors. Now I feel that he doesn't reciprocate. He gets so caught up in his life, job, and political career that he neglects my needs."

"Sexual needs?"

"Among other things," she halfheartedly replied. "I just don't want to delve into it. I could sit here and name a laundry list of things wrong in my marriage."

"Let me ask you a question." My voice became stern, and any sign of intoxication quickly vanished. "Do you still have sex with him?"

Gracie emphatically denied the implication. "Not at all."

Relieved, I exhaled. "How long has it been?"

"Way before I ever met you."

"Is that why you're here with me? Because you're feeling neglected at home?"

"No. It's not like that at all. When I saw you for the first time, I was captivated."

"Pah-leeze, you wanted to stab me."

Laughing, she said, "You sound like Anika with the 'pah-leeze.'"

"That girl's rubbing off on me with all her bad habits."

Suddenly our moods changed at the mere mention of Anika. Unspoken guilt loomed over both of our heads. We sat in silence for a few moments before Gracie spoke.

"What are you looking for?"

"What I've always been looking for . . . a woman like you."

"Anthony, I can't do this. I can't allow my feelings for you to escalate. I'm a married woman. You'll never respect me."

"Are you kidding me? Of course, I respect you. I've looked into your eyes when you said that I'm the only one, that there's never been anyone else, and I believe that. Things happen, and you can't question how or why. I'm feeling you, and that's all I care about. Gracie, can we just take one day at a time? I promise I will never hurt you or make a promise I can't keep. Can you do me a favor and trust me?"

"You're asking for a lot and taking me out of my element."

"That makes me feel good."

"Why?"

"Because you're doing something for me you've never done. It makes me feel special."

"I feel guilty just being out having drinks with you. What if somebody saw us?"

"Stop worrying about what-ifs and relish the moment. You only have one life and must do what's best for you. Remember I told you that."

"Okay, I will."

"Last question about your marriage: Do you ever plan on leaving him? Or are you just saying that? Because either way, I'll still be here but under different terms. If you just want it to be casual sex, then I'm game. But if you see a door at the end of your tunnel and you're ready to walk through it and start a new beginning, I'm game with that too. Don't lead me on, and I won't lead you on. We're both adults."

"This is God's honest truth. Next year my son will go to middle school. We're sending him off to Connecticut to a private boarding academy. As soon as that happens, I'm filing for an overdue divorce. I'll finally have my freedom."

When the check came, she insisted on paying—this time, I allowed her.

We sat there until Ed began calling.

"I have to get home," she said, and I silenced her with a kiss.

Her lips were soft and plump, her mouth wet and experienced. She pulled back from the kiss as I got more aggressive, and she finally persuaded me to let her go.

"I have to go…he'll be furious."

"Go to him. For now. But it won't always be like this. I won't be able to share you for much longer."

CHAPTER

16

MY CRUSH

IT WAS NEARLY 3 A.M. WHEN ANIKA WILLIAMS rolled into her Park Slope, Brooklyn apartment after partying in the city. One of her close friends, Brandi, came stumbling in as well. They were drunk, drinking shots of straight Hennessey at club Roxy's in Manhattan. Both girls were lucky not to be locked up in Central Booking. As Anika drove Brandi's Toyota Camry over the Westside Highway toward Brooklyn, they encountered a police roadblock. There were several police cars, parallel parked, and one police van to remove the perpetrators. The flashing lights dazed

Anika momentarily as her freedom passed before her eyes. She stayed stoic in the face of danger. Not only would she fail the breathalyzer, but Brandi had weed in her pocketbook. When Anika told Brandi to pass her the weed, they were five cars away.

"Huh? What are you talking about? You don't even smoke anymore."

"Just do it. No need for both of us to get busted. I'm more than tipsy, so this will be a DUI. Do you want me to take you with me?"

"Nah, I don't, but you're my home girl, and I don't want you sittin' in Central Booking by yourself. That ain't cool. I'ma hold you down and hold my own. Whatever happens, happens!"

Anika loved the Brooklyn "ride or die" mentality. Back home, she'd bet the ranch that any of her friends in Burlington would have let her go down alone. Thankfully, she would never find out because one of the cars in the lineup decided to break the chain and bolt out of the line, full speed, down the highway. Every cop in the area jumped in their cars and on their radios and gave chase. Both girls exhaled.

Inside, Anika kicked off her boots and climbed disappointedly into her bed, fully dressed. She lay across, looking up at the ceiling, while Brandi pulled a chair close to the window and lit her weed.

"Open the window," Anika snapped. "I don't want to smell that shit."

"What do you think I'm sitting over here for? And what's the matter with you all of a sudden? You still shook about the cops?"

"No, I'm stressing over this kid."

"Who?" Brandi asked and blew the smoke out the window.

"My boss."

"Your boss?! Doctor Cross?"

"Hell yeah."

"Y'all fucked?"

"No."

"Stop lying, bitch! I know you."

"I said no, for real, for real. It's like he doesn't want to get to know me. All he does is sleep around with skeezers who only want him for his money."

"What's wrong with that?" Brandi laughed.

"It's not like that for me with Ant. I don't care about how much money he has. He's so smart and funny and sexy...damn, I wish I was his girl."

"So tell him."

"Like he doesn't already know."

"Says who? He's not a mind reader. I say go for yours...." Brandi inhaled her blunt, blew it out, and then collapsed into the chair and stared into space.

"Can I tell you something strange?"

"Please don't blow my high."

"Bitch, please. I don't know how to say this, but I think Anthony and Gracie had sex."

"Old Gracie? Your friend?"

They both giggled.

"She's not old like that. But yeah...what do you think I should do?"

"That's messed up if she did sleep with him when her ass is married. I don't know...if she did, you can't fuck behind her. That's nasty."

"I know."

"So, scratch that. Me telling you to go for yours."

"But he said ain't nothing go down."

"Oh, you asked him?"

"Yeah, there was a rumor at work."

"Why didn't you say that in the beginning? If he said that he didn't hit it, then believe him. You two are so cool he wouldn't lie to you."

"You think?"

"Hell, yeah."

Anika held onto the hope that she had a chance with Anthony and fell into a deep, peaceful sleep.

CHAPTER
17

GRACIE LANE

THE STILLNESS OF MY HOME WAS SOMETHING I longed for. A once very calm woman turned into a nervous wreck. Since my sister-in-law moved in, my house has become chaotic between her antics and Ed riding my ass. And Tamara ran up bills as if my first name was Trump and my last name was Rockefeller. Not to mention George's threat. If he did plan on going through with it, I had two days to wire $20,000 to him. I felt like my life had been plagued by defeat, and I refused to allow something as trivial as money to hinder my new life as I knew it.

I sat in my kitchen at my granite island and contemplated dialing Chase bank for a wire transfer. My heart pounded and felt like it had risen to my throat as I considered my decision. If I wired the money, I didn't want George to think there was more where that came from. I didn't want to be extorted for the rest of my life. On the flip side, if I didn't give them money, then as George would say, my ass was grass! I realized that I needed to pay George's bounty over my head.

I called my brother to confirm if George's threat was real.

"Benjamin, what's George talking about?" I asked. I had planned to start slowly, but my brother jumped right to the point.

"He said that if you don't help him save his house, he's gonna put those people on you."

"What makes him think that I got that kind of money?"

"He doesn't care. All he cares about is himself."

I was enraged. I thought about how often George neglected and treated me like shit, only to cater to his boys. The same boys left him destitute and on the verge of homelessness.

"All he thinks about is himself? This is from the son whose mouth he put a silver spoon and practically held your hand through life. He gave you everything, and you pissed it away!"

"He may have helped me here and there, but I ain't the one who put him in this situation. Andre did. And he's long gone, and now I gotta put up with the bullshit."

"You got to put up with the bullshit, or do I have to put up with it? Look, Benjamin, I don't have any money. My husband and I are broke."

"Well, then, you gonna have a problem."

Like father, like son, I thought. My brother could give less than a fuck about me. He probably put it in the old man's head to go after me by any means necessary.

"Can't you talk to him?" I pleaded.

"Nope. He's stubborn," Benjamin exclaimed. "But if I were you, I wouldn't challenge him. He's as serious as a terrorist and will execute his plan."

"You sound as if you're cosigning his trifling behavior."

"I'm just stating the facts and trying to help you out. So, are you gonna pay?"

"Do I have a choice?"

"No."

"I'm considering borrowing money from my husband's retirement fund and a little from our credit cards. That'll leave us in debt for years…but I don't have a choice."

"Well, maybe you could get an extra job or do some overtime to make ends meet."

"What a thoughtful suggestion," I stated sarcastically.

"To make it easier on you, I can pick up the money if you'd like."

His slick maneuvering made my skin crawl.

"To make it easier on me, huh? You'd smoke up my husband's hard-earned money in a half day!"

"Listen, you better watch your mouth. I don't do drugs!"

"I'm going to say this once. Don't you ever call my motherfucking house again if you know what's good for you because I'll have my husband come down there and personally whip your scrawny, crack-smoking ass!"

I slammed down the telephone in an attempt to release some portion of my anger. It didn't work.

I ended my conversation with my brother more aggravated and annoyed than I initially was. My brother had put fear in my heart, and I had to stop and pray before I totally lost control. I needed to breathe, make a decision, and then stand by that. My future depended on my being strong. I knew my foundation was built on something as fragile and thin as a cracker, so I had to tread cautiously.

Reluctantly, I called back the bank and did a direct wire transfer into George's bank account with the routing numbers he'd previously given me. I tried to convince myself that everything was going to be all right. But for the first time since my life-altering incident, I was afraid. After transferring the money from my checking account, I felt somewhat relieved.

With my feet propped up on several pillows, a cool rag resting on my forehead, and jazz music playing in the background, I tried to relax after a long, stressful day. I contemplated not answering when my phone rang, but the number was private. Suddenly, I became curious.

"Yes, hello?" I breathed, exasperated.

"I'ma kill you, bitch," a woman yelled.

"Excuse me?" I asked. I sat up in bed, one hand holding my chest for support.

"Why can't you leave him alone?" the woman on the other end screamed like she was crazy.

"I think you got the wrong number."

"Listen, tramp, you called my man Anthony the other night, and I'm not going to tell you again that you better leave him alone!"

I weighed my options before settling on a response.

"He told me he had someone he was in love with, but I thought I'd give it a shot anyway. I don't want any trouble and won't call him again. But there isn't a need to threaten me. Nothing happened."

"If he told you he had someone, why didn't you back off?"

"Look," My tone was stern and unwavering, "I just said I wouldn't call again. So back off before I sleep with your man!"

The woman took a moment to process the threat before hanging up.

When I thought my day couldn't get any worse, Ed came home. These past few weeks, all he wanted to do was make love. Although his lovemaking skills were superb, there wasn't anything like the thrill of new, spontaneous, sneaky sex. Ed, whose penis was larger than Anthony's, wasn't as experimental as the doctor. The first night Anthony and I had sex, he took charge and sexually dominated me. On the other hand, Ed always wanted to make soft, sensual love. And that, after ten years of marriage, was dull.

"Hey, babe," he crooned all up in my face.

"Hey, Ed."

He sat at the edge of the bed and began massaging my feet.

"Elana cooked dinner. I've made a plate for you and put it in the microwave," I stated.

"You're not going to eat with me?"

"I'm not hungry."

As he massaged my feet, his hand crawled up my thigh until he reached my lace panties. Immediately I swatted his hand away.

"Do you not see me lying with a rag on my head? Isn't that a telltale sign that I have a headache?" I snapped.

"Watch your tone."

Now *his* tone infuriated me. He always wanted to have the last word.

"No! You watch *your* tone. This is my house," I said, throwing my weight around. "And I can speak in any tone I want!"

"Okay, okay, I see someone wants to be left alone," he replied, a lot less assertive. "I'll be downstairs until you cool off."

I rolled my eyes. I'd just about had it with any and all bullshit. I sat here fuming about how I'd had just shelled out twenty grand to save a man I despised, and my gut told me he'd be back. Then I thought about that silly bitch calling my phone and my husband, whose insecurities were smothering me. As if all that wasn't bad enough, Tamara came home. I could hear her loud, cheery voice booming downstairs. Dishes clanked together as Tamara prepared herself a plate of food—a plate of *free* food.

Crash! Another dish hit the floor, and I hit the roof. I leaped to my feet and ran downstairs to confirm my suspicions. Just as I suspected, Tamara had broken another dish. Looking at my expensive China on the floor, I could have sworn I detected a look of satisfaction plastered on Tamara's smug face. My sixth sense told me that Tamara was deliberately sabotaging Ed and me. For some reason, today solidified any and all ill thoughts.

"Something funny?" I glared at Tamara.

"Nope," she replied dismissively and turned her back toward me.

"Since when did you become so clumsy?" I pursued.

"Excuse me?"

"You heard me. I've been to plenty of your apartments on many occasions. I never recalled when you'd broken dishes or spilled so many drinks. Nor had outbursts of hot flashes, leaving numerous windows gaping open, and the list continues. But I want to know if your new habits are only reserved when you live under my roof for free?"

"This is my brother's home, too," she sassily replied, cutting her eyes at me in annoyance.

"Your brother's house?" I had had enough. I grabbed Tamara by the back of her head and pushed her, tossing her into the kitchen chair and table. Tamara fell forward and began screaming for Ed. I pounced on her and swung heavy fists into her back before my husband pulled me off.

"Get out before I drag you out!" I yelled.

"I'm not going anywhere," Tamara challenged.

"You're getting out of here tonight! I promise you that!"

Tamara began to sob, trying to play on her brother's sympathy.

"Didn't I tell you to keep it down because Gracie was upstairs nursing a headache?" Ed asked.

"I said I was sorry. Look, I'll pay for the plate."

"Get. The. Fuck. Out. Bitch!" I said through clenched teeth, looking at Ed and daring him to say otherwise. Tamara was also looking at Ed to intervene.

Ed knew when to throw in the towel. Sensing that our marriage had gone into left field out of nowhere, he didn't want to aggravate the situation. I'd tolerated enough.

"Tamara, don't look for me to bail you out of this. You did this to yourself. You've done nothing but disrespect our home and my wife, and we've had enough. You've got to go. Tonight."

"But where will I go?"

"Go to Aunt Linda's or Cousin Maggie's."

"But I don't like them," she whined.

"Then don't stay long. You should have enough money saved by now to get your own place."

For the first time in her life, Tamara was being shut down by her brother. Quietly she went upstairs and packed her things, vowing to get me back one day very soon.

I told her to take a number.

CHAPTER

18

ANTHONY CROSS

"YOU THINK I'M STUPID? That's your new bitch!"

Dakota leaped from the bed, naked, in a rage after I'd tried to discreetly make plans with Gracie for tomorrow. I thought she was asleep, but evidently, she wasn't. Since I told her about this "new woman," Dakota's behavior had changed drastically. She was now acting crazy and deranged, and it was unnerving. The old Dakota wouldn't dare scream at me, use profanity, or behave erratically.

"What are you talking about? That was Chris, and I'm making plans to play pool later. You're just paranoid."

"Don't lie to me because I swear I will bitch slap you here and now!"

Did I just hear her correctly? My petite, five-foot-two-inch, good, innocent girl would resort to violence because she was so in love with her man? The thought turned me on. I was drawn to her immediately. I grabbed her roughly and began to kiss her lips passionately.

"Baby girl, I'm not seeing anyone," I murmured through each kiss. Dakota started to respond, and I grew more excited. She started pulling at my boxers aggressively, and I ripped them off just as quickly.

We fell onto the bed, groping each other like undersexed college kids. Our foreplay was rushed and intense. I wrapped my hands in her massive weave and pulled myself inside her tunnel with force. She was slippery and warm as I eagerly mounted her. Dakota moaned in pleasure. She wrapped her legs tightly around my waist, and we moved together. My tongue explored the inside of her ear and the nape of her neck. I then sucked each finger, savoring the taste like an expensive delicacy.

As our passion increased, so did my stamina. I stroked harder and faster, sweat dripping down the small of my back.

"I want you to come all over me," she whispered.

Not wanting to break my stride, I ignored her request. Dakota tightened her vaginal muscles and then pushed my shoulders. I hoisted myself back on my legs and watched her massage her firm breasts. My penis was brick-hard as I grabbed it and jerked off all over her chest. The "new" Dakota squealed from enjoyment. As she rubbed the warm liquid over her erect nipples, breasts, and stomach, she stared at me intently, enjoying the moment.

When did my baby become such a freak? I wondered. What other things didn't I know about Ms. Dakota?

I knew she wanted more when she spread her legs open even wider.

We engaged in lovemaking twice that night, and I fell out of bed at a quarter after eight the following day. I had to move my ass to make it into the office before nine. Dakota had forgotten about my call to Gracie while she was channeling all her attention into pleasuring me. I was glad because I couldn't take another minute of arguing.

My affair with Gracie had begun to heat up. She was vivacious, caring, and secretive. But slowly, as time passed, she began to open up—just a little. She told me that she was originally from Philadelphia. Then her family moved to Burlington, New Jersey, hence the Jersey twang in her voice. She also told me that she had two brothers, and that was it. When I probed for more information about her parents, she shut down.

I don't know if it was a gift or a curse, but her time with me was always limited. Those stolen moments had me longing to hold her all night. Still, I wondered if I actually had that luxury and whether I would have appreciated it. Or if I would have clumped Gracie with the rest of the women, I'd gone through so quickly. For now, I decided not to analyze my relationship with her and to continue having a good time.

On this night, instead of my housekeeper preparing dinner, I decided to do it myself. I was a good cook but rarely did it for anyone.

Gracie came in wearing a conservative winter white dress with matching shoes. Although I didn't want to spend another evening in my apartment, Gracie refused to have an actual date outdoors. I wanted to take her ice skating at Rockefeller Center, but she said she was in the mood for a cozy dinner and a game, preferably, Backgammon. Her paranoia was the third person in our relationship.

Her tickling my back was indicative of what she wanted to do. She'd only been inside my apartment for ten minutes and was ready—I wasn't. I removed her hands from my body and put distance between us. I don't think she realized she was more to me than a booty call. I wanted to get to know her.

"Are we going to play Backgammon?"

"Sure. That would be nice. Where is it? I'll get it," she said and hopped up. I pointed her toward the hallway closet, and when she opened it, she saw a basket full of clean laundry I hadn't had time to put away. "What's this?"

"A headache," I laughed.

"There isn't a reason why you should live like this." She pulled the basket out, reached up for the iron, and pulled out the ironing board. "As soon as the clothes come out of the dryer, you should iron them and put them away. That way, everything will always be neat and organized. And if you can't do it, ask one of your girlfriends to do it for you."

Gracie put the iron in the living room and prepared to iron my clothes.

"You don't have to do that."

"I never said that I did."

"I'm not used to this. I mean, women usually did nice things for me like cook, but never has anyone taken time out to iron my clothes."

"Anyone can whip up a dish. If you want to know if someone truly loves you, see if she'll iron your clothes or clean up your bathroom."

Was she indirectly saying she loved me? I didn't want to play myself or challenge her at the moment. I watched as she ironed all my dress shirts, sheets, and jeans and folded everything into neat piles.

"Get up and put those away," she ordered once all my jeans were ironed.

"Yes, ma'am," I said and did a one-hand salute.

It took her almost an hour to iron all my clothes, and we had a pleasant conversation, talking about nothing.

"What's your favorite song?" I asked.

"Umm, let's see…I have a lot. But my favorite song is *"Father in You"* by Mary J. Blige."

"Really? I don't think I've heard that one. Why do you like it?"

"It's just a song." She shrugged off my question. "Are you ready to play the game? I'll have to leave soon, pick up my son, and then go to the market."

"Couldn't Ed do that?" She gave me a smirk. "I'm just asking."

We played Backgammon, and of course, I won. She was gracious about losing, though, and I couldn't help but have a little fun rubbing her face in my victory.

"I'm unstoppable!" I bragged.

"Wait until next time. Next time I'll win."

"Wishful thinking," I replied, then asked, "You aren't hungry?"

"My appetite is shot," she explained. "I don't know why."

Concerned, I decided to probe. "What's going on? Is it home or work?"

She hesitated for a moment. "It's a little bit of both," she finally said.

I poured us both glasses of wine. We were sitting on my sofa in front of my vast plasma TV. I popped in a *Dave Chappelle Show* DVD but kept it mute since Gracie seemed like she wanted to talk. She put her wine glass down and curled up on me. As her head lay in my lap, I began massaging her scalp, and her eyes drifted closed.

"I've been going through so much these past couple of weeks," she said. "Ed won't allow me to do anything but go to work and come home. If I'm not home, he calls my cell all day. He doesn't trust me."

"Why would he not trust you? I thought you said you'd never done anything like this before."

"That's why he doesn't trust me. What would be your initial reaction if your wife has had the same routine for over a decade, and suddenly things change?"

"I see what you're saying."

"You don't understand, Anthony. His family has done nothing but strain our marriage, and I can't take it anymore. Do you know that his sister and I had a full-on brawl the other night? I'm damn near forty years old and tussling like a school kid in the yard."

"Who won?" I joked.

"Yo, son, you know I handled mine," she said in a gangster-like voice.

We laughed, but I knew that wasn't enough to cheer her up.

"Is she still there?"

"No, she's gone, finally."

"So your husband has been on your back, and your sister-in-law has been making your life miserable. You've handled one situation; I'm sure the other one will work out independently."

"I know."

"Anything else?"

"A little trouble back home that I hope I straightened out once and for all."

"Is everyone all right?"

"They're fine," she replied, trying to end it there, but I took it one step further.

"Are you not close with your family? You never mention them, only Ed's relatives."

"Is it that obvious?"

"Not that obvious, but I'm quite perceptive."

"I had an estranged relationship with my family for years. I don't *hate* them, but there's no love there, if that makes sense."

"I guess you have your reasons, but family's the most important thing to me. I can't even imagine being estranged from my parents."

"My situation is not for you to imagine."

"You're right," I said and realized that until I knew the whole story, it was wrong on my part to lay claim that I could never be on bad terms with my family. Something profound had gone on, and she'd open up in time. "What are you doing on Saturday?" I asked, changing the subject.

"I'm not sure yet. Why?"

"I wanted to know if you wanted to come with me and meet my parents. My dad's cooking dinner and asked if I had a special lady I wanted to bring."

Her face couldn't hide her shock.

"Umm, how nice. What a sweet gesture…let me sort out my plans and get back to you."

"I figured you'd say that."

"How did you know what I'd say before you asked?"

"Nothing. Forget it. Listen, what about the holidays? What are your plans—Thanksgiving—Christmas."

"What about them?" She pretended to be clueless.

"How will we see each other? I don't want to spend the holidays alone, and since things aren't working out for you at home, I just figured you'd want to spend them with me. We could cook for Thanksgiving or go to my parents. On Christmas, maybe exchange a few gifts…I don't know. I haven't put much thought into it."

"Obviously. Anthony, I'm married. Must I keep reminding you of that fact?"

"I know that!" I snapped and startled her. "And you'll be filing for a divorce within the next year. Why wait until then to start our lives together? You could at least do the holiday with me. He gets you every other day after that." I was sulking like a child trying to get my way.

"Why are you always complaining? Why can't you just enjoy what we have? All I'm asking is that you be patient until I tell Ed I want a divorce."

"When?!"

"I don't know!"

"There isn't a need to travel at warp speed!"

"Well, I'm not getting any younger."

"You'll always be younger than me," Gracie said, rolling her eyes.

"You're so selfish and cavalier regarding my feelings."

She thought for a moment. "What about my daughter?"

"What, daughter?"

"I have a child, remember?" Gracie threw her hands up in surrender as if she'd been talking to a wall all this time.

"Clearly, I do. I remember you saying that you had a son!"

"What, are you crazy?"

"I know what I've heard! You said earlier that you had to leave early to pick up your son!"

"Why would I say I had a son when I don't!"

"That's what I'm asking you!"

We were in a shouting match, and neither wanted to back down.

"Okay, maybe I said, son. Perhaps I was being guarded with my daughter's identity. But you're acting as if I intentionally lied to you, and I resent that."

She began gathering up her coat, and I panicked.

"Look, I'm sorry if I came across that way. It took me by surprise when you said daughter when I already had in my mind how it would be to meet your son. I apologize for making you feel slighted or disrespected. It's the holiday season, and I'm a little stressed with bills and the office. "Please, don't go," I said, gently taking her coat from her arms and tossing it back over the couch.

Gracie began to relax.

"Can you do me a favor," she asked.

"I don't see why you think I should," I said, smiling.

"Can we not talk about me and my situation? I just want to enjoy you and our time together. We have so little time together."

I nodded my head and smiled slightly.

"What's this about bills and the office? Why didn't you tell me? You're always asking about me and my life, and I'm so selfish that I hardly ever ask about you."

"It's nothing really too pressing. I'm just trying to pay off my student loans while maintaining my practice and lifestyle."

"You're having money trouble?"

"I mean not like that. I'm not getting kicked out on my ass or anything. It's just that it'll be two years since my practice opened in March, and the first two years of any business are always tough. I do have a slew of patients, but my overhead's crazy. My mortgage on this apartment is obscene, and I still owe over two-hundred grand in student loans."

Any other woman would have never heard this information. I'm Dr. Anthony Cross, New York's most eligible bachelor. For some reason, I felt comfortable with Gracie and wanted to be who I was, not put on any fronts.

"How much exactly do you owe?"

I tossed my head in the sky, trying to remember the amount on my last statement. "I think it's $240,000. Why?"

"I'll pay half."

"Excuse me?"

"You heard me." When she smiled, I knew she wasn't kidding.

"What...why...how?"

"Don't worry about all of that. Just know that I'll help you. I want to help you. I want you to know that I'm in this for as long as you are, and I'm sorry that my situation has put you through any stress. I'll go with you next Saturday to meet your parents. That is if you still want me to."

"Yes, of course, I want you to come. But I can't take the money."

"Don't be a fool."

"Gracie, I'm serious. I'm a man who can't take another man's money! In five years, I'm going to be straight."

"I know, baby," she said and cupped my face. "I believe in you. You've accomplished more at your age than most. You make me so proud of you."

I blushed.

"And you won't be taking my husband's money. The money...it's mine to give."

I was floored. Gracie had more sides to her than an octagon. She was so mysterious, secretive, yet so vibrant. Just as much as she drove me crazy, she intrigued me. Of course, her response opened the floodgates for more questioning.

"You're worth enough to write me a check for over one hundred thousand dollars without speaking to your financial advisor?"

"Seems so."

"How? Are your parents wealthy? Was your money inherited?"

"Anthony, please, not now. I don't have much time here and want to enjoy you. Maybe, take a little stress off the both of us."

I knew what she needed.

I ambled to my bedroom with Gracie right on my heels. She stood back and let me undress her. I unbuttoned her shirt and let it cascade to the floor. Next, I unzipped her skirt, and she stepped out of it. There she stood with her hands covering her breasts, as sexy as any man could ever want a woman to be. She seemed bashful yet alluring, and I could tell she was playing a role.

My penis bulged through my jeans, and I hadn't touched her. Her sexual prowess was intoxicating. She sashayed over and stood on her tiptoes to kiss me. I leaned over and met her lips, and we began to kiss passionately. Her soft tongue expertly maneuvered inside my mouth and left me wanting to have sex all night. I pulled her in closer, pressed my pelvis against hers, and began to rock while gently cupping both breasts and playfully licking her areolas. She moaned her pleasure, leaned her head back, and seemed lost in the moment. I picked her up, walked over to my bed, and gently laid her down. As she lay looking up at me, I began to undress.

I looked directly into her eyes. They were talking nasty to me. Layer by layer, I removed each piece of my clothing and tossed it to the ground. When I was completely naked, my penis stood at attention. I stuck my finger in her sweet cave and felt her wetness. I grabbed her pedicured feet and began to lovingly suck each toe. I knew she could tell this would be a lovemaking session because I was sure the moment's intensity showed on my face.

I took my time as I made my way to her inner thigh and then to her clitoris. Expertly I performed cunnilingus in a controlled manner. Twenty minutes later, I was still tasting her sweet nectar. Her smell had me hooked. I could stay down there forever. She rocked her hips sensually and had to bite down on her hand to keep from screaming out. As her legs trembled, it turned me on. She made little love sounds like she was enjoying it just as much as I did.

When the feeling got too intense, she reached down and gripped my silk sheets as solid waves of pleasure came pouring out of her like a waterfall. I pleasured her highly aroused area and traced her erogenous zones with my tongue. Her body was hot and slippery as I tantalized and tickled her most sensitive areas, making her feel many new sensations.

Finally, I grabbed a condom and positioned myself to enter her.

"I'm just going to give you a little bit," I whispered in her ear. "I promise."

She lay passively as I applied pressure. I felt as if I was dominating her body as my pleasure intensified. She wrapped her legs around my waist, our limbs entwined, and we began making love. Each deep stroke opened her resisting walls. I gritted my teeth as I broke through.

I prolonged my climax because I wanted her to have multiple orgasms, and I was still maneuvering her through erotic positions. We made love until we had no bodily fluids left to excrete. Soon Gracie told me she had to go home.

"You hungry yet?" I asked.

"No. But I'll take a plate home with me."

"You sure?"

"Yes. I want to taste your cooking."

"That's why I made it, so you can see that I can throw down in the kitchen. You were supposed to eat it here with me."

"I know, baby. Thank you . . . next time. In fact, next, I'll cook for you. I'll bring the groceries and cook something. Would you like that?"

"Yes, I would."

I walked Gracie to the kitchen to make herself a plate of food, but she didn't make just one plate. Immediately pangs of jealousy shot through my body.

"Who's the second plate for?"

"Oh, I'm sorry. Am I taking too much? Did you want leftovers?"

"No, it's not that, but you won't eat both plates, right? I hope you're not disrespecting me and taking a plate home to eat with your husband." My insecurities were back.

"Come on now, that's not fair. I could never do such a thing. I was thinking about my little girl. Is that all right?"

"Of course, it is," I said, relieved and feeling dumb. "Not a problem. I just hope you like it."

As she fixed her plates, I began asking more questions.

"How did you and Ed meet?"

"It was a long time ago," she said, looking aloof at the ceiling. "I was in love with the idea of being in love."

"Was he your first? The first man you really fell in love with. Not puppy love. The real thing?"

"Who remembers?"

"You don't remember what he had to do to get you to walk down the aisle?"

"He sold me a dream, and I bought it," she replied sourly.

"If you had to do it all over again, would you?"

"I don't know. I've been so confused lately."

"So what type of men do you go after? What do you like other than handsome, successful men like me? Is your husband a good-looking guy by a woman's standard?"

Jeez, do I sound insecure? Am I prying too much? I wondered.

"How does my husband look? Is that your question?"

"Well, not like that. I'm trying to get to know you better. His looks are inconsequential."

"I guess I'm attracted to sexier than good-looking, but there has to be a mixture of both."

"Do all your men look alike and have similar characteristics?"

"All my men? What are you suggesting?"

"No, not like that. I'm just saying—"

"What?" she challenged, and I could tell I'd annoyed her.

"I'm wondering if someone saw me, whether they'd say I was

your type."

"Fuck what other people would say. This is about you and me."

"You're right . . ." I replied, letting my words trail off. It was time to end that conversation before I dug an even deeper grave of embarrassment.

"Baby, I gotta go." She planted a nice, wet kiss on my lips. "Thank you for the food. And before I forget," she reached inside her purse and pulled out her checkbook.

"Gracie, please, this isn't necessary." My plea was weak at best. She kept writing.

"I'll leave the top blank. One-hundred and twenty-thousand dollars…that should do it. I'll see you next week, Saturday?"

I slapped her on her ass.

"Don't play. You better get your ass back over here way before then."

"Anthony," she looked over her shoulder, "I'm trying. Can you see that…I am trying…to make it work. Please just work with me."

"I know, baby, I will."

I stared at Gracie's check for hours. What type of woman drops a hundred grand on someone she just met? What do I mean to her? Where's this relationship going? And if Ed isn't the breadwinner, why isn't she divorcing his ass? Maybe he'll stand to take a lot of her money, and it wasn't only about her daughter. Gracie confiding in me had only left me more confused.

CHAPTER

19

GRACIE LANE

I WAS RUNNING APPROXIMATELY FIFTEEN minutes late after leaving Anthony's house. I had made up an imaginary volunteer job at NewYork-Presbyterian Hospital to garner more time away from home. Still, I should have been home by now. And on the dot, Ed began calling.

"I'll be home in a few minutes," I said, slightly aggravated by his stalker-like ways. "I'm about to get off the highway as we speak."

"Okay, honey. Look, we should take it easy tonight. Elana had to leave early and left a note on the refrigerator that she couldn't prepare dinner. How about I order us Chinese takeout or pizza? Would you like that?"

"Umm, I got us something already. I'll see you soon. Love you."

"Love you, too."

The cold winter air inside the unheated underground garage froze my cheeks before entering the elevator and making it up to our house. Ed made a comment when I went to give him a kiss.

"You're frozen."

"I know, baby. Just from that short distance, too. It seems as though the temperature dropped from earlier this morning."

"It did," Ed said as he helped me remove my coat and noticed the food bag in my hand. "Where did you get this?" he asked.

"Anika stopped by and brought us a couple of plates. Wasn't that nice?"

Ed grunted. "Maybe we should test it for poison."

Ed didn't like Anika. He couldn't understand why she was always hanging around me. He hated that she came over, borrowed money, wore my clothes, and ate our food. And she washed and dried all her clothes as if we owned and operated a laundry service—the nerve when his sister, Tamara, did the same thing.

Ed set the table as I removed my clothes and returned downstairs in my pajamas for dinner.

"This looks great," he commented as he looked at the T-bone steak, mixed vegetables, and sweet potato. "Since when does Anika cook like this?"

"You'd know if you allowed yourself to get to know her better."

He flicked a fork full of vegetables at me, and we laughed at his silliness.

I thought about how great of a catch Anthony was. He was

successful, he could fuck, he cooked, he was handsome, he had brains, and so on. But he wasn't Ed.

Later that night, before we went to bed, Ed stepped out of the shower, naked, and asked, "Babe, am I getting fat?"

I laughed. "You mean those love handles?"

"You see them too, right? No matter how hard I work on them in the gym, they won't disappear."

"Edward Lane, what's wrong with you?" I asked. "You have a perfect body."

He stood there for a moment, dripping wet, staring at me. Then he cracked a small smile.

"You still think I got a perfect body?"

"Did you hear me complaining?"

"Well, no, but I just wanted to be sure. I don't want you leaving me for no body-building jock."

I cocked my head back and laughed.

"We're gonna be old and gray, swaying on rocking chairs, before you'll get rid of me."

"'Til the end?" Ed asked and kissed me full on my lips.

"'Til the end, babe. I wouldn't have it any other way."

T.G.I.F. was all I could keep repeating in my head. I promised to meet with Anthony and his parents tomorrow, although that wasn't my scene. Luckily, I had my fingers crossed when I committed. I sat back and thought about how George had never even called to bid me a thank you for the $20,000 I'd dumped into his account to save his sorry ass. George and his gang of sons were the most fallible, stubborn men I'd ever met, and I was sure that if God didn't grant me immunity for my sins, then I'd meet them in Hell.

I was working a double shift today and wouldn't get off until eleven P.M. I didn't come in all week, but the supervisor called said they were short-staffed and asked if I could. It was just nearing 3:00 P.M., and I still had another shift left before I could go home and relax for the weekend. I had a facial and massage scheduled on Lexington Avenue this Sunday afternoon and was looking forward to that. A day of pampering myself was always enjoyable.

At this hour, my job was bursting with noise. All the consumers—the name the workers used for the mentally challenged residents—were back from school, and all my coworkers were busy finishing their daily duties. My Brad Pitt look-alike coworker, Skipper, had arrived at work earlier than usual. He wasn't due to come in until the 4:00 P.M. shift. He grabbed me by my hand when he saw me and hustled me into one of the empty rooms.

"Sexy, I need you," he said, groping my hips and ass. My adrenaline started pumping at the prospect of getting caught.

So this explains his early arrival, I thought. I had been having an affair at work with Skipper for over a year. Although he was a white boy, he packed a nice package. We'd have hot, sneaky sex in the most peculiar places around our job, from outback near the woods to the basement where they stored the food to the laundry room. None of our coworkers had ever caught on to our fling.

Keeping a fuck buddy at work was the smartest thing I could have ever done. Ed was none the wiser about my liaison. I had always made it home on time, and the affair with Skipper never spilled over into the outside world. It was strictly confined to our workplace.

Just as I began sliding up my skirt to give him access, Jessica yelled for me to come into the foyer.

"Gracie, could you come here for a moment?"

"Okay," I yelled out, "In a moment."

"Skipper, stay and wait until I come back. Keep it hot for me, baby."

I did a slight trot down the steps to where Jessica stood, her hands perched on her hips.

"Come with me inside my office."

I walked behind my supervisor, and when I entered, she closed the door to give us privacy.

"Did you ever get that situation straightened with your social security card?"

"No, no, but it most likely concerns my stolen wallet. I have a fraud alert filed with all the credit bureaus. This must have to do with my identity being stolen."

"Well, I don't know how or what you'll do to straighten this out, but the IRS called today. They said you and another person named Gracie Ferguson are filing their taxes under the same social security number. Here's a number that they want you to contact them at."

My heart dropped into the pit of my stomach after hearing that news.

"Human Resources called back," Jessica continued. "And we'll have to lay you off until you get this situation straightened out. At this point, you don't exist."

"What?! Jessica, no! This is my life. This is what keeps me from going insane," I pleaded.

"You're not even getting paid for this. Why are you so upset?"

"I'm benefiting in my own way. Look, it's personal. You

obviously wouldn't understand."

Jessica stared at me awkwardly. "This wasn't my decision. Do you think I want to be short-staffed? Today will be your last day until we get a letter from the IRS clearing you as the authentic Gracie. Vanessa has agreed to cover your second shift."

I sat there, shell-shocked. Why was everything crumbling around me? What did they know? Were those people getting closer? Is it over for me? I realized that I was paranoid. If they were coming, there wouldn't be any warnings.

"Okay, I'll get this whole matter straightened out, and hopefully, I'll be back to work next week," I replied with false bravado.

I hoped Jessica couldn't see the fear in my eyes as I slowly got up. Never telling Skipper I was leaving, I grabbed my keys and coat and bolted out the door without looking back.

On the ride home from Long Island, I felt sick. The IRS and Human Resources were both after me. Things were moving too quickly. I had to think of a way to slow down everything. I knew I had until Monday morning to think of something before calling the government. I decided not to tell Ed about the layoff. I'd just look for another fulfilling volunteer job and use the excuse that I no longer wanted to travel the distance to Long Island.

Instead, I called Anthony on his private line at work and told him I'd been laid off. He couldn't understand why I was upset when it was "only" volunteer work.

"Because I'm giving back to the community."

"Oh, I see. Well, I'm sorry about your situation. Anything I can do to help, just let me know. In fact, if you'd like to put in a few hours around here, we could certainly use the help."

I thought about it for a moment.

"That's a really nice offer, but it's not the same. I spent ten-hour days helping adults who couldn't bathe or feed themselves. I helped them get dressed in the mornings and fed them dinner at night. They needed me. They depended on me, making me feel as if I mattered and was making a difference in someone's life. Working for a plastic surgeon whose patients were vain, snobby whores—"

"Weren't you just in here a couple months back?"

"Exactly. Your patients are vain, snobby whores!"

We both laughed.

"I understand. I'll call around and see if anyone in a more *worthy* practice is looking for someone as caring as you. Just note that I'm only calling female practitioners!"

I didn't tell Anthony the actual story; I told him they were phasing out their volunteer department due to office politics. He was so sympathetic that he told me to go to his place, and he'd call security in his building so I could get in and relax until he arrived. As I drove there, I poured out my little heart. He gave me all his attention, telling Anika to hold his calls. I sobbed like a baby as I told him my fears. I couldn't understand why it was so easy to talk to Anthony. Maybe it was his smooth voice, or perhaps it was that I didn't care if he judged me. Although I didn't tell him anything incriminating because I trusted no one, I told him bits and pieces of my past, which was somewhat cathartic.

"They're looking for me," I cried.

"Who, baby? Who's looking for you?"

"These crazy people...they hate me...they hate me...."

"Are you in danger? Huh? Is someone trying to harm you?"

"It wasn't my fault...If I could take it back, I would...but I can't...."

"Baby, what do you want me to do? Tell me how I can make it better." His voice was shaky; I detected his panic. I got my composure together.

"No, I'll be all right. I'll explain when I see you. I love you," I said out of habit in a crisis. I didn't know what made me say it, but it was too late for correction. I didn't mean it, and I hoped Anthony realized I'd only said it under duress because I felt vulnerable. He never voiced his feelings, and I was happy.

I was inside Anthony's apartment for less than an hour before there was a knock on the door. Hesitant to open it because I wasn't expecting anyone, nor did I live there, all types of thoughts went through my mind when I heard the head of security, Bruce, call out to me. I recognized his voice and opened the door. The aroma hit me first—a variety of smells, from food to flowers. Several delivery men and women came hustling into the apartment. Anthony had sent an enormous flower arrangement of lilies, long-stemmed roses, violets, and orchids with a card that said:

SORRY BUT I HAVE TO WORK LATE.

I LOVE YOU, TOO.

A.C.

So much for thinking that he missed the *love you* thing. He also sent a gourmet dish of steamed lobster, vegetables, and a tossed salad. Finally, a masseuse was equipped with her own massage table and oils. I was treated like a queen for the next hour, and my stress was finally dissolved.

After a brief nap in Anthony's apartment, I had to leave. I'd only come to get a quickie. I called him at work to thank him, but he was in surgery, so I left him a thank-you message on his cell phone. Before leaving, I wrote a note, sprayed it with my perfume, and signed it with a kiss.

On my way home, I ignored a call from Vanessa, who was undoubtedly nosy, and called Anika instead.

"Hey, girl," I said.

"What's up?"

"Don't say anything, but I lost my job today."

"What? How can a volunteer lose her job when they ain't paying you? Pah-leeze, I wish someone would try to fire my ass when I'm technically not hired. I'd tell them to shove—"

"Anika!" I had to stop her because she would have gone on for hours making threats.

"What happened?"

"Please, just let me vent."

"Oh, my bad. Why did they let you go?"

"My past. Need I say more?"

"Are those peoples close?"

"No, it's not anything like that. There's a mishap with my social security number, and I was flagged."

She exhaled. "Damn, Gracie, what's Ed gonna say?"

"You know I can't tell him."

"I know. Well, if there's anything I can do, let me know. You know I got your back."

"Yes, I know," I replied. "Listen, I'm on my way home. I'll call you tonight."

"Gracie—"

"Yes?"

"I know this is a bad time with you losing your job. But as I said, they weren't paying you anyway. But I wanted to know if I could borrow $2000 to catch up on some credit card bills."

"Sure, that's not a problem. Do you want to come over and pick up a check?"

"Umm, could you put it into my account as you did before?"

"Done. And you don't have to borrow it. Consider it an early holiday gift."

"Thanks, Gracie."

I was minutes away from home, and reality began to sink in again.

I told Ed that I was going to the Metropolitan Museum of Art to have an interview in hopes of securing another volunteer job. Ed worked 40-hour weeks at Verizon and was happy I used my free time productively. Unbeknownst to him, I used my free time to help maintain my affair.

I arrived at Anthony's early enough to make breakfast. I scrambled an egg white omelet with peppers and mushrooms, and then we climbed back into his bed for a quickie. When I went to shower before preparing to leave for his parent's home, I glanced in the mirror and noticed that Anthony had left a hickey on my back. *Kinky*, I thought. And I loved it. As I lathered my body, I replayed our sex session and wondered if Anthony could be more to me than just a fuck buddy. He'd begun to show signs of wanting more from me other than sex. We spoke on the phone, having long, meaningful conversations. He loved to do romantic things for me and kept referencing my leaving my husband. No, Anthony had definitely moved from fuck buddy to histress. *And what was a histress?* I thought. It was a male in a long-term relationship with a married woman. He was the male version

188

mistress. Yes, he was my histress.

Fully dressed, I met Anthony at his dining room table, where he was drinking a mid-afternoon coffee. He'd poured me a cup.

I blurted, "Can we talk?"

Anthony looked up with fear in his eyes.

"Sure, what's up?"

I grabbed my coffee cup and sipped the rich, hot liquid. "I know I'm not an open book, and I'm sure that can be tiresome. But I've put up a wall around myself for legitimate reasons."

"Of course, you have. But I also know I must earn your trust, and I hope I've done that."

I nodded. "I've been awful to you." My eyes began to well up with tears.

"Shh, baby, what's wrong. Why the tears?"

I spewed, "I'm so confused lately. I don't know what I'm doing anymore. I don't want to hurt Ed because he's a good man. And I don't want to hurt you, either. I know I'm in a precarious situation, and everything won't end amicably." I was sobbing uncontrollably.

Anthony raced over and grabbed me into a tight embrace. His strong arms felt comforting as I clutched his forearms.

"You know it's over, don't you. With your husband and marriage, you're afraid. You're afraid that you may trade in your husband for me and that I may turn out to be your worst fear. Is that it? Is that why you've been so emotional lately?"

"I want to leave him. I want to leave him now, but I don't know how. We both said we were in it forever, but my forever has turned out to be ten years. What kind of wife am I?"

When did I become such an actress? My lips were trembling, and for a split second, I actually believed my words. Truth be told,

I was scared shitless about my situation. When I walked out of my apartment building today, I looked over my shoulders. A man came up to me in a trench coat and asked whether I had a light for his cigarette, and I thought my world as I'd known it for two decades was about to end. And then, finally, I thought about Ed. I loved him more than I could ever express, and I didn't want him to get caught up in my past. I even considered packing up and fleeing. Leaving everything and everyone behind. I'd done it once and was sure I could do it again, so why was I still here? The heat was definitely around the corner....

"Gracie, don't beat yourself up. You're human with feelings and emotions, and values. Don't be this martyr for married women. People get divorced every day. Your daughter will understand, and your husband will get over it. Let me ask you a question."

"Anything."

"Am I the reason you're getting a divorce?"

"Truthfully?"

"Please."

"No."

"No?"

"No," I repeated.

I don't know if my response was what Anthony wanted to hear because he didn't probe further. The awkward moment was tempered by his home phone ringing.

"Yes, hello...hey Dad...is she all right? Okay, no problem...we'll reschedule...tell Mom I love her."

Anthony hung up and turned to me.

"Is everything okay?"

"Yes. That was my father. My mother isn't feeling well today, so he thought it best to cancel our plans. I really wanted them to meet you."

"They'll be other times."

"So, what are we going to do today? Any suggestions? And please don't say that we should get back in bed!"

"Okay, you didn't have to say it like that. As if that's all we do," I said, giggling. "Hey, I got an idea. Why don't we go to the shooting range and let off some steam."

"Shooting range?"

"It'll be fun."

"I've never handled a gun before."

"Stop being a punk. You're only shooting at targets. We can go to the shooting range in Bay Ridge, Brooklyn. You in?"

"Yes, I'm in. Sounds like a plan."

"I'll need to borrow one of your shirts. This shirt is too dressy," I said, looking down at the silk blouse I planned to wear to Anthony's parents.

Anthony drove us to the firing range, and we stopped along the way and got frozen smoothies from Baskin & Robbins. I hated to admit it, but I had a fantastic time doing nothing more than hanging out.

We both showed our licenses and were told to pick out our guns when we arrived. I chose a 9mm Glock, and Anthony chose what I considered to be a more personal gun—the revolver. Anthony paid for four cartridges, and we were given our eye and ear protective gear. And after we holstered our guns, we proceeded to our target areas. Only paper targets at 25 ft distances were allowed at Bay Ridge Gun Club.

I took aim at my target and began to shoot. I must admit I was a little rusty. I hadn't been at a range in over two years. Once I pulled the trigger, my heart began palpitating. I can't quite explain the adrenaline rush or sense of satisfaction I got. I would almost compare it to your anticipation when slowly climbing a rollercoaster track and the drop your stomach feels when you plunge. It was euphoric.

Anthony went through his four rounds quickly and didn't want to re-up his cartridges.

"What's the matter?"

"I don't like this."

"You don't? Why not? I'm having fun."

"It's not stimulating. This isn't my idea of a fun day with my girl. You and I don't have any contact, and my mind isn't doing much but focusing on a stupid piece of paper and trying to see how close I can land a few bullets. I can't believe you like this sport."

"No big deal. This just isn't for you. I'm sorry I wasted your time. I was being selfish."

"Any time I get to spend with you isn't wasted. And believe me, I'm most grateful. But I'd preferred to do something I suggested, like ice skating in Rockefeller Center. We can hold hands. We can fall together. You know, couple stuff."

Anthony was really trying to make this work. I impulsively said, "Hey, I got a better idea. Why don't we go away? Let me plan a trip for just the two of us. We'll go right after the New Year. Would you like that?"

"Hell, yeah, I'd like that."

"So that's what it is then."

CHAPTER

20

ANTHONY CROSS

"YOU'VE GOT TO BE KIDDING ME, MAN," I told Chris. He had just gotten a check in the mail with his return on his first investment.

"This guy's a pure genius," he bragged. "A financial guru who could triple my net worth in two years if I played my cards right."

"I hate you right now!" I could have kicked myself for not getting in on that deal. Although I was doing all right for myself with the help of Gracie and a few new customers this month, it would have felt great to have earned a return on investment. My common sense told me I needed to check out Gabriel before investing.

"Haters never win," he replied in his ordinarily soft voice. "Would you believe he has something else in the pipeline? A bigger deal. Same margin for return."

"He wants me to get in on this one?" I asked skeptically.

"You can't."

"Not even with the lowest investment? The twenty-grand?"

"Nope. Gabriel's got all the investors needed. If he and I weren't cool, I wouldn't have gotten in either."

"So why are you calling me bragging and shit." I was pissed. Although I didn't want in, I was upset that I wasn't afforded the opportunity. And it seemed that Chris only called to gloat.

"I'm not bragging. I'm calling my man to share my good news, thinking he would be happy for a brother. But, again, it's always only about you!"

Chris hung up. I shrugged it off; he was too emotional.

Two hours later, he called me back. His tone was cavalier.

"Gabriel has invited us to his art gallery on some top-secret shit. You down or what?"

"I was on my way out to the gym. Why does he want me to come along, and what's this about?"

"Again, I just said it's some top-secret shit. Either you're in or out. No one's going to beg you. Gabriel said he's sending his car and driver to pick us up."

"Okay, sounds like a plan. I'll be ready in an hour."

Gabriel's chauffeur-driven Bentley arrived, and I must admit that Gabriel impressed me. Sitting in the backseat and smoking a cigar was Chris. I openly smiled as I got in.

"Hey, man, I didn't know you smoked cigars."

"No, you didn't know I could *afford* cigars...the good shit," he replied, and I detected tension.

"So, did Gabriel tell you why he wanted me to come?"

"You're only invited because of me. Don't think that Gabriel's really checking for you like that." Chris repeated, "You're here on the strength of me!"

"Gabriel's your man. If you're taking my relationship with your friend personally, don't. It's purely business, and you should get over any hang-ups."

I needed to set Chris straight. He was acting as if I owed him something.

"C'mon, you're my man, and Gabriel's my man," Chris said, pretending he wasn't just giving me attitude. "I don't have anything but love for you guys, and I want all of us to get that money. I'm only going today to purchase some art from him. He bought a few pieces from Christie's two years ago and sold them at a sixty percent profit."

"Really?"

"Yes, really. This time next year, my bank account will look like yours."

"You wish," I said and punched him in his arm. "So this is about art?"

"Yes. He has some good pieces and thought you'd be interested."

Only I wasn't. Chris should have said this before he dragged me out of the house. I decided to keep quiet. There wasn't anything I could do now.

In the middle of our male bonding, my phone rang, and it was Dakota. I wasn't in the mood for her now, but I knew she'd call and leave a million messages if I didn't pick up.

"Hey, Ant," she said.

"Hey, Dee. I have to be in surgery in ten minutes. I'll call you as soon as I'm done."

"Promise?"

"Without my fingers crossed?" I joked. "Never."

"Okay, love you."

"Okay."

"Say it," she whined. "Say you love me."

"Goodbye, Dee."

I really needed to cut Dakota loose so she could find someone deserving of her because I genuinely felt little to nothing. Everything she did and said irked my nerves. She could barely hold my attention for more than a few moments, and those moments usually involved sex.

We pulled up in front of an upscale art gallery on Long Island. It was huge and took up most of the block. Gabriel's black Maserati was parked in his RESERVED spot. I started to seriously feel poor compared to this guy's wealth. I began to wrestle with the idea of investing a small portion of my money. Gracie had paid a chunk of my debt, but I didn't want to start mooching off her, as I'm sure her husband was. If I invested my money wisely, perhaps I could repay her even though she said the money was a gift. I think I'd feel better about myself as a man if I could give Gracie back her money.

Maybe I would invest a conservative amount of money if I wanted to play with the big boys.

Several people were in the gallery, admiring the art. I crept up behind a woman staring intently at something that looked very abstract. She was an ordinary-looking white woman with a Black girl's shape. That StairMaster was every white girl's savior. Finally, they, too, had a butt and thighs.

"What do you think about the painting?" I asked her out of curiosity.

"Which one?"

"Ahh, this one." I pointed to a picture of a house and grass.

"It's a post-impressionist piece—*Restaurant de la Sirene at Asnieres* by Vincent Van Gogh."

"Van Gogh, huh? I prefer Monet," I lied and then switched the subject so as not to make it too apparent that I was a novice art observer. "My friend Gabriel owns this place."

For once, I used another man's credentials to impress a lady instead of mine.

"I've seen him around here but never met him. Do you think you could make an introduction? I'd love to discuss art with him."

I looked at this small-framed, assertive woman going for hers. She looked around twenty-five years old and was possibly looking for a husband, but not just any husband: a successful husband. I admired her for knowing how to play the game. You want to meet successful men, then go to the right places. I told Anika that all the time. She always ran out to the nightclubs thinking she would find something worth marrying there. There were a bunch of wannabe rappers, record producers, drug hustlers, and wannabe single men who were married.

"I'll see what I can do," I responded as Chris called me into the back for our business meeting.

Gabriel had a huge office, several paintings on canvases propped up against the walls. He was sitting behind a massive mahogany desk with an oversized leather chair. His Breitling watch glistened, peeking out from the sleeve of his cufflinked shirt.

I shook his hand.

"Man, thank you for inviting me here today. This place is awe-inspiring."

"Don't mention it. I'm glad you could come down."

"I want to hear about these paintings," Chris said, taking the focus off me and putting it on himself.

"I'm auctioning off three paintings from my collection at Sotheby's and Christie's next week. I bought them a handsome price a couple of years ago and will sell them for a profit. I'm willing to sell them to you for my asking price minus the fee that the auction houses will take. So it's a win-win for everyone."

"Well, how much are they worth, and how much do they cost?"

Gabriel tossed Chris a book with Post-It notes marking three pages. Chris flipped through the pages and saw the three paintings with descriptions. Then Gabriel walked us over to three artworks.

"This one will go on the market for $250,000," Gabriel said, pointing to the first painting. "This one for $285,000, and finally, the last one will go for $320,000."

"Are you sure these will sell for those prices?" Chris asked.

"No."

"No?"

"Correct. It's an auction. They will sell much higher to the highest bidder. Those prices are what I'll take from you, but I could potentially sell for much more."

"So why would you make this direct sell and not try to get the maximum amount?" I asked. I was curious. It seemed risky.

As Gabriel educated us on art, he turned over paintings and

showed us their Certificate of Authenticity. I gained a new respect for something I knew virtually nothing about. Art was like fine wine. You bought it, held it, let it marinate, and then sold it at a profit. Easy. You had to keep some paintings longer than others, but all were worth the investment. When you held the painting, you placed it on your wall and discussed it at dinner parties.

When Gabriel was done talking, I bought *View From The Artist's Window at Eragny* by Camille Pissarro for $280,000. I almost had to pry it out of Chris's hands. He didn't even have all the liquid to purchase it, but he didn't want me to have it, which only made me want it more.

When the deal was done, I knew I'd messed up. I used all the money Gracie had given me and most of my liquid in the bank. Although I felt there was a light at the end of my tunnel with the potential profit I'd make at an auction, I hoped I hadn't made a grave mistake. This deal seemed less risky than the investment deal Gabriel had spoken about before today. These paintings were authentic, and Gabriel had the Certificate of Authenticity to prove he was the rightful owner. And Christie's had a picture of each portrait, which was exactly what I was staring at.

After the art deals, Gabriel detailed his next business adventure. He explained that he owned $1.2 million shares of Microsoft stock that had accumulated over two decades and that he was now optioning those shares at $85.00 per share. Chris quickly told him that he was in for 5000 shares. Where the hell was Chris getting all the liquid to keep investing? I decided to intervene on behalf of my friend as a precautionary measure.

"Chris, why don't you have Gabriel send over the prospectus and have your lawyer review the documents before you proceed?"

Instantly, I realized that I had ruffled a few feathers.

"I assure you I have nothing to hide," Gabriel remarked dryly.

"Ant, I know how to handle mine. You just worry about yours. I got this. I've been doing deals with Gabriel before you came around."

"So be it," I said, relenting.

"So be it."

In the car, I called my baby.

"Gracie, I miss you!"

CHAPTER

21

SECRETS

CHRISTOPHER WILKENS WANTED MONEY so badly that he thought he could almost do the unthinkable. No one knew this, but he thought about robbing a bank right before meeting Gabriel. He had the plan down to the last-minute detail and his alibi. He hated that he owned a co-op in Brooklyn and Anthony owned a condominium on the Upper Eastside. He had to bail out criminals, and Anthony had a distinguished career as a plastic surgeon. Most importantly, he hated that it was hard to get women because they thought he was gay and living on the down low.

The two men were in Gabriel's plush home in the Hamptons on Long Island. They drove up for the weekend at Gabriel's request. He wanted to show Chris the location of a new hotel he would build once he gathered all the investors.

"What's going on with your friend, Anthony?" Gabriel asked.

"What do you mean?"

"I thought you said that he had a lot of money."

"He does."

"And he doesn't want to invest any of it?"

"Didn't I say I didn't want you letting him in on any deals until I've made a good chunk of money?"

"Why? I thought he was your friend."

"He is, but you wouldn't understand our relationship. I've always had to stand in his shadow since I've known him. He grew up in a two-parent home; my dad was a deadbeat who never came around. I had to study twice as hard in school to get Cs; he got As without breaking a sweat. Then to add insult to injury, he announced when we were in high school that he was going to medical school!"

"And?"

"Don't you hear me? He never wanted to be a doctor. That was *my* dream! He'd said he would be a lawyer so he wouldn't be a cliché and follow in his dad's footsteps. However, I wanted to follow in his dad's footsteps. I wanted his dad to be my dad!"

Gabriel looked at the pathetic man, who he figured had hit a low point in his life. Or maybe he'd lost his mind from all the drugs he was doing. Gabriel had supplied the grade-A quality of pure, uncut cocaine that Chris was sucking up his nose like a Hoover vacuum cleaner.

"You can't be serious."

"But I—" sniff, sniff, "am serious. I fucking can't—" sniff, sniff, sniff, "stand him."

"I understand," Gabriel empathized. "And you said Kevin and Lance wouldn't have any money to invest. Is that right?"

"Those two are freeloaders. They definitely don't have any investment money." He summed up his two friends in two sentences. "Kevin's living off his wife, and Lance ain't shit!"

"So, are you ready for this big deal I got going? I told you that I wouldn't just let anyone in on this, but I want you to be able to compete with Anthony. I want you to be able to throw your weight around and make him live in your shadow for once."

"That's what the fuck I'm talking about!"

Gabriel ambled over to Chris, put his hands on his shoulders, and massaged him. "Just relax and take it easy."

Chris swatted him away and continued to do his expensive powdery white substance line. Gabriel was unrelenting. He watched Chris fall into his own zone and collapse back into the plush sofa, eyes closed, while surfing on his own high. He began tapping his feet and snapping his fingers while singing a song Gabriel didn't know. Slowly, Gabriel touched his face. Groggily, Chris's eyes opened lazily. He wasn't sure if he'd really felt the touch or if he imagined it. As Chris's eyes opened to their full potential, they were shocked to see Gabriel's paper-thin lips approaching at warp speed, ready to plant a wet kiss on him. Chris went nuts.

"What are you doing, man?!"

"I thought you and I were cool?"

"We are, but not like that! I'm not gay!"

"Okay, okay, calm down. It's not a big deal."

"If you ever pull that fag shit again, I will fucking end you!" Chris reached into his oversized jeans, pulled out a large gun, and flashed it before Gabriel to prove he meant business. As a licensed bail bondsman, Chris had a gun permit and wouldn't hesitate to use it; on anyone. "I'm no queer, alright. I'm just a regular Black man trying to get that paper, and you'll help me. Do I make myself clear?"

"Crystal."

CHAPTER
22

GRACIE LANE

ED WAS BEGINNING TO BECOME A PAIN in my ass, I thought. Every day and night, he was screaming about something or another. "You're not spending enough time at home," or "You don't do anything with me." How was I supposed to want to do anything with him when he constantly complained? His nagging was running me out of the house. I planned on going home early some nights, but then I thought about Ed's constant bickering and detoured to Doctor Good Dick's house.

I didn't understand Ed's problem. I micromanaged our housekeeper, kept a clean house, did the laundry, and most times, went food shopping, made love to him when he wanted to make love, but still, he wasn't satisfied. He wasn't approachable anymore, so I kept my distance.

This was the first time I had had an affair with someone and took the chance of staying out the entire night. But I wasn't sloppy about the situation. I told Ed I would drive with Anika to her hometown and stay overnight. He hit the roof and said he didn't give a damn about Anika or her hometown and that I'd better bring my ass home!

I refused. When I awoke the following day at Anthony's, I was scared to death. But then I convinced myself that Ed really didn't know anything. He only *suspected* something, and that was a huge difference. I wished that Ed would just relax and let all this blow over. Suppose he allowed me to get out my fantasies in my system. In that case, we could monogamously live the rest of our lives together. Sometimes I just wanted to leave for a while and tell Ed to wait. I'd soon come back.

When I went home the next day, Ed was seething. I tried explaining that we had gotten drunk and neither could drive back impaired. Ed was belligerent as his voice rose to levels I'd never heard before. He was irate. I would have seen him masking his pain if I had looked deeper into his eyes. I realized my husband could think I was sleeping around. But could he prove it? For all I knew, he was running up inside some chick half my age.

"Ed, you're going to have to trust me. If I say I'm out with friends, then that's what it is."

"Who are you?"

"What?"

"I don't even know you anymore! You're not the woman I married ten years ago. You've changed."

"I've changed? I've changed," I asked perplexedly. "You're the one who's gotten all insecure about me! You used to walk around here with a swagger. Now all you do is nag and complain like a little bitch!"

"Fuck you!" he bellowed, and I was temporarily dazed. I can't recall ever hearing him curse at me. Ever. I was insulted.

"No, mother fuck you! You piece of shit. Get the fuck out of my house," I roared.

"I'm not going anywhere! You want me out—put me out!" I guess he got his swagger back.

"Since you won't leave—I will."

The next day I went home and tried again. To me, it was like training a dog. I walked through the door, and Ed was silent and solemn. I thought he was trying to make me feel guilty, but he gave me an ultimatum instead.

"If you ever disrespect me, our marriage, or this household again by staying out the entire night, I'll divorce you. There won't be any discussion, no mediation, no marriage counseling—just an old-fashioned, no-nonsense divorce."

From that moment, I put things back in the proper perspective and began acting as the doting wife again. Ed didn't have to ask for a cold beer because I'd already placed one in his hand. He didn't have to wonder about dinner because it was prepared, hot, and waiting when he arrived home. His threat was exactly what I needed. It took me a couple weeks to sneak off to see Anthony again, and now *he* was furious.

"You can't just walk out of our relationship without provocation," he screamed. "Where have you been? I've been going crazy!"

"I went home, and after spending overnight with you, Ed started yelling. He even threatened divorce."

I took off my jacket and slipped off my shoes.

"You sound as if you're surprised. What did you think he'd do? Perhaps run you a hot bath to wash my scent off of you. Maybe, buy you a douche to wash my semen out of you!"

Anthony was facetious.

"Is that really necessary?"

"When you come in here talking crazy, it is."

I exhaled. "I really hadn't thought ahead that far. I didn't know how Ed would react because knowing and suspecting were different things. And I was so consumed in my own pleasure that I never stopped to think about Ed's pain."

"Whoa, let's not make this a *poor Ed* story. What about me? And my pain?"

"I'm doing the best I can," I exclaimed. Anthony stared at me intently.

"Do you love me?" he asked.

"Of course, I do," I said without hesitation.

"Well, I love you, too. I'm in love with you, and I know you're not in love with your husband. I can tell by how you touch me and make love to me. It started out as just sex for us, but we both know it's way beyond that now. I want you to leave him. Leave him and marry me."

Anthony's words were so sincere that I got lost in the moment.

He continued. "We could be a power couple!"

I hated it when people said that. Ignoring his last remark, I told him what he wanted to hear.

"I want a divorce but don't know how to tell him. I cannot hurt Ed. I just can't." My eyes began to well up. "But I don't want to lose you."

"You won't lose me, baby," he soothed. "But Ed has got to go."

CHAPTER
23

ANTHONY CROSS

CHRIS AND I TOOK A CAB TO THE WAVERLY INN to grab food. I was in love with their banana shakes and chicken pot pie. And occasionally, you could get a glimpse of a celebrity. On those nights, it was tough getting into the semi-private restaurant.

Once we arrived, we laughed and caught up on each other's lives. The prospect of new money entering our hands had us both giddy. I was stoked about the painting I'd purchased, Gracie's impending divorce, and my practice. And Chris was excited about his investments and a new outlook on life.

Chris really looked better lately. The telltale signs of a coke user weren't as apparent. The bags of stress around his eyes from work and gambling were gone. He looked like a new man on the verge of owning the world. I confided in him about my feelings for Gracie. I spoke of her with great respect and adulation, and Chris gave it to me raw.

"How could you respect a woman who would leave her husband for you?" His dark eyebrows furled together, forming one line and making me uneasy. "You always fall fast for a pretty woman, but that never lasts. Pretty women are your Achilles' heel, but then you dump them and move on to the next. What's so different about Gracie?"

"She's everything I've always looked for. She doesn't like drama. She has a nonchalant attitude that I admire. She's funny, strong, and whenever she hears about the problems other women put me through, she says she'd never behave like that."

"That's easy for her to say because she's not your wife. At the moment, she's another man's headache. Do you know how stressed her husband must be right now? I can't even imagine all the shit you got her doing in your place. Imagine if she was married to you. You could never trust her. A ho don't change her stripes for no one!"

"It's not an act. I know acts. Dakota—act! The girl from the gym—act! Gracie's the real thing. She jeopardizes so much just to be with me, which should never be taken for granted. She's not even having sex with her husband, and before you say it, I know she's not lying."

"Did you get smacked with the *dumb* stick because you sound dumb as hell right now? I know her husband's hitting that.

There's no way she's lying next to him 24/7, and he's not hitting that. From what you tell me, she's a superstar."

"That she is…." I retorted while thoughts of my baby danced in my head.

"And the way she throws it right back and takes it from the back like no other is amazing, but you don't—"

"Excuse me?"

"What?" Chris asked.

"How do you know how she throws it back or takes it?"

"You told me."

"No. I never did."

"Shit, well, then I got her mixed up with one of my jump-offs."

"You wish you had someone like Gracie."

Chris shook his head.

"What?" I asked.

"She's playing you like we play bitches, and you can't see it. I bet I can run down her whole game because it's something we've both done regularly. I thought game recognized game!"

"I'm telling you, I got this."

"Just tell me if I'm right," he urged.

"All right, proceed."

"Okay, I bet it started out with you both knowing it was going to be a one-night stand—"

"I told you—"

"Let me finish, and don't interrupt. You both knew what it was when you took Gracie home. You knew she was married, and neither of you thought you'd want to take it further than one night, but you didn't realize there'd be chemistry. There was a spark…at this point, she loves the danger of the affair, but she's smart enough not to play you too close. She wants to be nice enough to you to keep it casual but not too nice, whereas you think she wants more. So, when she came over for a while, she'd make it clear it was only about sex. Maybe, in the beginning, she'd verbally display this. But as time went on, she did it with her actions. Like she'd never stay much longer after sex. Cuddling was out of the question. Just hit it and leave.

"Then she realizes you no longer think it's casual. You start putting demands on her because your ego's kicking in, and your mind's playing tricks on you. You start to think you really have feelings for this broad. Your girlie ways come out, and you start saying shit like, *'fuck him, stay here with me.' 'Leave that man.' 'You don't ever spend any time with me.'* Your mind's asking you what he has that you don't, and you begin to make more demands on her, so now she resorts to plan B. Which is she's getting a divorce. But let me guess—it's complicated. Am I right? She can't do it because of the kids?"

My face was stone as my gut twisted into knots. I wanted to punch Chris in his big blockhead.

"Nah, it's not even like that." That was the most I could muster up.

"Well, either she's used the kid or money excuse, but I know she's used one."

"I just said it's not like that."

"Then why do you have that sour expression on your face?"

I looked at Chris and needed him to feel where I was and how much I thought I'd grown mentally.

"Listen, man. Remember when we were in college, and all we pursued were the girls with the big asses?"

"Yeah, so?"

"And we'd say that when we got married, our wife needed long, soft hair because we didn't want any nappy-headed rug rats running around."

"Yeah, I still feel like that. You know I love me, a Puerto Rican girl."

I shook my head.

"See, I've been taking an introspective look at who I am. How I really am and what type of man I want to be. I've realized that I'm too judgmental and childish. Life's too short to be judging a person about their past. I don't care who she was with before me, her skin color, how long her hair is—all I care about is that she loves me and that I love her."

"I hear you, but a person's past is what defines their future."

"I don't buy that. Not anymore. Not after meeting Gracie."

Chris began gawking at me. "You're whipped."

"I don't know why I even bothered to sway your opinion. I'm so vexed I wanna punch something."

"The man in the mirror, perhaps?"

"Keep it up, and I'ma whip your ass in here."

"My Glock says otherwise," Chris replied.

"Yeah, okay."

"Don't you realize that she can't give you any more than she's given her husband, which is a bag of lies and deceit? Why would you want that for yourself? You're a smart and successful man. Why are you belittling yourself and willing to take someone beneath you?"

"She won't do me like she's done her husband. Gracie would never cheat on me. Look at me…I'm a great catch. He works for a telephone company. Clearly not on my level."

Chris shook his head. "And to think, I used to look up to you. For women, cheating doesn't have to do with who looks better or has a bigger bank account. Cheating has to do with character or lack thereof. Gracie's a person of low-moral character and incapable of commitment. Bottom line. Come to think of it, it sounds as if I just described you. Maybe you two are made for each other."

"Fuck you."

"What's the point? Like, why are we even discussing her?" Chris took a large bite of his turkey burger.

"We're discussing her because I brought her up. We're discussing her because she means a lot to me. Can't you see that I'm different? I've changed?"

He huffed, "Changed? The weather outside just changed. You're still the same Anthony I've known almost all my life. New York's most eligible bachelor who's a hypocrite. You're still sleeping with that young chick, and how many others? So stop preaching to the choir because I know Anthony Cross. The *real* Anthony Cross."

Chris's words had me stunned. Was I a hypocrite talking about all this love when the woman I'm saying I love is married? And I'm washing different vaginal juices off my penis any night of the week?

I needed to clean out my closet and figure out what was really good.

I changed the mood. "Gracie's a slightly used sistah with a recently refurbished body. She's well groomed, educated, and independent…how could any man give that up?"

"Don't. Don't give it up…lease it…don't buy it."

215

We sat around the Waverly Inn for another hour when a few women we'd met this past summer at a Keyshia Cole concert came strolling in. I could tell that they had spotted us and were easing over to our table. Usually, I would have stayed and fucked around, but not this night. This night I was going home. Alone.

CHAPTER

24

GRACIE LANE

THE NIGHT AIR WAS BRISK AS I WALKED through the underground garage leading to my home. It was almost eleven o'clock. I hadn't spoken with Ed since I had left the house that morning, pretending to go to work. I was back to my same tricks. I gave him a call during lunchtime, but he'd skipped lunch and was out in the field working on mainframes. I thought I'd call him later, but it slipped my mind.

Anthony and I had made love five times that night. He was an absolute beast, matching my stamina thrust for thrust. I thought a lot about loving two men, though. It was a conflicting thought. But my love for Ed had pulled me out of Anthony's bed to return home. I missed my husband.

Anthony gave me a long, succulent kiss goodbye that lingered on my lips. Once I told him I was ready for a divorce, he began helping me to be careful about our affair. He was a gentleman and didn't want the divorce to get ugly due to our entanglement. He was also an idiot for thinking that I would leave my marriage, my husband of ten years, for a fling. It didn't surprise me, though. My actions were saying that we had something. That, combined with his massive ego, we were damn near engaged in his mind.

I've been thinking I may have to put Anthony on time out because he's getting beside himself. Or maybe I should use another angle and tell him that divorce isn't an option. Last week I was in Anthony's apartment, on the phone with Ed. As I told Ed I loved him, Anthony decided to answer his home phone and converse as if I wasn't there or on the phone with my husband. Of course, I had to tell Ed I was over Anika's; the voice was her maintenance man. Anthony gave me the cold shoulder when I got off the phone until I was forced to leave—without sexual intimacy. He actually had an attitude. His lips were poked out, he had this distant look in his eyes, and when I reached for him, he pulled away.

The ride home was slow. I had deliberately driven the speed limit. I needed the time alone to clear my head. I said a silent prayer before I put my key in the lock, asking God to please let Ed be asleep, so I could just crawl into bed and hold him all night.

God was definitely on vacation because the moment I walked through the door, I heard, "I was about to have the police post an all-points bulletin for your whereabouts. Did you forget where you lived?"

"Ed, please don't start. I've been with A—"

"I know you were with Anika. Only I called Anika, and she hasn't seen you all day."

"I wasn't with Anika. I was with Van—"

"Vanessa? Try again."

"You tell me where I was!" I screamed.

"Typical. Go ahead and scream hysterically because, once again, you're busted."

"Busted? What have I gotten busted doing? Staying out and getting fresh air instead of being stuck in the house all day? Busted, having a life outside of you? What have I gotten busted doing because it sure ain't having an affair? Please show me some evidence of that."

The calm Ed was back. I guess he was going through phases.

"Good night, Gracie. I'll see you in the morning."

When I finally went upstairs a couple of hours later, Ed was in bed, and all the lights were out. I quickly slid off my clothes and climbed into bed. He turned to face me when I wrapped my arms around Ed's back. I didn't say a word. Nor did I want to fight anymore. I just stared into his eyes. They were consumed with hurt and pain. He touched my face gently and then brought my lips to his. We started to kiss, and it was an *I-want-to-make-love* kiss. I backed off slowly, but he reached for me, and I gently pushed him away again. I hadn't taken a shower before I left

Anthony's because Ed would smell the soap on me, which would have been another argument. And I could feel Anthony's DNA ready to ooze out of me. Yes, we'd begun having sex without any condoms. Although I knew it was foolish—not because of potential pregnancies—my tubes were tied. But because I was married, this was sooo disrespectful. Both Anthony and I took regular H.I.V. tests, but again, I knew better.

Usually, when I pushed Ed away, he'd turn over angrily, leaving me alone. But tonight, he came back a little more aggressively. How long had it been since I'd made love to my husband? I was becoming careless. What was I going to do? I couldn't sleep with him now, with remnants of Anthony still present.

Ed slid under the covers to try to persuade me. I gently pulled his head back up.

"Not tonight…I'm tired," I said and tried to get up to go and sleep in the guestroom.

His subsequent movements were swift. Ed grabbed me roughly by my shoulders and pushed me back onto the bed. Shocked as I lay on my back, he positioned himself atop me.

"Get off me!"

"You can't fuck your husband anymore? Huh?"

I tried to squirm out of the position, but his strong arms had me pinned down. He started to aggressively kiss my lips, face, and neck. He was a wounded man out of control. I tried to reach up and slap his face, but he grabbed my hands and pinned them by my sides, with his thighs holding them in place. I wanted to kick the shit out of him, but my legs were also immovable. I knew where this was heading, and I refused to let my husband do something I was sure he'd regret for the rest of his life, which was rape his wife. I submitted completely.

Ed had his way with me and then cried to sleep in my arms....

Ed was on me like a hawk. It was Christmas Eve, and I'd promised Anthony I would spend the day with him. It was a beautiful morning in the city as the first snowfall of the year began to drop. The news forecast said we were going to have a white Christmas. We sat on our vast windowsill, sipping hot apple cider. We watched last-minute shoppers brave the weather as we listened to Patti LaBelle's latest Christmas CD. She had a fantastic rendition of *Every Year, Every Christmas,* that I fell in love with. At that moment, I knew I wouldn't make it over to Anthony's. I was having a relaxing, lazy day with my husband. I didn't want to ruin our holiday by disappearing for a few hours. Ed would hit the roof. Besides, I loved spending the holidays with him. He was my only family. I'd only agreed to be with Anthony on Christmas Eve because he went ballistic when I couldn't get away during Thanksgiving. The nerve of him. He knew he was asking the impossible, but his ego wanted to see if he could pull it off. He wanted to know if he could get me to disrespect my husband even more.

I realized that the year was flying by. We were already heading into 2008, and I was still up to no good. I had started the year off wrong. I'd already booked a South Pacific vacation on the Fiji Islands for Anthony and me. A little getaway that I'd promised him we'd take. Ed doesn't know anything about it, nor have I come up with a sensible lie to cover myself for three nights, four days. Sometimes I'm so stupid. When I'd made the obligation, I felt that Anthony deserved it for tolerating so much from me and my situation.

We'd decided to have our old neighbor, Gloria, over for an early afternoon lunch. Ed had also invited Tamara, but she declined. She was still furious with her brother for cosigning with me and tossing her out. I told Ed that she was grown and would eventually get over it. After lunch, we planned to watch old movies and lie around in our pajamas. We'd bought *Wuthering Heights*, *Casablanca*, and *What Ever Happened to Baby Jane?* All the old black and white classics.

Gloria beamed as she walked through the door. She was positively radiant. She'd taken my advice and walked away with millions after she cashed in her jewels and landed a seven-figure advance on a tell-all book deal. She'd bought me a little gift; a journal. It was a keepsake for all the help and advice I'd given her. Gloria didn't stay long. She didn't want to run into her estranged husband; the divorce was being finalized the next month.

As our evening died down, we both looked out the window, and the snow looked to have reached at least ten inches. We turned our thermostat to 69 degrees, started a fire in our fireplace, curled up on our sofa, and began our movie marathon. It was so cozy as our feet touched, and Ed ran his fingers through my hair. Earlier, I felt a little guilty for ignoring Anthony. And not having the common courtesy to call and tell him I couldn't make it. But I knew he'd have a fit, and I didn't want to hear his mouth. I'd shut off my cell, but that didn't stop him from calling my landline. Yes, another stupid move on my part. He had the house digits. Ed had picked up, and no one said anything. My first inkling was that George was calling to harass me, but when I called George—no one answered. George and Benjamin were quickly ruled out. Anthony's the only other culprit to consistently call here and hang up.

I'd just started to doze off when our intercom phone rang. I nudged Ed to get it, but he was snoring like a big bear. Groggily, I went to answer.

"Yes, who's there?"

"Mrs. Lane, this is Albert."

"Hi, Albert. Is someone here for us?"

"We have a problem in the garage. Could you come down? It has to do with your car."

"I'm on my way."

Quickly, I threw my overcoat over my pajamas and scurried down to the parking garage, where I met Albert. I took one look at my car and gasped.

"What happened?"

My beautiful Mercedes Maybach had been vandalized. Each tire had been slashed, and someone took a sharp, heavy instrument, pounded, and cut deeply into my car's exterior. All the windows were intact, but they could have smashed those too.

"We've pulled the surveillance cameras, and they're working on finding out who did this. Don't worry, Mrs. Lane. We're on it."

"Now you're on it? This should never have happened. What are these cameras for?" I pointed toward the ceiling, where at least a dozen cameras were installed. "You're supposed to be watching in the security booth to stop something like this from happening! I could have been killed!"

"You're right, ma'am, and I take full responsibility. But it's a holiday, and we're understaffed—which isn't an excuse. I'm very sorry, ma'am."

"Where's the tape?"

"Back in our office. Do you want to come with me to see if they found anything?"

We returned to the security room, where they found the perpetrator. I saw a clear image of Doctor Anthony Cross going berserk on my innocent car. After he banged it up, he looked around to see if he'd been caught and then scampered off. I could not believe my eyes.

"Don't call the authorities or give them this tape. Please call and have a towing company get my car out before the morning at any cost. Have them take it to the parking garage around the corner, and I'll handle everything after the holiday. I don't want my husband coming down and seeing my vehicle in this condition. If my orders aren't followed, jobs will be lost. Do I make myself clear?"

"Yes, ma'am. I'll take care of it."

I decided not to mention my car to Anthony. It was the cost I had to pay to be the boss. He was a wounded puppy and needed to vent his hostility on someone or something. Besides, it was only a car. His heart was worth more than that.

CHAPTER

25

ANTHONY CROSS

"MMM, HMM, DADDY...fuck this pussy!"

I was making love to Gracie on my dining room table. I had her on her back with her legs spread-eagled. It started to get really good when she said, "I want you to pee on me!"

My eyes flew open in horror, and not even two seconds later, she slapped the shit out of me and said, "Do it!" I felt like a little bitch that wasn't up for the challenge.

I pulled out of her, and I swear I didn't even have to pee, but the fear she'd instilled in me got my juices going. I let out all I had and gave her the infamous R. Kelly—a golden shower. As I watched my piss physically assault her delicate skin, she stuck her finger inside her cave and gave me a freak show. She thrust more fingers inside herself, then put them into her mouth, moaning and groaning as if it was the best experience in the world.

"Fuck me!" Gracie demanded.

Quickly I reentered her, and my senses were heightened.

"Is this all mine?" I asked as I banged her back out.

"Yours, baby . . . it's all yours." Then she started screaming. "Fuck me harder . . . fuck this juicy cunt harder . . . harder . . . harder!"

Those words were music to my ears. I pumped in and out with vigor. I loved it when she spoke nastily to me. It turned me on, although I had to admit that she could sometimes be a little controlling. She flipped over and let me enter her from the back. The sensation was sooooo good. She had me babbling like a baby.

"Sweet Jesus!" I screamed as I came hard.

Exhausted and sex sweaty with an exaggerated case of the munchies, we somehow managed to make it to the bedroom, where we both collapsed face down on my king-sized bed. After ordering Chinese takeout, I finally regained the wind in my lungs.

I was a satisfied man, and she was a satisfied woman. Or so I thought.

"You like making love to me more than your husband, right?" I asked. She just smiled and languorously stretched but said nothing. "Answer me."

"I thought it was more like a statement. You know how you make me feel in bed."

"That's not an answer to my question," I retorted. My voice was stern and demanding. The situation started to become uncomfortable.

"It's different," she stated honestly and then continued. "When I make love to you, it's hard, exhilarating sex. There's always an element of surprise. When I'm with my husband, it's soft and loving. He treats me like I'm his baby who needs nurturing. He makes love to me like he *needs* me. Also, inside, you two feel different. He's much bigger than you—thick and long. It feels as if his penis doesn't end when he's inside me. From the moment he enters, he stretches me to limits that every woman should be blessed to experience. I feel each and every thrust. But his bigger manhood doesn't allow me to do what I can do with you. It's just too much. When we make love, your penis allows me to explore different positions easily."

Whatever pleasure I'd felt only moments earlier was gone. I was physically sickened by Gracie's answer. No man—I don't care how secure he is in his manhood—wants to hear about someone with a bigger penis sleeping with the woman he loved. I didn't care if he was there first. I hated it each time she mentioned his name, regardless of whether she was bashing or praising him. Immediately I got upset. The mere mention of Ed always triggered an adverse reaction inside my body. I wanted to kick her ass out. But I couldn't. I was in love, and at that moment, my feelings were defined.

I turned on my side to see her face to face. Looking into her eyes, I didn't say anything for a long while.

"You're still having sex with your husband?" I finally asked.

"Well, I am married. That's what married people do."

"That's funny because I remember you saying you were no longer intimate. That your sex life with your husband was done. Over."

"It is."

"Then what are you talking about?! *You two feel different; he's bigger.*' What type of shit is that to say to a person?" I said, mocking her voice. I was livid.

"Oh, grow up! Do you know what I got to go through to be here with you?"

"You should eagerly walk through hell and back to be here with me!" I spat.

"Anthony, don't go getting insecure about me. I love making love to you. You two are just....different. There's no other way to say it. And you can't get mad because you asked the question."

"Insecure? Is that what you think this is about? I'm just trying to keep things in the right perspective. I'm the most sought-after bachelor in New York. I got dime pieces at my fingertips— educated, articulate, gorgeous women. I wanted to see where you were at because I didn't want to hurt your feelings if I started seeing other women."

"That's silly. Thank you for thinking about me, but how could I ask you to be exclusive when I'm married? That would be selfish, and I couldn't do that. I love you too much." That last line made me feel somewhat better—not totally, but a little bit. I also felt like she was running game.

She got up to shower, and I stayed in bed. When the water came on, I decided to call Dakota. I needed a distraction from Gracie. I was getting caught up and needed to level the playing field.

CHAPTER
26

GRACIE LANE

THE REDDISH-YELLOW SUNRISE BURST through my Venetian blinds while the rays playfully kissed my face. I sat back on my bed, surrounded by massive pillows and a goose-down comforter, staring at the sun and loving the tranquility it brought me. It's incredible how a little thing like watching the sunrise can make you appreciate life. I dragged my body from my bed and walked over to the window. The house had that winter chill in the air. I stood there looking at the sun for nearly ten minutes before going downstairs to grab *The New York Post*. We had weekly delivery. I shuddered at the brisk morning air and realized Ed had turned down the thermostat to an unreasonable 68 degrees when he knew I couldn't survive under 80. I hated to be cold, and he knew it. He was being evil. I turned it back up, ran upstairs, and hopped back in bed.

After me and Anthony's heart-to-heart, he put a little distance between us, but it was all good because sneaking around took a lot out of me. Constantly keeping up with my lies and having enough energy to satisfy two virile men was draining. After a week or so, though, Anthony finally gave in, and we made plans to see each other later that afternoon.

I exhaled as I arrived at Anthony's apartment. I was bored. Although the sex was good, possibly the best sex I'd ever had, I was looking for more thrills. It started off as a fleeting thought and emerged as a strong possibility.

"I want to mix it up a bit," I told Anthony.

"Mix it up? What do you mean?" he asked.

"It'll be something you'll like. Don't worry."

"*Should* I be worried?" he asked cautiously.

"Why do you take everything so seriously?" I asked, laughing at him mockingly.

"Babe, I'm just asking. What do you mean by mix it up?"

"I want another companion to join us."

Anthony wasn't shocked by my admission, but he seemed disappointed. Perhaps he couldn't understand what provoked this discussion. Immediately his manhood was in question.

"Am I not satisfying you?"

"Why would you ask that?"

"Why would you ask what you did?"

"Because that's what we do for each other. We make each

other happy."

"I am happy, baby. I don't need another woman added to the equation to feel happier. You're all I need."

I walked over to Anthony and kissed his lips softly while I ran my fingers over his chest. "Aww, Anthony, that's so sweet. Can't you do this for me…peeeaassss," I said in a baby-like voice.

He kissed me again. "Oh, all right. Since you insist, I'll do it, but I'm telling you she better not be too sexy. You better be worried because there's a chance she might take your man."

I slapped him hard on his ass. "I'm not worried."

"You're not worried, huh?"

"Nope. But you should be."

"Why should I be worried? I said I didn't want another woman in our bed—that's all you."

I burst into laughter at his humor and then got serious. "Anthony, we're both adults, correct?"

Sensing that my mood had shifted, Anthony almost didn't want to answer me. He looked deep into my eyes and couldn't read me.

"Yes, we are, so spill it. What are you getting at?"

"You were presumptuous when you assumed I would want a woman in our bed. I was talking about a threesome—with a man—my choice."

The thought sickened Anthony. His mouth immediately stopped salivating, and his throat dried up.

"Did you think . . . you *really* thought I . . . wanted a woman to join us?"

"Why would I ever think that?" he sarcastically replied.

"Stop being a big baby," I clowned him. "I thought you said we were adults."

Anthony went berserk.

"You're going to cause me to have an ulcer! I feel like I've aged ten years. What female asks to have another man in the threesome? That's asinine! Wasn't that against protocol? Ethics? Morals? Code? Something…who's wearing the pants here! Am I your bitch?"

"Calm down with your sexist, dated rhetoric."

"Fuck that! There isn't any way I'll allow another *naked* man in my bed. That's some real gay shit, and I'm not down. Not even for the big butt and pretty smile that you got!"

"What about for a blow job and a hundred thousand?"

"Are you kidding me!" he growled.

"Yes, but not about the threesome."

"Listen, listen, listen," he snapped, "Go take that fag shit to your husband! Don't you ever come up in my house with your soft voice, trying to play me like a bitch. I like you, but I don't love you."

Anthony was lying. I knew he was in love with me. A blind man could see he was in love with me. He was only saying those harsh words to hurt me because he was hurting.

"Okay, so we don't love each other. Now back to the threesome. Can I count you in?"

"Get out!"

"For good?"

"You heard what I said."

"So, it's over?" I pressed.

"Yes, it is!"

I shrugged and tried to give Anthony a parting kiss on his cheek, but he swatted me away.

"It's been real," I said and made my dramatic exit.

I spent all morning and most of the afternoon in my home library, plotting. I needed to research legal matters, but after six hours, I finally realized that I'd have to have access to a law library. Determined not to have a pity party for myself, I decided to prepare something nice for my husband. I went to the market, ordered a couple of red snappers, picked up a bottle of white wine, stopped at Barney's New York, and bought Ed a pair of gold cufflinks. I planned a romantic dinner for him and wanted to prepare it before he came in from work. Growing up with three men, my cooking skills came easily.

After dinner was prepared, I still had about thirty minutes before he came home, so I hopped in a warm shower and put on my Vera Wang's *Princess* perfume. Since I was doing this whole seduction thing, I put on my trampy, scarlet-colored silk teddy. I then lit twelve candles and put the wine in the fridge to chill. I flipped through our enormous CD collection and put on some Billie Holiday. I decided Billie would best represent the melancholy mood I was in.

As time passed, I realized Ed was an hour late. Perhaps he was working overtime. I called him on his cell, but he didn't pick up, so I decided the mood wasn't quite right. I quickly dressed, hopped in my car, went to the local neighborhood flower shop, and bought a dozen long-stemmed roses. When I returned home, I plucked the petals off and made a trail leading to the bedroom. I thought I'd wait for Ed, naked, in bed. I had been feeling very horny since the doctor and I broke up. He hadn't even bothered to call me to see how I was doing—I never called him, either.

Finally, after almost two hours of waiting, I walked downstairs toward the front of the house as the door opened and slammed.

"Is that you, Ed?" I asked. I waited for Ed to show his gratitude for my gestures by making love to me for hours upon hours.

"Who lives on east 69th Street?" he asked instead.

"What are you talking about? I don't know anyone who lives there."

"You're a liar, Gracie."

"Babe, please, not again," I said, "I don't know anyone who lives there. Who's supposed to live there?"

"I don't know. That's why I'm asking you! You got a ticket in the mail for your car with this Upper Eastside address."

"Ed don't do this. Not now, not today."

"Why are you ruining our marriage?"

"Look, I'm tired of this shit, Ed. Okay?" I exploded.

"You're tired of this shit? No, I'm tired of *your* shit!"

"Well, leave then. Yup, get out!" I had reached my breaking point. I was tired of his paranoia.

"You want me to leave?" His voice was a haunting whisper.

"You can do what you want. If you're so tired of my shit, as you put it, leave!" My voice was stern and unwavering. I ran upstairs and began frantically getting dressed, only to return downstairs.

"Where are you going?"

I didn't respond. I was fully dressed and heading out the front door before Ed could do anything. He had the stupidest expression when he realized I was leaving him alone. And that was how I left him standing there—dumbfounded.

I wanted to go to Anthony's house but realized we had broken up. I detoured to the mall to do a little shopping when, to my amazement, Anthony called. I was shocked, but I really wasn't. I knew it would be a matter of time before he swallowed his pride.

"Hello." I had the sweetest voice, syrupy and soft.

"Hey baby, don't hang up."

"Yes…"

"I need you. I love you. And most importantly, I'm sorry. This is all my fault the—"

"You—"

"Let me finish. Please, I've been working on this for two weeks. The way I spoke to you was uncalled for. You're a lady, and you deserve respect. My respect. If you give me another chance, I'll promise not to be such an ass."

"I've missed you."

"I've missed you, too. Gracie, I was so angry and filled with rage because something inside me kept telling me you wanted something casual. That I was only good for the moment, and that bothered me."

"You mean more to me than I could ever express. You're too good for me, Anthony."

"You're the reason I wake up in the mornings."

"Aww, baby, I'm sooo glad you called," I said.

"Are you having a bad day?"

I released a breathy, "More than you'll ever know."

"So, fill me in."

"It's nothing…it's all right. Forget it."

"Why won't you let me know you?"

I thought about his statement and wondered if he really knew me, would he still love me? We decided to meet for coffee at a Starbucks near Broadway and patch things up.

$$\infty$$

Ed had threatened me a few more times over the next couple of weeks, telling me that if I didn't get my act together, he'd divorce me. I used to believe his words, but now I knew they were just that—words. He wasn't going anywhere.

$$\infty$$

This girl is driving me crazy, I said to myself a few days later. I had been trying to get my beauty rest, but Anika wouldn't quit calling.

"Hello?" I asked groggily.

"You home?" Anika asked.

"Yes, I'm asleep."

"I'm on my way to you."

I was confused. I didn't invite nor want Anika over; I was tired and annoyed.

The heavy banging on the door should have indicated Anika's mood, but my senses were dulled from just waking up.

I could barely click the locks open before she pushed through the door.

"Did you do it?" Anika asked.

"What? Do what?"

"Sleep with Anthony!"

I looked around suspiciously, afraid that Ed was home.

"Ed?" I called out. No response.

"It's a Wednesday morning. He's at work," Anika concluded. "Now, what were you saying?"

"Did you sleep with Anthony?"

"Yes."

"How could you?!"

"Because I wanted to. What do you mean? How could I?"

"You know how I feel about him!"

"Well, obviously, he doesn't feel the same way about you."

"But you're my mother! You're not supposed to be this way!"

I hadn't heard that word in two decades, which sounded odd. From the day Anika was born, I hadn't raised her. I rarely saw my daughter, and by the time Anika was three, I was already heading to New York.

Anika knew most of my murky past but didn't know everything. Four years ago, I went looking for Anika—she was an easy find. I told her who I was and wanted to foster a relationship with her. But under any circumstances, could she ever tell anyone—not even Ricky, that I'd been in contact with her. I was amazed that Anika didn't harbor any resentment toward me. She wanted to develop a relationship and get to know me better. I laid down my rules when she said she wanted to follow me back to New York. No one could know that we were mother and daughter, especially Ed. She agreed to be my friend, and so it began—more lies in my web of deceit.

"Anika, we both know I'm a lot of things, but 'mother' isn't one of them. I love you, but I don't *know* you, and you don't know me because if you did, you wouldn't be here, in tears, asking questions."

"I hate you," she declared.

"Come on now, don't do this. I'm doing the best I can."

She glared at me with contempt and hatred.

"I will never speak to you again. You're nothing to me. You

no longer exist!"

"Anika, let's be reasonable. All this over a man?"

"If he's not worth my anger, then he shouldn't have been worth your deception!"

I nodded and then acquiesced. She was absolutely right.

Anika pushed past me, bumping my shoulder as she exited speedily. I had no idea that she would take the news so hard. And how did she know? Did Anthony tell her? More importantly, did Anika tell Anthony that she was my daughter? I panicked as I called his office.

"Anthony, did you, and Anika get into an argument this morning?!"

"An argument? No. She asked me numerous questions about you and then excused herself. She said she had to leave early to take care of something urgent. Why? What's up?"

"She just accused us of having an affair."

"How . . . how did she know?"

"She hasn't told me any details, but she's distraught. I'll straighten everything out and call you back."

"Perhaps I should call her."

"No. If Anika doesn't mention it, then you shouldn't. She may be embarrassed about her feelings for you."

"Okay, you're right. But I'm worried about her. She must be so disappointed."

"Yes, she is. I have to go."

"Are you all right?"

"I'll be fine."

I didn't know what to do; it was one dire situation after another, and I couldn't take all the drama. I felt a knot rise in my chest as a troubling possibility emerged. *What if Anika went to the authorities and exposed me?* After drinking a cup of green tea, I sat on my sofa with my knees pulled closely into my breasts, staring blankly off into the distance. I started to remember my past.

Ricky couldn't be anymore happier than he felt at that present moment. His first day on his new job as an armored-car driver had gone off without any hitches. He proudly wore his gray and black Brinks uniform. He had his wife, Marie, iron and starch his shirt, and his new patent leather shoes were shining. He felt like a king. This new job would give him a steady income to care for his wife and hopefully get his baby girl back. They had to put her into foster care because they didn't have enough money to raise her properly.

He was eighteen, and his wife, his girlfriend at the time, was only fifteen. He told anyone in the listening distance at the hospital where Marie gave birth that he planned on getting his baby back one day, and he knew he would do just that. He figured it would take him one year in his new position to save enough money to prove to the court that he and his wife could support their child.

Initially, he wasn't due home for another hour or so. But he was let go earlier than expected on his first day. His boss told him to go home and study his routes and defensive driving manual, and Ricky obliged, although he didn't need to study. He had committed practically every word in that manual to memory. Still, he figured his boss only gave him good, sound advice. Ricky wanted to prove himself to many people, especially the naysayers who thought he'd never amount to much.

The sounds coming from the back bedroom were familiar. Ricky had heard them on more occasions than he could count. He'd made those noises, moans, and groans when making love to his wife. Only

Ricky wasn't making love to his wife—some other man was. He pushed the flimsy door open and saw a significant figure pumping his naked ass up and down. His wife's hands were bound to the bedpost, and he couldn't see her face. Panic and rage consumed his body.

"What the fucks going on?" he yelled in a loud, maniacal voice.

"Ricky! Help me!" she screamed. "He's raping me!"

Shamefully relieved at the word rape, Ricky braced himself and defended his defenseless wife.

CHAPTER
27

ANTHONY CROSS

GRACIE WOULDN'T LET UP. I WAS LEARNING that she was the type of person that would do what she had to do to see it through when she had something in her mind. She was constantly nagging me about her threesome. I knew it was every man's dream to have a ménage à trois. By the time I'd reached seventeen, I'd had two. But now it was sort of like been there, done that. Truthfully, I was over that whole scene. I couldn't get Gracie to understand that it wasn't the "average" threesome. She wanted me to be near another naked man—the mere thought gave me the creeps. So why did I agree?

Mike, Chris, Lance, and I played high-stakes poker in my

living room. We had nearly $50,000 on the table, and I was losing my shirt. I couldn't concentrate.

Anika had never returned to work, and the phone went to voicemail when I called her. Finally, Samantha told me that Anika had sent in her resignation letter. For a moment, I thought she was taking it too far. You didn't mess with your livelihood over a man who was never yours. That young girl had bills to pay. And even if it wasn't Gracie, it would never have been Anika. No matter how much we kidded around with our sexual banter, which was all it was to me — sex talk.

Then the more Anika sent me to voicemail, the more I got it. She was hurt. Maybe in her mind, our conversations were the prelude to something concrete. I sent her a bouquet of flowers with a note that said simply: I MISS YOU, KID. Although small, I hoped my gesture was enough for her to return and work for me. I needed her.

"Man, I don't want to share my bed," I protested to my boys as I took a swig of my Corona beer. It was my third one. I bent the truth and told them Gracie wanted a threesome. Naturally, they assumed it involved another woman.

"Or is it you don't want to share, Gracie?" Mike asked.

"That too," I retorted.

"Man, are you kidding me? This woman's giving you pleasure on a platter. I wish I could double up. You're missing the whole point," Lance commented.

"Lance, I'm not married. This isn't a hall pass. I'm a bachelor. I can always double up if that's what I want. I'm saying that's not what I want."

"This isn't the famous Doctor Anthony Cross that I grew up with," Chris said, shaking his head. "Man, you're going soft."

"Soft? Never that. I mean, I still do me. I still got the stable full, but Gracie stands out."

"How are you going to take her seriously? That chicks married. You gotta go with the flow. Any chick, shit, my *wife* can tell me she wants a threesome with another woman, and I'ma go-with-the-flow. We're men. This is what we do!"

Mike had gotten himself all worked up with the fleeting thought that his wife would come to him and ask to bring in another woman.

"Are you kidding me?" Lance asked. "My wife be on my balls. I can't breathe around that motherfucker, let alone her offering me another woman. All Gracie wants to do is have sex—exciting, kinky, uninhibited fucking. Something you used to know about. Now you want to *make love.*"

I could see that the joke was on me. Maybe they were right. I was taking the threesome situation too seriously. As long as he didn't brush up against me, and I knew it would be meaningless to Gracie, I should be fine.

Gracie's got me under pressure, I thought. Who was she gonna get for this threesome? I didn't want her asking anyone she knew, but who wanted a strange, unknown male inside their bed? The very thought was making me berserk! I thought asking one of my homeboys would be a good idea. At least I could trust them to not fall in love with my baby and not try to come for me in bed. But then I realized that it could jeopardize our friendship. I didn't know if I would ever feel comfortable around them, knowing that they helped me make love to my baby. Anonymity was best.

Gracie and I headed for a night out on the town a few days later.

She could roam the nightlife with me because her husband was placed on the 12-8 A.M. shift at work. At Verizon, they were on rotation, and it was his group's turn. Once inside the club, I saw many men checking her out, and I got nauseous.

"What's wrong?" she asked as her hands ran up and down my back.

"Every man in here's checking you out," I replied.

"You seem surprised you're in here with the hottest lady," she challenged.

I cracked a smile. "Am I? Because I thought that little cutie over there had you beat!"

Her dimpled smile was on full display. "Maybe next time she could join us, but for tonight I want him."

She pointed to a light-skinned, pretty boy with triceps, biceps, curly hair, and a goatee.

"Why him?" I asked.

"Because he's not my type," Gracie said, and I felt more at ease. He was on the dance floor with a nice-looking girl twirling her hips to Beyonce's *"Upgrade You."* I watched as his lady friend twisted her hips in figure eight, dropped to the floor, and ground her way back up. She danced like she could fuck. I almost wanted to ask for a foursome.

I turned to Gracie, and I could see she was turned on. She reached down and grabbed my manhood. It was brick hard— proof that I was turned on, too.

It was on. Gracie stood up and walked hesitantly toward the couple. She began dancing just as seductively—outdoing the obviously younger woman. The guy was absolutely amused at Gracie's antics and started showing her attention. He eased away from the younger girl and began grinding on her from behind.

Deep pangs of jealousy shot through my body, and I had to keep composure.

Gracie whispered something into his ear, and they both looked at me. He nodded quickly, and they both exited the dance floor. Gracie whispered in my ear, "Let's go."

When I hesitated, she cheered, "You can do it, baby."

As we exited, I glanced over my shoulder at the woman I was having an affair with and smiled. She was anything but ordinary. We were in a nightclub, and she looked like she was attending church. But, oh boy, what she did behind closed doors would make the pastor in any church pray for her soul.

Gracie made introductions, and I could have choked her quiet, but then I realized we never discussed the particulars.

"Anthony, this is Nico." Damn, she should have used an alias.

"Nice to meet you," I said, extending my hand.

Eagerly, he grabbed my hand and replied, "I've seen you on *E News*. You're famous!"

"Somewhat."

"My name's Nico."

"So, I've been told."

With that, we all left and headed to the W Hotel. There wasn't any way I was taking this groupie dude back to my place.

I had them wait in the taxi while I secured the room. When I returned to get them, I noticed they were conversing as if they'd known each other for years. Both seemed relatively calm in light of what was about to happen. I think I was the only one on edge. They both slinked ahead of me into the hotel holding hands, a gesture that briefly infuriated me.

Inside the hotel room, Gracie took charge. She roughly pulled Nico's shirt, and they began kissing. My stomach felt squeamish as I watched Gracie's hands grope his chest and move toward his ass. She tugged at Nico's pants and helped to remove his clothes. I sat on the hotel's dresser and watched as each was stripped of their clothing. I honestly didn't want to join in.

Nico had velvety, light skin, tight, athletic body, and a massively hairy chest. His six-pack abs were experiencing Gracie's well-skilled tongue.

My eyes cut to Gracie. Her honey-brown-colored skin glistened in the moonlight that illuminated the room. Her new body was that of a woman half her age. Her ample breasts were a feast for Nico, and he sucked on my baby's areolas, turning me on.

"Come here, baby," I said, and she came over to me.

Gracie and I started off kissing slowly, and Nico soon joined in. He began kissing her back and ears and licked her earlobes. Gracie caressed my chest and massaged my manhood, which had become erect. I could feel that Nico wanted to experience all I had to offer, but I aggressively pushed his hands away, and he got the message. I pulled her over to me.

"Sit on my face," I told her.

She climbed on top of my face and spread her legs wide. My long tongue slithered inside her cave like a snake. She was now facing Nico. He fondled her as she sat on my face and kissed her passionately. When he leaned over and began to caress her breasts, Gracie didn't stop him.

As she was about to climax, I gently began to bite Gracie's clit just the way I knew she liked it. This drove her crazy. Her legs began trembling as I anticipated hot waves gushing through her body. She began grinding her hips methodically until she reached her peak.

"I'm getting ready to come!" she murmured.

I gripped her hips and felt her body shutter. We all switched positions. I sat on the edge of the bed, and Gracie got down on her knees and deep-throated me as Nico wrapped up his penis and entered her from the back.

She moaned in pleasure mixed with pain, but she took all of him fully engorged.

"How does it feel?" Nico asked.

"Fuck me harder," she said between licks of my manhood.

After Gracie came for the second time, she was ready for me. I pushed Nico to the side and climbed on top of her. Gently, I eased inside her deep cave.

"You're so tight," I crooned in her ear.

We started off slowly until our bodies were in sync. Gracie wrapped her legs tightly around my trim waist as I pumped in and out. Her fingernails gently dug into my muscular shoulders as I sunk deeper and deeper, prolonging each stroke. Tiny tears escaped her eyes as she nibbled on my shoulder blade. Nico kept trying to get in, but we wouldn't let him. We both came with such intensity that we moaned in ecstasy. We lay there for long moments, breathing heavily, unable to speak.

"I'm ready to go again!" she said finally.

This time we allowed Nico to rejoin us. After our last round, we were exhausted. Gracie fell asleep, wrapped tightly in my strong arms.

When I awoke a few hours later, Nico was gone. So were my Rolex watch and my wallet. I knew no good could have come from that situation.

CHAPTER

28

GRACIE LANE

I HADN'T HAD A DRINK IN WEEKS, AND the very fine, single malt scotch, although it burned going down, had also opened up my sinuses and unclogged my cloudy head.

I would be one agitated woman if it weren't for my newfound, thrilling sex life. I was turning forty in a couple of weeks and noticed that I was at my sexual peak. If the wind blew too hard, I was horny. Despite all my issues—estrangement with Anika, looming extortion, and losing my volunteer job—I was still trying to keep a positive outlook on my future.

My ruse that I still had a volunteer job also started to affect me. That, coupled with Anthony and his constant requests to leave my husband, was daunting.

As I walked through the door from my imaginary day at work, Ed handed me the phone.

"Who is it?" I asked.

"It's the service department at Honda. They said your car's due," Ed replied as he gave me the phone, leaving the room.

"What? I just had service," I said. "Hello?"

"We gotta talk."

"I thought I told you not to call me here again," I whispered.

"They were here, and they're not playing. They're kicking in doors looking for you."

"What did you tell them? Why do they care about this old case?"

"His family won't let it go. They're screaming for justice."

"Justice? It was a mistake, a bad judgment call."

"That's neither here nor there. The old man said that you better be here in the morning or else."

"I'm not ever—"

"He's dying."

"Don't start that bullshit again. Aren't you the one who said he'd outlive us all?"

"He's messed up and swore on his death bed that you're gonna pay for your shit!"

The following day, I took another drive to George's house. I decided to sport a red wig and a ton of makeup to disguise myself. Again, I drove around to the back of the house, got the spare key, and entered.

No surprise to me that the house was still in disarray. The

surprise was George's appearance when I finally found him in his bed. He'd aged forty additional years in a matter of weeks. He looked at least one hundred years old. His already frail-looking body had shriveled up, and his features were even more pronounced. His gaunt face was sunken in, and his eyes bulged. His salt and pepper hair had turned a silvery white and looked woolly, like cotton.

"George!" I gasped. "What's happened to you?"

"They lookin' for you," he whispered, struggling to talk. "They gonna get you soon. They hot on ya tail."

"Why do you take pleasure in my unhappiness? Why?!" I screamed. "I never got one full hug, no kind words, nothing! All I ever wanted was for you to love me."

"It wasn't my place to love you. I had two boys to raise."

"What about me, you crazy bastard!" I yelled and began to beat my frustrated fist into his weary body. He was too weak to fight back. When I couldn't beat him anymore, I collapsed on his chest.

"You can hate me all you want, but I ain't the one who did you wrong. Your momma did you wrong when she messed up your birthright."

"What are you talking about? Stop talking in riddles."

"You not mine," he stated in a matter-of-fact tone. "You're my brother's chile; he didn't want you either. I told you, ya mother was a whore. She dipped out on me with my brother and had you. She left when I told her I ain't want you 'cause you not mine. My brother didn't want to take you, either. He had a wife and kids, and you woulda ruined that for him. So, I was stuck with you, and all you caused me was aggravation."

I stared down at George without emotion. And at that

250

moment, all the pieces to my life's puzzle were answered—the neglect, the harsh treatment, the lack of love, everything. Always being the outlier of the family but not knowing why. My aunt, my natural father's wife, wouldn't allow me to come over and play with my cousins, and the list in my head went on and on.

"You're like a scab over my heart that keeps breaking open," I said. "I want to walk out of here and leave you for dead, but I'm better than you. I'm calling an ambulance."

"Chile, I'm a dead man talking. All that ambulance will do is leave someone with a bill. Look" —a lung-rattling cough made him pause, and then he composed himself— "go in that dresser drawer and hand me that stack of my important papers."

I pulled out a clear plastic bag of old papers and brought them to George.

"Benjamin has finally done it and killed me," he declared.

"What? You're not dead."

"Yet. But I'm about one day from it. I think he's been poisoning me for the insurance policy."

"What insurance policy?"

"I had one for over four decades. It used to be payable to Andre and Benjamin, but after Andre disappeared with my money, I changed it to be for Benjamin only and made the mistake of tellin' him. Those drugs done got his mind, and he was desperate. He pulled the money you put into the checking account and went through that in a few hours. He came in here and beat me senseless. I just recovered, but he broke my ribs."

George lifted up the covers and his shirt to reveal an awful sight. His bruised and broken ribs were protruding.

"Oh my gosh, George, how can you stand the pain?" I was aghast at my brother's cruelty.

"This pain's nothing compared to the pain I feel inside my heart for my boys and how they've betrayed me and how I betrayed you. I'm sorry about how I've treated you, but I'll only say it once. The hate and betrayal I felt inside my heart were dished out to you. Every time I saw your face, I saw the mixture of my brother and my wife. I'd imagine them in bed makin' love, and it was slowly killing me. I thought that my boys could dull my pain. I'd finally win the brotherly rivalry if they were successful and you weren't. It was foolish. I was foolish."

"George, Benjamin could never harm you."

George pulled out the $250,000 life insurance policy.

"I got two hundred and fifty thousand objections. But Benjamin's no longer my problem. He's yours."

"Mine? How's that?"

"After I got ill, I changed his name to yours. You're now my new beneficiary, and when Benjamin finds out, he'll sick those boys on you. You're not safe. You gotta take your family and go."

"But I don't want your money."

"Too bad. It's yours."

Again, he began coughing incessantly and holding his stomach, trying to squash the pain.

"Why have you done this to me? You had to know what Benjamin would do when he learned about the policy. My life, as I know it, is at stake."

"Take the money and run. It should be enough to start you over with a new life."

I was frantic. A million thoughts ran through my head.

"You've ruined me, and you don't know if Benjamin has done anything to you! He's a crackhead, not a murderer."

"He's a dumb criminal. And his drug use has made him

dumber. Look in the kitchen, check the food, and I'll bet you'll find something incriminating down there."

I charged downstairs on a mission. It was pretty tricky trying to search the refrigerator for poisoned food. Everything was spoiled. Maybe Benjamin was feeding George spoiled food, which got him sick. I searched for another fifteen minutes until I stumbled upon a bottle of thallium. It was a silvery substance in a clear jar. I put the bottle to my nose and smelled it. Nothing. *Could he be using this?* I wondered. I didn't have to wonder long. In the back of the refrigerator was a small bowl of what looked like ravioli, on the top was what appeared to be thallium. He hadn't mixed it up yet. Perhaps he planned on feeding this to George later. I ran back upstairs to George. I was getting him out of there tonight while he was still alive.

Only he wasn't. When I pushed through George's bedroom door, George was still on his bed, eyes open, and papers tossed on the floor. Tears streamed down my cheeks as I picked up his paperwork, kissed his leathery forehead, and crept back to my car. There wasn't anything I could do. From my cell, I called 911 and waited in the shadows of the night for the police, ambulance, and finally, the coroner to show up. I waited hours, but my brother never came around.

On the drive home, I wrestled with whether I'd tell on my brother and, if so, how? I couldn't just waltz into a police station, trying to give him up for murdering his father without sealing my fate. Was I selfish? What did I owe George?

No matter what, he didn't deserve to be murdered slowly by his son. I no longer felt safe in my own home. Danger was looming ahead, and it was only a matter of time before it showed up at my front door.

CHAPTER

29

ANTHONY CROSS

TMI. TOO MUCH INFORMATION.

I was forced to listen to Elizabeth talk about a night of wild sex with a local firefighter she'd met.

"He was soooo good in bed," she squealed. "The best I've had in months. When he stuck his tongue in my—"

"Elizabeth, can we finish this conversation later? I have a Grafenberg-Spot enhancement in an hour, and then I'm leaving early to do some last-minute shopping for my trip."

"What trip?"

"My lady and I are going to Fiji. We're leaving tomorrow morning."

"How nice. Who's going to take care of your patients?"

"Well, I don't have any surgeries planned, and Samantha can do any follow-ups."

"What's this about a Grafenberg-Spot enhancement? What's that about?"

"It's something I'm sure you don't need," I laughed. "But it's a simple procedure, whereas we locate her G-Spot with the patient's help. I inject a small needle, making her G-Spot hypersensitive; therefore, it's easier for her to have orgasms. The injection usually lasts around 3-6 months."

"Anything involving a better sex life, I'm all for it."

"Elizabeth."

"Yes?"

"Please leave."

"My pleasure."

After surgery, as planned, I left the office early with promises to bring everyone back souvenirs. I went to Bloomingdales men's department and bought two pairs of Ralph Lauren Polo swimming trunks, a couple of RayBan shades, and a pair of Gucci sneakers. I had already packed my other outfits, and the only thing left to do was go and get a shape-up.

Before heading to my barber, I wanted to buy Gracie something nice. Something sentimental to give to her while we're on our trip. I went into David Yurman's jewelry store and perused a few gorgeous pieces. Flashbacks of the expensive jewels Gracie had worn on several dates came gushing back. How could I compete?

"May I help you, sir?" The friendly, middle-aged saleswoman

asked.

"Yes, you may. I want to get something nice for my lady friend to show her how much I care about her. We're going away tomorrow to Fiji, and I thought it would be a nice gesture."

"Do you have something in mind? Earrings, perhaps?"

"Well, she has a lot of expensive jewelry. Earrings, bracelets, necklaces…she has everything but nothing from me. If you get what I mean."

"Yes, I do. Come here and look at these charm bracelets." She opened up one of the display cabinets. "Charm bracelets are nice for a few reasons. They're sentimental, dainty, and rarely go unnoticed on anyone's wrist."

I looked at the gorgeous white gold bracelet dangling with diamond and ruby charms. It was absolutely stunning. I couldn't wait to see her face when she opened the gift. I bought the bracelet and then called Gracie. I hadn't heard from her all day. Her phone immediately went to voicemail, and I left her a brief message. I'm sure she's doing last-minute errands just like I am.

It was almost midnight, and I still hadn't heard from Gracie, which didn't sit well with me. Surely, she's gotten all my messages. I reassured myself that everything was all right and that she'd be here at seven o'clock in the morning. Just as she said, she would.

CHAPTER
30

GRACIE LANE

I MIGHT HAVE WARNED ANTHONY THAT he didn't need to pack for our trip if I wasn't a desperate, inconsiderate woman. Not that it was canceled—*he* was canceled. I decided that my future was no longer crystal clear and that I needed to repair my marriage. If the boys in blue came knocking, loyalty to me would lie in my husband. Anthony was flighty at best and wouldn't hold up under the pressure of my past for more than a season. Ed and I took vows, and he'd hold me down forever if I didn't give him a reason to walk away. I offered Ed my credit card to buy him a few things for our trip, and of course, he declined.

"Babe, you know I'm not taking your money," he sang in an upbeat mood. "How long have we been together, and never once have I asked you for anything?"

He was speaking the truth. Ed has never taken my money for granted. He didn't require special treatment—high-end vehicles, lavish spending sprees, all my money could afford him. In fact, Ed was the one who kept me grounded. When he asked to marry me, he told me it wasn't about my money. He truly loved me and would pay his own way until death do us part. When my lawyer prepared the sixty-page Prenuptial Agreement, his hand never wavered as he signed on the dotted line.

"What's a few hundred dollars amongst millions," I said jokingly.

"Well, since you put it that—"

"Yeah, right."

We both laughed and felt jovial about our impending, impromptu trip. Ed thought it was a trip to celebrate our love. Truthfully, it was a trip to clear my head. I honestly didn't want to deceive him, but it wasn't in my nature not to. Not only did I lie about a few things—well, more than a few things—if the shit hit the fan, my husband could be in for the shock of his life.

Ed and I had to take a plane into Miami, where the ship was docked for departure. The ship was huge, bigger, and more intimidating than I thought it would be. I was a little nervous about being surrounded by only water for days but was used to facing my fears. We were going to the Bahamas, St. Thomas, and St. Martin. I contemplated taking Ed to Fiji. But when I called to change Anthony's name to Ed's one week later, they still had Anthony Cross as the second passenger. I couldn't take any chances that we'd get there, and there would be a voucher with

Anthony's name on it. Mix-ups such as those happen all the time. And with my luck, I decided not to take any chances.

We slept for most of the three-hour plane ride in our first-class, luxurious leather seats. When we awoke, we were in Miami. It was 2:30 P.M., and the sun was beaming brightly. We both looked out the window from the plane, and huge grins covered our faces. I realized that we only traveled twice a year—once for Ed's yearly family reunion—once for Ed's yearly accumulated vacation time from his job. My money allowed us to travel spontaneously, but Ed was always reserved.

My heart was racing, and eagerness showed on both our faces. Soon we boarded the larger-than-life vessel and were ushered off to our first-class cabin to unpack.

It was a beautifully decorated cabin with a small window and a large marble bathroom. The ship had an outdoor and indoor pool, and the outside was heated with a waterfall. There was also a swim-up bar and all types of water sports. We didn't stay long in our room. I took a shower first and wore a sexy, two-piece Gucci bathing suit; Ed hopped in the shower after me and put on the Nike swimming trunks he'd purchased.

Ed was amused with every aspect of our getaway vacation. I knew that was partly due to the strain I had put on our marriage. To him, the trip was a gesture on my behalf to say that I was sorry for any and everything I'd done over the past few months.

Our four-day, five-night trip flew by. Once we touched the ground on each island, we rode horseback, explored a bat cave, and windsurfed. I was the doting wife and felt so alive during our escapade. I was happy the trip had brought us closer together from all the nonsense I'd put our marriage through. Ed asked me again on the first night if I had anything to tell him. My response was that I loved him. He never brought the subject up again. When it was time to leave, we both were sullen. We discussed our time together and realized we needed to get away more often to keep the spark in our marriage.

∞

We arrived Saturday evening, and Ed didn't have to return to work until early Monday. Reality was kept at bay for the rest of the weekend. I didn't turn my cell back on until after Ed left for work on Monday.

The first phone call was from Anthony, and my heart dropped. One week prior, I could have cared less what Anthony thought about my taking off on vacation with Ed instead of him, but today I was concerned.

"Hello," I answered.

"Who did you go on the vacation with?" he asked. His voice was icy.

"My father," I lied, taking Anthony off guard.

"Your father? But you never talk about him."

"We were estranged. Hopefully, my gesture will help mend our quarrels."

"Did it?" He was putty in my hands.

"No. We're no closer now than when I was a child," I replied glumly and tried to portray defeat in my voice.

"Don't you think you should have told me I was no longer going? I had blocked out my calendar for that week, canceled all surgeries, and told my staff that I wouldn't be in. Don't you realize how much money I lost out on behind your being inconsiderate?"

"Yes, I'm sorry. I do apologize. Everything happened so

suddenly...."

"I see...you needed to take your father...and to think I thought that you went with your husband."

"Why would I disrespect you like that?" I asked.

"That's what I've been trying to figure out."

"There's nothing to figure out because it isn't true."

"Bitch, are you trying to play me!" Anthony roared. His anger rattled me through the phone.

"Did you just call me a bitch?"

"You heard what I said! I know you were on a cruise with your husband because Anika told me!"

"How would Anika know when she isn't speaking to me!"

"She went looking for you, and your doorman told her that you and your husband went on a cruise! Are you going to continue to lie to me, or are you gonna give up now?"

"If you couldn't take the truth, you shouldn't have gone looking for it!"

"This is what I get? After all, I've done for you?"

"Well, what do you want to do? Do you want to end it?"

"Damn right, I'm ending it."

"Well, thank you for the courtesy call."

Determined not to allow my conversation with Anthony to ruin my day, I decided to take a taxi into lower Manhattan and have lunch with my husband as a surprise. I would try really hard to stay faithful and repair our marriage. We had done some serious bonding on the trip, and I felt I needed him now more than ever. So much was leaning on my weary shoulders.

I knew that I would need to pick up and go one day, very soon. Whether Ed would run with me depended on the stability and love in our marriage.

I took one last look in the mirror, ensuring I looked great. My new tan had given my already honey-colored skin a nice glow. I knew Ed would show me off to his boss and coworkers, so I was determined to look my best. I wore a conservative, form-fitting, dark blue dress with matching pumps. My hair was loose, with curls dangling seductively around my face. The weather report said that it would be sunny and relatively warmer today. That was a plus.

My lobby was buzzing with early-afternoon activities. Housekeepers, chauffeurs, tenants, and deliveries were being made.

"Mrs. Lane." I turned to see John. He sat at the front desk during the morning shift.

"Yes?"

"This delivery's for you." He pointed toward a dark chocolate, 6' 3", incredibly handsome man. All my tension faded as he walked toward me.

"Mrs. Lane, I have a package for you. I'll be on my way if you just sign here." His pearly white smile was endearing. He looked no older than Anika.

"Sign my name here on your pad?" I asked, playing dumb.

"Yes, Ma'am."

"Please, I'm no 'Ma'am.' Call me Gracie."

He just smiled.

"What's your name?" I pursued.

"Who me? My name's Michael."

"Nice. Michael, how long have you been working for UPS?"

"For about four months. I'm working my way through college. I want to open up a chain of restaurants. I'm majoring in Business Administration."

"How nice. How old are you?"

"I'm twenty."

Yikes…a little young.

"I may have a few connections in that field. Why don't you give me your number and I'll see what I can do? Do you have a card?"

"No, Ma'am…I mean, Ms. Gracie. But I have a cell phone."

I smiled at his innocence. I took Michael's number and stored it in my phone as "Michelle." I'd begun to get tired of Anthony. He was too clingy and temperamental, and I needed a new distraction. Someone younger and easier to mold into the man and relationship I wanted.

I trudged along as I stepped out of my building and maneuvered down the block. I listened intently as the traffic rumbled, horns honked, and tires drove over the dilapidated New York City streets. I was suddenly accosted by a deranged-looking woman.

"I told you, but you didn't listen!" the woman screamed.

My heart was pumping with fear. My eyes darted around for help. Ironically, the street became desolate within seconds. I looked out and made brief eye contact with a passerby in a car. My eyes desperately sought help. The young, dark chocolate woman had rage in her eyes.

"Are you talking to me—"

The punch was swift and exact as it landed directly on my nose. The force temporarily blinded me. My breath emptied out of my lungs. I stumbled back, fell into a parked car, and began to shield myself as best as I could until I could refocus. The litany of angry punches dazed me as I cowered on the ground, screaming. Every nerve in my body went slack as my body grew numb. Soon

I began fighting back with all my strength. I got back onto my feet and began matching each blow with newfound power. I was now fighting for my life. I reached up and gouged her face with my sharp fingernails leaving long whelps oozing with blood. We fell back onto a parked car, and she began pounding my head into the car's hood. I heard a sickening thud as I almost lost consciousness.

"I hate you," the angry woman kept yelling. "I hate you!"

The crazy woman reached into her pocketbook and pulled out a four-inch kitchen knife, swinging it wildly. I instinctively grabbed the woman's wrist as we tussled for the blade. I bit the woman's arm, and she screamed in agony, dropping the knife. We both scuffled on the ground, scrambling for the deadly weapon. I got to the blade first, but the woman, who had more determination and strength, pried it out of my hand. Just as the woman swung it in the air to bring it down to my back, my doorman and a neighbor's friend, who happened to be a detective with the NYPD, came to my rescue. The detective grabbed the crazed woman, tossed her against the car, and then forcefully tossed her to the ground.

"Don't move! You're under arrest!" He twisted the woman's arms behind her back and handcuffed her as she squirmed and screamed.

"Ma'am, are you all right?" he asked me.

The experienced detective had everything under control in a matter of seconds. He helped me to my feet, secured the scene, and called for backup.

I was in shock. I stayed numb as I was led back to my home. My head felt like I'd been hit with a bat, knuckles felt like they'd gone through a cheese grater. My swollen eye was half-closed, and a thin line of blood slid out from my nostril.

"Ma'am, my name is Detective Brown. Do you want me to call an ambulance, so someone can take a look at your injuries?"

I was seated on my living room couch while the big, burly detective hovered over me.

"No, sir. I'll be fine."

"What's your name?" He took out his small notepad and began jotting down notes. My heart started beating rapidly.

"Gracie Lane."

"The lady taken into custody has refused to give us a statement. Can you tell us what happened?"

"I . . . I honestly don't know," I said and began massaging my temples. "One moment, I was going to meet my husband for lunch, and the next, I was being attacked."

"Do you know her? Was there a recent argument?"

"I've never seen her in my life."

"Really? Did she try to steal anything? Your pocketbook?"

"Nothing."

"Well, her identification says her name is Dakota Blair. Does her name ring a bell?"

"No, nothing."

"What did she say exactly?"

"She didn't say anything. She just began beating on me," I lied.

The detective's eyebrow rose.

"Are you married?"

"Yes. As I've said. For ten years, happily," I added.

"Mrs. Lane, I really hate to imply this, but do you think this has anything to do with your husband? Could he be having an affair?"

"No!"

The firmness in my voice was indicative that I no longer wanted to discuss that theory.

"Okay, fine. I'll need your husband's telephone number to speak with him."

"You'll do no such thing. He wasn't here, so there isn't anything he could do to help you. Now, if you would please leave, I would like to lie down for a while."

"I'll be in touch."

"Why?"

"We've arrested Ms. Blair for your assault and possibly attempted murder. The DA will need to speak with you."

"Good day, detective," I said dismissively.

"Good day, ma'am."

I knew that the incident had nothing to do with my husband and everything to do with Anthony. How foolish was I to have called Anthony from my home phone without blocking my number? That would be the only way the woman could find out where I lived. But how did she know how I looked? There were a thousand people who had access to this building. Had she come around snooping? Perhaps gotten up to my floor? Negative. This building was Fort Knox with our security when fully staffed. Anthony would have to answer that question. I'd gotten careless, and now the drama had landed on my doorstep. What if the woman came back? What if she succeeded in hurting me next time? What if this lady told my husband about my affair? I knew I needed to contact Anthony and have him put his woman in check, but for now, I needed time to think. Too much was at stake.

When Ed arrived home, I felt like a bulldozer had run over my body. Every joint, muscle, vein, and bone hurt. Damn, even my skin hurts. I'd opted not to tell him about the incident while he was still at work because I didn't want him to worry. I called out to him when he pushed the front door open.

"Ed, don't worry, but I had an accident at work," I said.

"What kind of accident?" he asked, removing his boots and hat.

"This type of accident." I appeared in the doorway, and his eyes grew wide with concern. He rushed to me.

"Baby, what did they do to you?"

"You know those wild consumers are always pumped up on that Ritalin we give them, making them unstable and strong."

"Which one of them did this to you? I'm going there tomorrow to kick some ass!"

"You can't do that. They're mentally challenged."

"So what! Look at you. Look at your beautiful face."

I stared at my husband and fell in love again. Although my body was beaten and bruised, I walked over and kissed him. We fell into bed and made love for hours. And although I knew that I felt safe and secure at that moment, I knew problems were just around the corner.

CHAPTER

31

ANTHONY CROSS

I DID EVERYTHING IN MY POWER TO get over Gracie. I had a string of women in my bed, was on the straight Vodka diet, and partied with my boys almost every night, but I just couldn't shake that cavalier temptress. At the beginning of our affair, she pursued me aggressively. She was in my bed nearly every night, passionately loving me whenever she could get away from her husband. Soon things slowed down to a moderate pace, and now, after the trip fiasco, she didn't call at all. I hated to admit it, but I feared our relationship could end. I'd called it off numerous times, but we always seemed to get back together.

I called her.

"Yes," she answered.

"Gracie, I need my shirt."

"What are you talking about?"

"My shirt. I need it. You wore it out of here one day, and I need it."

"Anthony, you can't be serious."

"Oh, I'm serious. So if you could bring it by my apartment tonight, I'd really appreciate it."

"Listen, I'm not bringing any shirt tonight or in the future. I'm not coming anywhere near your residence!" Gracie screamed. "Your crazy-ass girlfriend came to my home yesterday and tried to kill me with a knife!"

"Who?" My heart began to beat. "Are you all right? Which girlfriend?"

"You have that many?"

"No, no, I told you I'm not with anyone."

"Well, she's claiming you and tried to kill me. Her name's Dakota."

The color drained from my face. *Dakota?* Sweet, innocent Dakota was trying to kill people? She could have been the mother of my child. The news had me stunned.

"Gracie, I truly apologize. She and I have been over for some time now. She can't take the rejection."

"Make her take it because I cannot go through another ordeal of this magnitude. She's a few cards short of a full deck, and her anger is directed at me. Only me. So, I'm begging—no, I insist you handle her."

"Where is she? Do you know?"

"Why do you care?" Her jealousy began to show.

"So, I can help."

"She's in jail, Anthony."

"When can we meet so that we can discuss this situation?" I knew it was a cheap ploy, but I was desperate.

"There's nothing further to discuss with me. You need to check your bitch!" I could feel her anger seeping through the phone.

"What about my shirt? I need that back," I snapped.

"Is it that serious? Your shirt? Because you're acting as if I stole something."

"Jeez, Gracie, I know this isn't the time, but I truly miss you. I need to see you."

"You're right. Now isn't the time."

I called Chris a little later to vent.

"Yeah, Gracie keeps calling my phone," I told him.

"You're not picking up, are you?"

"Nah. I keep letting her go to voicemail. I don't have anything to say to her. She's lucky I'm not that type of dude to go upside her head for the shit she pulled!"

"That was some bullshit. How she gonna take her husband on your trip? She played you like a little *bitch*," he said and made my skin crawl.

"She's begging to make it up to me, but I'm not going for it, right?" I asked.

"Of course, you're not going for it! Who does this woman think she is?"

"Whoever she thinks she is, I'm not that dude!"

"Man, you should change your number on her. You know

how chicks get. She's nothing but a whore, and I would leave her where she stands. Give that back to her husband."

"All right, man, thanks."

"Anthony!"

"Yes?"

"You're slipping. No woman's worth your pride."

I thought about Chris's words, and although each word was correct, I couldn't just write Gracie out of my life. How could she take her husband on our trip? How could she do that? There had to be an explanation. Maybe she took him out of guilt. Maybe she felt guilty about our affair. Maybe she felt guilty because she was in love with me. There could be many reasons for her actions, and until I sat her down and had a face-to-face, I couldn't just give up on us.

CHAPTER
32

GRACIE LANE

IN THE WEEKS AFTER GEORGE'S MURDER, I sat on pins and needles. I didn't want to provoke my brother Benjamin by calling and accusing him of murder. I had been careful not to leave any evidence that I'd been by the house. But my intuition told me that Benjamin would call when he found out he was no longer the beneficiary. I had taken all of George's paperwork and predicted this would slow my brother down in connecting the dots. Sure enough, it took him about three weeks after George's death to call.

"Hey, sis." It was shortly after eight in the morning when I got the call.

"What do you want, Benjamin? Because if you or George is calling about more money, I don't have it!" I screamed, hoping to deflect any suspicions my brother might have.

"Nah, I'm not calling about any money. George is dead. I just thought you should know."

"Dead?" I mustered surprise. "When?"

"A few weeks back."

"George died a few weeks back, and you're just now calling me? What if I wanted to pay my respects at his funeral?"

"Well, for one, we both know that you could never do that because those people would snatch you up faster than you could put your car in park. And second, he ain't buried yet."

"You've got to be kidding me!" I bellowed. "Let me guess, you're calling me to pay the expenses."

"Don't nobody need your money!"

"Well, then, bury your father!"

"They won't let me. The coroner has requested some big-shot forensic pathologist to run some tests on the old man. He's still at the morgue."

Benjamin's ass was in deep shit, and I was relieved for the moment. He was going down for murdering his father.

"Tests? What kinds of tests?" I probed.

"I don't know, and I don't care. They won't find anything."

"What are they looking for?"

"Didn't I just say that I didn't know? But I guess that response didn't register to your stupid ass!" he snapped. "You always were slow."

Benjamin had inherited his father's rude mouth, but I had

grown numb to their disrespect long ago.

"Again, what is it that you want from me?"

"Do you remember the name of the insurance company Momma had her policy under?"

"Why would I remember that? I didn't receive any of the payouts."

"I just thought that you would. I'm trying to find Daddy's insurance policy papers, which seem missing. If I knew the company, I could call them up. I swear, I think the old man burned all his paperwork just to spite me. But I'm going to get the last laugh."

I was disturbed by the phone call. What kind of family had I been born into? Was I just as cuckoo and remorseless as my siblings? The one positive aspect that I had been able to glean from the conversation was that my brother had no clue I was the policy's beneficiary. So he had no reason to turn me into the police. I already knew that George hadn't been buried. I had called trying to get the death certificate to submit to the insurance company to get my name off as the beneficiary and restore Benjamin's. But legally, I couldn't do it. They said that once the coroner stated the manner of death and released the death certificate, it was my decision to do whatever I wanted to do with the payout. Of course, I wasn't accepting one penny of that blood money.

After ignoring several telephone calls from Detective Brown and the front desk, a heavy knock landed on my front door hours later. The heavy knock turned into a thunderous boom as I decided whether to answer. I rushed to the door and flung it open.

"Yes?"

"Sorry to disturb you—" It was Detective Brown.

"No! You're not! I've already told you that I don't want to press charges. It's over."

"Ma'am, this woman could have killed you, and we'd rather not have someone like that out on our city streets."

"Listen, Detective, please come in."

I led the detective into my enormous, stylish living room. He sat on the couch, and I sat directly across from him on my husband's recliner. Looking directly into his eyes, I began my story, hoping he'd understand my plight and stop harassing me.

"Detective, I've been happily married for ten years, as I stated previously. A couple of months ago, I met a man and had a brief affair. I was lonely and feeling slightly neglected. I'm not offering that as an excuse. I'm simply stating the facts." I suddenly dropped my eyes into my lap and began twirling my fingers. "We both thought it wise to end the affair, so when I was attacked, I had no clue why. If my husband ever found out I'd been unfaithful, he would divorce me. I'm asking that you please make this go away."

Detective Brown shrugged and shook his head.

"Sorry, I can't do that. This is my case, and I plan on seeing it through to the end, whatever that end may be."

I let the detective out, not feeling any better about what my future might hold. I decided to lie down and try to get some sleep.

"You've made a horrible mess of things," George declared. "Now that Ricky's locked up, possibly facing a death sentence for killing that

fella, what you gonna do? Cause you not gonna come back up in here to live."

"I don't know. It wasn't supposed to happen like this. Whyyy did this happen?"

"You make me sick to my stomach. You done ruined two good lives! And what about your chile? What that baby gonna do?"

"I can't think about that now. My baby will be all right. Some good family will adopt her, and she'll have a better childhood than I did!"

I awoke from a frightful sleep; the dreams were back. My past was back.

CHAPTER
33

ANTHONY CROSS

EVER SINCE DAKOTA WAS ARRESTED AND bailed out by her parents for assaulting Gracie, she'd been out of control, a total lunatic. So, it wasn't a shock when Dakota showed up at my office unannounced. As I sat at my desk, totally consumed in paperwork, I looked up, and there she stood. She was still wearing the same clothing from the previous night; her hair was tossed about, and her eyes were puffy as if she'd been crying.

"What are you doing here?" I asked. It took all my strength not to totally lose it.

"You didn't say you loved me." She had the strangest look in her dark eyes as if she was permanently out to lunch.

"What are you talking about?"

"You didn't say you loved me when you left."

At that moment, I realized that I'd made yet another mistake. Still down over Gracie, I called Dakota. She came over, and I had sex with her, trying to see if I could recapture something from the past. A feeling, something, anything to feel nostalgic about when we first met. Of course, no sparks flew. My feelings for her were dead and buried.

"Dakota, listen. We need to talk, but unfortunately, now is not the time. I'll swing by your place after work. Is that good?"

"It's over, isn't it?" she asked, looking aloof. For some reason, I couldn't bring myself to be straight up. I wanted to tap dance around the topic.

"I'm working more than usual. I just think that we should cool it for a while. It wouldn't be fair to you."

"Stop it, Anthony, and be a man for once. Tell me the truth. I need closure."

Her plea forced my hand to be straightforward. "I'm not in love with you."

"I love you with all my soul," she began and collapsed into an empty chair. "But it wasn't enough. I wasn't enough. What was it that you wanted from me?"

Her eyes pleaded for me to say something that would make our breakup seem logical in her mind.

"Baby, I'm just not ready for the type of commitment you want."

"I've sacrificed my life for you and risked my freedom!"

"I had nothing to do with your choices. I thought you were

better than that. Your actions were deplorable."

During my heated discussion with Dakota, I heard a loud commotion coming from my waiting area. I jumped to my feet and ran to the door, just as it was pushed back into me. I fell back and regained my composure as several police officers busted into my office. My heart started to palpitate for Dakota. What had she done now?

"Doctor Anthony Cross?" one police officer asked.

"Yes?"

"Turn around and place your hands behind your back. You're under arrest for illegally selling and distributing pornography. You have the right to remain silent. Anything you say can and will be used against you . . .."

I was stunned. I couldn't speak. I assumed the position in a daze. I could see Dakota's mouth moving, all my staff running to my defense, news cameras being thrust in my face.

Am I really under arrest? I wondered. *Are they leading me out of my high-end office into the back of a seedy police car?* Things like this didn't happen to guys like me. Finally, the realization sunk in as I was stuffed into the back of the police vehicle.

"Call my lawyer," I belted out, and Samantha, my RN, nodded rapidly. At that moment, I missed Anika more than ever. She would have handled the situation and done what was in my best interests.

One thought entered my mind as I was carted off. *Who the hell called the news?*

My ordeal ended just as it had begun—ambiguously. I had no idea how or why I was charged with selling and distributing pornography. The police told me very little once I invoked my rights and requested my attorney. I was shipped to Central Booking, where I was processed and awaited a judge to set bail. The cell was disgusting and quite intimidating. I stood up for most of the seventeen hours there with wild thoughts going through my head.

Yes, I have a vast video collection of women I've taped without their knowledge. That's trifling, I know. But I never, ever thought about selling those tapes. And since I didn't do it, who did? I wondered. I was determined to find out.

I called Anika from the holding pen collect, half expecting her to deny my charges, but she didn't.

"Hello."

"You have a collect call from '*Anthony*,' an inmate at a correctional facility. If you would like to accept the charges, please press 1. If you'd like to deny charges, please press 2," the automated system stated.

I was put through.

"I heard what happened," she began, her voice depicting concern and bewilderment. "What's going on?"

"I have no idea," I stated honestly.

"Did you do it?"

"Of course not!"

"I'm just asking. I'm not your number one fan anymore."

"I know I've hurt you, but you're a good friend, and I need all my friends right now."

"What can I do?"

"I need you to call Gracie and tell her what's happened—"

"This is about Gracie? You're actually calling me so that I can call that bitch!"

"Anika, please, this isn't about you right now. Did you forget I'm in jail? And Gracie's been through a lot lately. Dakota went to her house, beat her up, and tried stabbing her."

"Tell me when I'm supposed to care!"

"You do care. You care about me, and you care about Gracie because that's who you are. Under your tough exterior lies a soft heart. I know you."

"Know this!"

Those were her last words before she hung up the phone. I called all my boys, but none of them were home. Kevin's wife picked up, sounding concerned, and said she would get the message to Kevin to show up in court and have funds available just in case the DA asked for bail.

I expected Dakota to sit in the courtroom's front row, crying her eyes out while waiting for me to be arraigned. Still, to my surprise, she wasn't anywhere around. I looked into the audience and saw no one there—not one friend, staff member, or special lady. It was five o'clock in the morning, but was that really an excuse? My life was on the line.

Jeez, this is the treatment I get when I'm in a fucking crisis, I thought.

They brought ten of us into the courtroom at one time to appear before the judge. Samantha did get in touch with my lawyer, Vallerie Mallore, and she was there, looking great, I might add—if you were into white women. Her long legs, blue eyes, and svelte figure were a welcome sight after my ordeal. She got right to the point.

"I wasn't able to get a lot of information. But it appears that someone has been selling and distributing pornographic tapes with titles such as *Doctor Good Dick and Nurse Betty*," Valerie whispered. "They show you and several women engaging in different sex acts. Most of these women have been contacted. Although they're furious with you for taping them without their consent, only one thus far has agreed to testify against you—Ms. Dakota Blair. I pulled her name, and she has a criminal record. She may want to plea bargain with the DA, giving her testimony in your trial for leniency in her case."

Again, sweet Dakota had rocked my world. I now knew that I never knew her at all.

There wasn't anything I could do at that moment but concentrate on getting out. Valerie asked that I be let go on my own recognizance. The judge declined and set bail at $50,000. I heard a familiar voice as I was led to the back of the courtroom.

"Anthony," she called.

My head spun around, only to see Gracie. She had come for me. My heart filled with so much emotion that I almost cried. My eyes spoke what I couldn't. Valerie noticed her and went to talk to her. As they were conversing, I saw my father and Anika come through. Anika swallowed her pride and held me down. Although I was overjoyed to see my father, I didn't want the stress of my situation on him. He had a lot on his shoulders to deal with concerning my mother. That's why I didn't call my parents. And who was watching my mother? My Pops' eyes were worried, and he called my name as soon as we'd made eye contact. "Anthony!"

"Quiet in the courtroom, sir!" The judge hit his gavel, and several court officers went to tell him to either take a seat or leave the court. I gave him a smile and a nod to let him know I was all right. I could take on the world with my Pops and my girl by my side.

Three hours later, Gracie posted my bond, and I walked out

of my holding cell and was on my way back home in a taxi with her by my side.

CHAPTER

34

ANTHONY CROSS

AFTER THE PORNOGRAPHY SCANDAL, I felt like a bad boy, like I had more flavor than the average plastic surgeon. Not only that, but my already blossoming practice had suddenly almost tripled with patients. So many freaky women were vying for "Doctor Good Dick." You couldn't plan better PR. I was now busier than ever. I hired a private investigator to find out who copied each tape from my house and sold them online.

My relationship—or lack thereof—with Dakota was officially over, and my relationship with Gracie had resumed. We still had to be very discreet, but more and more, I wanted to marry her. I wholeheartedly wanted her to leave her husband. She wasn't happy there—I knew it, and she knew it.

"Doctor Cross, your ten o'clock consultation is in examination Room Two," Samantha told me.

"Thank you. Give me five minutes."

I finished my third cup of coffee and headed to examination Room Two with Samantha. There stood a reasonably good-looking man with funny-looking twists in his hair; he was slightly taller than me and probably stood at 6' 4.

"Doctor Cross, this is Edward Lane."

My face showed no recognition when I heard his surname. Could this be Mr. Lane, Gracie's husband? If so, why was he here? Did he know? Was I in danger? Then my fear subsided. He didn't look intimidating. He looked like I could take him down if he tried any bullshit.

"Doctor Cross, you operated on my wife, Gracie."

Bingo! I was right.

"Yes. How may I help you today?" I asked in an agitated tone.

"Well, you did a great job on my wife, and I wanted to surprise her and get liposuction on my stubborn belly fat."

Was he serious? I gave him another look. His funny hair twist, lanky body, and uncoordinated clothing were far from what I expected Mr. Lane to represent. His wife was worth millions, and he looked like a poor man walking. I couldn't see one characteristic that would convince me he was Gracie's type. I couldn't understand what she saw in him. My observation of her husband had plucked my nerves. If he wasn't the money man and couldn't hold a candle to me, then why was she holding on to her marriage? He looked like a loser.

"If you could open your examination robe, I can begin your consultation."

One week later, Mr. Lane was under anesthesia and at my mercy. I could have ended it for him right there if I wanted to, and no one would have been the wiser. Ha! That was all bullshit. If I tried anything, they'd have my ass in jail—no bail.

I couldn't resist peeking at his *Johnson* after Gracie had done all that bragging about how endowed her husband was. Inwardly, I'd hoped she was lying. But to my dismay, she wasn't. Her husband was huge.

Despite how I felt about his wife, I did a superb job on this guy. My ego kicked in and wouldn't allow me to do a botched surgery. I thought he was getting his fat sucked out because he felt my presence in his marriage. He struggled to hold on to a wife who no longer loved him. She had one foot out the door and the other walking over my threshold when we married.

I visited Mr. Lane in the recovery room and gave him his filled prescription. He was in minimal pain and coherent, but his speech was slurred.

"Mr. Lane," I said softly, "I've filled your prescription, and in an hour, you're free to go. Can you hear me?" He nodded.

"Than-nnk, you," he struggled to say. I pushed a small, brown paper bag in his hand with two bottles of meds and their instructions. He had to come back in five days for his follow-up.

I chuckled at my devious behavior. Gracie would have long divorced Edward Lane before realizing what I'd done.

As time passed, I thought about calling Anika. That was my friend, and it seemed senseless that she would carry my affair with Gracie to this extreme. After she rallied everyone to support me in court, she was back to not speaking to me. I thought we were better than that. I mean, who did she think she was? She couldn't lay claim to me. I was her boss, and she was my subordinate.

Each day I wished she'd walk through those doors so we could kick it again. I missed talking shit to her and bragging about the plethora of women that came and went in my bed. Anika was so stubborn that I wanted to choke some sense into her. Before I got arrested, I was so close to getting her to come back to work. We talked a few times weekly, and she entertained the thought. Now, all that was gone.

My cell vibrated, and I saw that I'd missed thirteen calls. I scrolled back to see that they all came from Chris.

"What's good?" I asked.

"Turn on the news!" he blurted out.

"Why? Which channel?"

"Any channel!" He was in a panic, and it only took me a few moments to understand why.

I watched the TV screen as the police taped off Gabriel's art gallery. For a split second, I thought he'd been murdered until I saw him being brought out in handcuffs. He didn't hide from the media. He walked proudly as the detectives escorted him to their squad car. As cameramen thrust microphones in his face, he was asked one question.

"How could you do it?"

He stopped and looked at the officer to see if he could answer the question, and then he said, "I'm innocent. I'm being framed!"

"What's going on—" I started to ask.

"Shh, keep watching," Chris demanded.

The news reporter began speaking.

"Gabriel Copa was arrested today in what the FBI has named the biggest fraud in art history, for selling fake post-Impressionist works. He's accused of duplicating the Certificate of Authenticity on early nineteenth-century, modern, and Impressionist paintings. He took the Certificate of Authenticity from original illustrations. He placed them on reproduced copies, and then he would order another Certificate of Authenticity for the actual paintings from Sotheby's or Christie's auction houses. The auction houses wouldn't give him a problem because he owned the originals.

"Mr. Copa hired Mexican immigrants to paint the counterfeits. He gave them free room and board to duplicate upward of ten forgery paintings per original.

"Mr. Copa grossed his first million from this fraudulent business by selling to overseas buyers. But Mr. Copa's biggest mistake was greed. He began selling his fakes in the United States, which is how the FBI caught this thief. Copa made more than $14 million with his art scam," the reporter finished.

I was speechless. How could this have happened? Immediately I blamed Chris.

"You vouched for this dude," I accused. "I would have never done business with him if it weren't for you!"

"Don't blame this situation on me. You wanted in!" Chris barked.

"All I know is that I'm gonna break my foot in somebody's ass if I don't get my money back! Do you think that he swindled us? I mean, you're his boy. Better yet, do you think he'd swindle me? I'd hate to find out that the painting on the wall in my living room is worthless, and I just got conned out of three hundred grand."

"How am I supposed—"

"You should know because you've been riding his ass for six months!"

"So, what! Oh God, no, my investment..." His words trailed off.

"You've been paid on your investments!"

"Don't you get it?! He's a con man. I was paid for my first two investments. Both were very small. This last investment was all the money I owned. I cashed in my 401K plan and IRAs and took the equity out of my apartment to have enough liquid to get in on this deal."

"Didn't I tell you to wait? That I wanted to do more research on this guy? How could you be so foolish?"

"The same way you walked in and dropped three hundred on a painting, and you know nothing about art! Greed! We're both guilty of it. Are we the only educated people in America to get swindled? It happens to the best of us...bankers, celebrities, and Ivy-league graduates have all been victims. So don't come down on my bail-bondsman ass because I wanted to make a few extra dollars."

"I guess you're right." I thought about what he'd said, and nobody forced my hand regarding the painting. Stupidly, I jumped into the deal without any background check on the guy. I was more suspicious of the women I slept with than my finances. I think one part of the blame is that I had just gotten that large check from Gracie. I was feeling myself as if her money was my money.

"Anthony, listen, man. If anything jumps off, you have to tell them I didn't have anything to do with it."

"What are you talking about?"

"You know—"

"No, I don't know, so why don't you tell me?"

"I'm just saying that although Gabriel's my boy, he could lie to those federal agents and say I was down with him."

"Are you crazy? You're as much a victim as I am. Listen, I need to contact the FBI so that they can come and get my painting and investigate the transaction I've done with him. I suggest you do the same."

I legitimately had no liquid assets if the news reporter and my gut were correct. Anthony Cross was officially broke.

CHAPTER
35

GRACIE LANE

THE RIPPLE EFFECT OF MY AFFAIR WAS beginning to rear its ugly head. I stood in front of my mirror, under the fluorescent lighting, and noticed I had aged these past couple of weeks. I fingered a few crow's feet around my eyes that weren't there last week. I saw fine lines on my forehead and thick creases around my mouth, known to many as laugh lines on closer inspection. I was worrisome, nearly forty years old, and on the brink of a mental breakdown from the stress.

I called the coroner's office for the umpteenth time.

"Hello, this is Gracie Lane. I'm calling to see when you'll release my father, George Perry, so we can give him a proper burial?"

"Mrs. Lane, your father's body was released to your brother, Benjamin Perry, this morning. Our findings were turned over to the police department. We found thallium in his system. His death certificate reads homicide. Detectives will be in touch with you."

"With me?" I shrieked.

"They asked, I answered. They wanted to know who, if anyone, contacted us about releasing the body. Your name came up several times."

"Because I wanted to bury him!"

"That's not what you said. You said you wanted to get the death certificate for the insurance money."

My body went numb. *How could she have twisted my words?* I wondered.

Today was a bad day for me. Little did I know that it was going to get worse. I wondered whether I should call the insurance agent and get his take on the situation because I knew I shouldn't be a suspect. I didn't kill George, and most insurance policies were only null and void in the case of suicide. Or if the beneficiary was the prime suspect in the insured's death. Perhaps I should call the police and tell them what I knew.

I decided to probe the insurance company first. As I went to pick up the phone, it rang.

"Hello?" I snapped.

"Mrs. Lane?"

"Yes, who's this?" My patience was growing thinner by the second.

"This is Detective Delgado. I'm Detective Brown's partner. He's off today—"

"Listen, Detective, I've already explained to Detective Brown that I don't plan on testifying. And that the state will have to try Ms. Blair without my help."

"Yes, we have that information, but there's a problem."

"Your problems are your problems," I barked. I'd finally had it with tiptoeing around the cops and allowing them to harass me daily.

"Maybe," he said. He spoke slowly and softly as if my outburst couldn't rile him. "Maybe not. The problem could very well be yours."

"How so?" My curiosity was piqued.

"Ballistics pulled two fingerprints off the kitchen knife. One was traced back to Dakota Blair, the other to a felon. Does the name Marie Perry sound familiar to you?"

The name silenced me.

"Mrs. Lane, are you there?"

"Uhm, yes. Someone's at my front door. What was that name again?"

"Marie Perry. She's wanted for murder!"

"No, I don't know that name."

"Okay, thank you."

"Goodbye, Detective."

"Mrs. Lane?"

"Yes?" I said and exhaled.

"We need you to come into the precinct so that we can run your fingerprints."

"I'll do no such thing! I'm not a criminal. I'm a taxpaying citizen, and in case you've forgotten, I'm the victim."

"I understand that Mrs. Lane, but I'm not asking. I'm telling you that you need to come down here, so we can clear you. I'm sure you have nothing to hide."

With a tight-lipped resignation, I replied calmly, "Very well."
My life imploded.

"NOOOOO!" I screamed and let out a haunting wail filled
with anguish and fear.

I sobbed for hours, cradling myself on the floor in my kitchen.
When Ed walked in, he found me crouched near the refrigerator,
in a trance-like state, shivering and mumbling, "No, no, no, no,
no...."

I began making plans to leave. I called the illustrious Jill Stuart,
top realtor to the stars, and placed my apartment on the market.
I told her that I wanted a buyer and to close within the next 30
days. I put my apartment on the market for 20 percent less than
its appraised value. All the wolves would come out for this steal. I
decided I wanted to head west, and it would also be wise to start
stashing my money in an offshore bank account. It wouldn't take
the police long to connect Marie Perry and Gracie Lane, so Gracie
had to die. All traces of her existence had to go. The only way that
would happen was to put my money in an untraceable account
and disappear from all I knew. I did this two decades ago without
any money. Surely my wealth would afford me a better escape
route.

I knew my husband wouldn't run with me in my heart, and I
loved him too much to ask. How could I subject him to a life on
the run? That would be the most selfish thing I'd done in my
treasure trove of selfish things. What stumped me was that I
thought it would be easier to walk away. I felt the heat hot on my
ass, but it wasn't making me bolt as quickly as it should've.

I felt my husband might be having an affair to worsen matters.

He no longer wanted to make love, and it was driving me crazy. He kept blaming it on his recent operation, saying his body wasn't built for surgery because he now felt like an old man.

That afternoon, I drank more than the legal level of alcohol and then drove to Anthony's house. I felt alone and neglected and wanted to feel a stiff dick and fuck my blues away.

Again, I flirted with his doorman, who allowed me up without announcing. I didn't know why it gave me the thrill to get my way like that, but it did. Although I was heavily intoxicated, my walk was steady. By the time I reached Anthony's door, my hormones were blazing. I knocked, only he didn't answer.

"Well, hello, Gracieeee," a man sang.

"How do you know my name? And where's Anthony?"

"He had to stay late tonight at work. He had emergency surgery. Some woman's stitches burst open because she didn't follow his orders."

"Are you going to invite me in?"

"Sure, sure, come in," he replied, leading farther into Anthony's plush apartment. "My name's Chris. I'm Anthony's friend."

"Pleasure to meet you."

"The pleasure's all mine."

It never occurred to Chris to call Anthony and tell him to rush home because he had company. He was too busy flirting with me.

"What's your poison?" he asked.

"What's your pleasure?" I retorted.

"Excuse me?" He didn't understand my personal joke.

"Scotch on the rocks."

"No chaser?"

"Not tonight."

I was pretty drunk and feeling awfully naughty. I didn't factor into my conscience that Chris was my histress's friend. Maybe I didn't care. We sat close on the sofa, *very* close. Quickly I slid my tongue into his mouth. He tried to resist, but I was too much for him. All the passion I had bottled up inside of me came bursting out. My tongue explored the inside of his mouth and his earlobes, then I moved down to his neck. I sucked gently until I heard a faint moan. I ground my hips up and down and felt a bulge, which excited me. I got more aggressive and reached inside his boxers. Once my hand touched his penis, it grew to a decent size—nothing to brag about, and I almost backed out. But my hormones wouldn't allow me to stop.

Chris started to respond to my gestures and began exploring my body. He gently caressed my back, then his hands traveled to my bra. Chris unclasped it, and my ample breasts spilled out. He opened his mouth and took a mouthful. He sucked until my nipples were like two ripe fruits. We switched positions until we were on Anthony's designer sofa, with Chris's body wedged between my thighs. I parted my legs slightly, slid up my skirt, and he eased off my silk panties. He looked into my eyes, and lust consumed his face.

"Fuck me," I said. "Show me what you can do."

Chris steadied himself on top of me and gently slid inside. I was so wet you could hear soft noises as he pushed in and out. With steady, consistent strokes, he completely penetrated me. Each thrust brought me closer to my climax.

"How does it feel?" he crooned in my ear.

I ignored him.

Again, he asked. "It feels good?"

"Please, be quiet," I whispered.

I was grinding my hips to his rhythm, and the feeling was incredible. When the feeling got too intense, I bit down hard on my bottom lip and kept throwing my hips back.

We slid off the sofa, and I assumed the doggy-style position. Chris reentered me and began giving me back shots. I gripped the couch as he pounded into me, slapping me on my juicy ass so hard I screamed out. I loved every minute of the abuse.

"Yeah, this is how you like it! From the back! You like it from the back, don't you! You wanna suck me off how you suck—"

"Please, shut the fuck up!" I screamed. This guy was a lousy lay.

Before I could climax, Chris shuddered and came without warning, collapsing on my back and breathing heavily. Annoyed, I pushed him off me.

"What was that?" I asked, standing and towering over him.

"That was five solid minutes of good loving!" he said boastfully.

"That was three minutes of weak dick! You're too young to be operating on old man energy!"

"I got mine. Don't be mad if you didn't get yours. I hope you didn't expect me to wait on you!" Chris had already jumped up and adjusted his clothing.

I was furious. I slid on my panties and couldn't resist picking up my glass and tossing my drink in Chris's face.

"How 'bout that?" I asked and stormed into Anthony's bedroom, closing the door behind me.

"Bitch!" he screamed.

"All day," I retorted.

I showered, climbed into Anthony's bed, and fell asleep within moments.

CHAPTER

36

ANTHONY CROSS

"SO, ARE YOU TELLING ME YOU'VE traced the internet site to my best friend, Christopher Wilkens?"

"Yes, that's correct."

After hours, I was in my office with Brian McDonald. The private investigator I hired to find answers about who set me up, duplicated my whole DVD collection and made a profit. The news stunned me.

"How long has this been going on?"

"At least eight months. Chris was uploading small clips of your DVDs to Pornotube.net. Customers can see a 30-second clip, and if they like what they see, they can buy the whole video. All the money's going into an offshore, joint bank account. Once the funds are put in, it's being funneled back out—"

"Let me guess. The other partner is Gabriel Copa?"

He nodded. "I did a little investigating, and they both have serious cocaine habits. Still, Mr. Wilkens also has a large gambling debt owed to the Irish Mafia."

"Irish mob? I didn't think shit like that really existed." I was perplexed. How could my best friend have betrayed me like that?

"It does exist, and the Mafia is more dangerous than any myth could portray."

"Did you see the scandal on the news regarding Gabriel and the art?"

"Yeah, I caught that."

"Well, guess who got mixed up in that, too? He got me for nearly $300,000 on a painting."

"Well, if it makes you feel any better, I did some investigating when I made the connection between your friend Chris and Gabriel. Chris didn't have anything to do with your getting swindled with the painting. He got duped as well. It seems as if Gabriel used Chris to bring you and others in. He's a professional con man and didn't exempt friends or family. If Chris had money, then he wasn't going to be excluded.

"I'll have my report in your inbox in two days. Also, I have a friend high up in the police commissioner's office. He'll also get a copy of the report. Steer clear of your friend, and don't mention anything. He'll get a knock on his door early next week."

"Thanks, man. Any chance I'll get my money back when all this is over?"

"Your chances are slim to none. It'll be difficult to recover all the money bilked by Gabriel. Whatever is recovered, the payout line will be so long that it's unlikely you'll receive pennies on the dollar. Most of his take went to expensive cars and lavish living for Mr. Copa."

"Why would Chris conspire with Gabriel to cross me...." I wasn't really asking Brian this question, but he answered anyway.

"I have no idea. Only Chris knows."

The news hit me below my gut. I felt betrayed. As I walked Brian out and began closing the office, I got a knock on the glass door. I looked up, and it was Ed, Gracie's husband. Immediately I was aggravated. If he'd burst open a stitch or wanted to bust my balls about his surgery, I swore on my mother that I'd choke his life out. I wasn't in the mood for any bullshit tonight.

Aggressively I opened the door.

"What is it?" I asked.

"May I come in?" he asked in a level voice.

"Quickly. I don't have a lot of time. I'm busy and need to get home."

"This won't take long."

The frail-looking man entered my office with his trench coat draped over his forearm. His eyes were cold and distant, and his breathing became erratic.

"I went to my medical doctor last week because I wasn't feeling like myself after the surgery," he began, and immediately I knew where he was going with this. "He took a series of tests, and I'm sure you know the results."

"Amuse me."

"Amuse you, huh?" If he was upset, his voice showed no sign of that. But the glare in his eyes gave him away. "Well, I guess it would be amusing for everyone hearing the story except me. See, I haven't been able to get an erection and make love to my wife in weeks because my plastic surgeon gave me 500 mg of Finasteride to take twice daily. Can you imagine that?"

"Why would I give you that? You must be mistaken."

"I figured you'd say that, and that's what you're supposed to say because you're protecting your practice. But I'm not a snitch-ass dude. You don't have to worry about me filing a lawsuit or reporting you to the medical board. But I am going to whip your ass in here tonight. You can believe that. I'm gonna whip your ass for hating! You're not God. If you're a man and you're fucking my wife—fuck my wife! Don't come after me. I work every day, and I don't bother anybody. I can get another good woman. Gracie knew from the beginning that I would never tolerate cheating. If you want her, she's yours."

"I *had* your wife. I don't *want* her," I replied. I had to snap on homeboy, who thought he was putting me in my place.

I looked at the six-foot-four male who stood before me. His lanky, lean, frail body wouldn't be a match for me—I bench-pressed 300 lbs. four times a week. It was time I started to throw my weight around and take out some of my anger on him.

"Look, get the fuck out before I throw your Black ass out!" I yelled.

I went to grab him by his collar when he seized my hand. He twisted my arm around my back and forcefully slammed me against the wall. The force of my head hitting the solid surface resulted in a speed knot over my left eye. Before I could get my bearings, he spun me around. He began an aggressive assault, lashing out a litany of punches to my upper body. He was as fast as Ali in his prime. I tried to ward off each jab with half-assed blocks and semi-ducks, but he was too quick. Almost all his punches landed at their destined locations. He was making weird noises and doing Tae Bo moves and karate chops. Ed gave me one-and-two-piece combinations, uppercuts to the jaw, and a succession of rib shots. One last punch to my gut leveled me. I fell back over a waiting room area table. I was out for the count. Ed walked over to me and spat in my face.

"Bitch-ass punk!" he yelled before exiting.

Could my day get any worse? Finally, I got up and made it to the phone.

"Operator, please send the police here. I've just been assaulted!"

CHAPTER
37

VENGEANCE IS MINE

BIG MOMMA MORALES WALKED UP the stately steps of the Burlington Township Police Department with an undeterred conviction. Her steel walking cane supported her weight as she took baby steps toward her destination. Dozens of grandchildren hovered around, all at her beck and call. Each collectively thinks the same: *I can't wait for her to kick the bucket to get my inheritance.* Big Momma smelled of old money. The expensive sable fur coat was large enough to make three smaller versions out of the skins. She wore gaudy gold and diamond rings on each finger, including her thumbs. Her fat hands could barely close to make a fist.

Everyone in the precinct knew her well. Big Momma had been coming to that precinct consistently for twenty-one years, five months, and eighteen days. She inquired about the senseless murder of her grandson, Emmanuel Morales.

Detective Ryser was on his way home from a double shift when he spotted the family's matriarch. He had been handling the case since the original detective had retired nine years ago. His heart went out to her, and he respected her determination.

"Detective, when is Marie Perry going to get apprehended. My poor grandson cannot rest until that hussy is behind bars! That trashy tramp will regret the day she said a Morales raped her dirty little ass!"

"Mrs. Morales, we're doing everything possible to assist in her recapture."

"Do you realize I've spent over one million dollars on private detectives throughout the years searching for clues leading us to her arrest! I'm afraid I will not be on this earth much longer. I'm old, and I'm tired. And I want to go on and be with my husband. But I can't until I see that murderer behind bars."

"Well, we've got good news from New York. Her fingerprints came back on a knife—"

The whole clan began giving high-fives and sighs of relief. They were sure their grandmother would die when Marie Perry got arrested, just as she'd promised for the past decade.

"When? When were you going to tell me! Is she in jail?"

"Let's everyone calm down. Marie's not in jail yet. That's why you weren't contacted. But I'll fill you in on every detail."

"Let me speak to your captain!" The cantankerous Big Momma yelled, and Detective Ryser wasn't moved. She did the same routine three times a week, every week. Captain O'Malley, who blames his premature balding on Big Momma, came over to placate the situation.

"Yes, dear," he soothed. "What can I do for you?"

The elderly lady cut her eyes. She was genuinely smitten with the Irish captain.

"This young fella here has been withholding important information regarding my grandson's case. Did you know that?"

"Detective Ryser has been putting a lot of man-hours on this case. He feels we're going to make an arrest soon."

"Soon? Did you know I've spent well over one million dollars doing the job for the police?"

"I told you years ago to stop giving good money to those crooks. All of those leads they gave amounted to nothing. All those sightings of Marie Perry in Amsterdam, London, and Prague were false intel."

"What about my reward? The $100,000 reward. Do those cops in New York know that there's a reward for information leading to her capture?"

"Yes, they know."

"You're looking at me as if you want me to leave!"

"You? Never...you're my favorite lady. But you should go home, and I'll personally call you when we get her."

"I hope I'm not dead!"

"You're gonna outlive us all," Captain O'Malley replied, giving her a firm hug. She loved it.

CHAPTER
38

GRACIE LANE

IT WAS CLOSE TO ELEVEN AT NIGHT when I heard Anthony's key maneuver the locks. It took him at least ten minutes to make it to his bedroom. By this time, I had already slept off my intoxication. Anthony screamed into his phone, but I couldn't make out his conversation. Soon he walked into his bedroom and was startled by my small figure curled up in his bed.

"Jeez, you scared me," he admonished.

"Where've you been? I've been waiting forever," I said in a baby-like voice.

"How did you get in?"

"Chris was here and allowed me to wait for you."

"That slimy bastard!" he spat. "Are you all right?"

"Yes, I missed you."

He walked farther into the room and flicked on the lights. I gasped at the sight of my lover.

"Baby, what happened to you?" I ran to him, put my arms around his waist, and lightly kissed his face.

"It looks worse than it really is. I don't want to talk about that right now. I got a lot on my mind. Shouldn't you be home, being wifey?"

"I don't want to talk about that, either. Maybe we could talk later."

"Sounds like a plan." He looked deep into my eyes. "Whatever happens, I need you to know I love and want you. But I want you to want me, too."

"I do want you," I said. "I want you, and I don't want to go home. I want to stay with you forever."

Those were the words he'd been waiting to hear.

"Let's get in the shower," he suggested. "I've had a miserable day."

The hot water cascaded onto our faces as we submerged our bodies underneath the powerful showerhead. The steam was so thick that we could barely see each other. I let the soothing water drench my hair and face as Anthony stood behind me and pressed his hard body against my backside. His masculine hands started lathering my back in circular motions, and I got lost in erotic pleasure. As the soapy rag traveled along the nape of my neck, tracing my hips, my plump ass, and then lingered between my thick thighs, I shuddered. I turned around to face him, and we began kissing passionately. Anthony slowly licked my earlobes while massaging my erect nipples with his fingertips.

He pushed me against the shower wall, got down on his knees, and parted my legs. He put my right leg on his shoulder and opened my nether lips with two fingers. My swollen clitoris entered his warm mouth eagerly. As he began sucking my clit, I held on to the shower walls for support. He traced the creases outlining the walls of my vagina with his tongue, causing me to quiver involuntarily. Anthony nodded as if to say he knew he'd hit the right spot.

He pulled back, stuck his finger into my stimulated cave, and began twirling. Warm juices seeped out onto his hand. I encouraged him by moaning. He stood up, positioned me in front of him, and bent me over. Spreading my ass cheeks, he began easing his manhood into my resisting backside.

He didn't say a word as he aggressively massaged my breasts in a circular motion while placing wet kisses on my spine, driving me crazy. I sucked in my breath. Inch by inch, his girth penetrated me anally. The sensation was exquisite. I started rocking my hips seductively as the feelings filtered through my body. Finally, he had entered me wholly. The pain mixed with pleasure was a little overbearing for me as our slippery bodies became one. As Anthony held tightly onto my hips, pushing in and out, we both moaned in pleasure.

"You . . . like . . . this?" he asked, moaning. "You . . . like . . . this . . . big . . . dick?"

"Oh, yesssss," I agreed. "Yessss, baby, fuck me good."

"Tell me what you want."

"I want you to fuck the shit out of me," I demanded.

"I can do that," he replied through clenched teeth as he mercilessly pushed his penis into me.

"Yeeessssss," I screamed, gripping the shower door for support.

"Tell me you love me!" Anthony commanded.

"I . . . love . . . you . . ." I purred.

He continued expertly guiding his manhood, each stroke deeper than the last. The combination was explosive as I felt intense waves of pleasure cascading through my body. I braced myself as my muscles tensed and began to contract. We both exploded and screamed out together.

For long moments, we tried to catch our breath. Soon Anthony eased out of me and continued to do what he had initially started to do: wash my body. He enjoyed washing my fingers, arms, feet, and intimate parts. I was his baby, and at the moment, he felt like I was his and *only* his. After washing my body, he carried me back to his bed, laid me down, and slid his tongue into my mouth. We began kissing softly, which soon progressed to slow, passionate kisses.

I was yearning desperately for him to enter me again. I arched my back as he aggressively sucked my breasts until my nipples were erect. I wrapped my shapely legs around his trim waist, and he entered me gently this time. I pushed back my hips as he pumped his pelvis, meeting each thrust. It felt like his penis was expanding inside me as I dug my nails deep into his masculine shoulders. I began to nibble on his neck before I pushed him over and mounted him.

I expertly rode him while his hands guided my waist. I looked and saw pleasure all over his face. Sliding up and down while contracting my Kegel's muscle drove him crazy.

"Is it good?" I asked.

"Yeah, baby," he said, moaning.

As my vagina began to contract involuntarily, I sped up my rhythm.

"I'm about to comeeee," I yelled as Anthony grabbed me tightly. We both exploded for the second time. Sweat poured from our bodies as I collapsed on his broad chest.

We'd made love from the shower to the bed four times that night. We were physically drained and exhausted as we snuggled together and drifted off peacefully.

CHAPTER
39

ANTHONY CROSS

GRACIE WAS STILL IN MY BED IN THE MORNING, and I felt a sense of victory. Could I wake up to her every day? I thought so. All I knew was that it felt good, and I liked it. I prepared my sleeping beauty breakfast in bed and woke her up with kisses.

"What's all this?" she asked with a grateful tone as she struggled to get up.

"It's the start of a new beginning," I said, crawling into bed with her. I felt it was time for us to have a heart-to-heart talk. There was a lot that I didn't know about her. "Tell me about who you are."

"What do you want to know?"

"Whatever you're ready to tell me."

She exhaled.

"I'll tell you as much as you can stomach."

Her voice was weak, and she didn't look me in the eyes. She put her head down in shame and began her story.

"Growing up, I never knew my mother. She left us when I was still very young. Living in a house full of men—my father and two brothers—was hard on a young girl. Especially when my father despised me. My daddy, who I recently found out is my uncle, always insisted that I go out into the world and find my own way. If I wanted a pair of shoes, he'd encourage me to go out and get them however I could. So be it if that meant sleeping with the dirty old man at the corner store.

"I didn't want to whore myself out, so I figured I'd do as my mother did. I'd marry young and have someone take care of me. I fell in love with Emmanuel. He and I snuck around for years. His family was one of the wealthier in our area and thought I was trash. His parents would have never accepted me. He promised to marry me when we were old enough, and I believed him. He wanted me to have an abortion when I got pregnant, but I refused to kill his baby. I loved him. I was numb when he suggested I sleep with someone else to blame the pregnancy on that person. He, too, was whoring me out. But I did as I was told. I didn't know any better.

"It was easy enough to find the perfect scapegoat in my town. His name was Ricky. He didn't come from wealth, but he was a hard worker. I slept with him once, and it was a 'miracle.' I was pregnant. He was the proudest man walking the earth. After I gave birth, neither of our parents wanted another mouth to feed, so we had to put the baby in a foster home. Thus, my telltale stretchmarks." She laughed as tears streamed down her cheeks. I caressed her face, which encouraged her to keep talking.

"Take your time, baby," I soothed as she began to sob.

"Three years after the birth of my daughter, I was still attached to Ricky in the town's eyes, but I was sneaking behind everyone's back with Emmanuel. I had just turned eighteen, and Emmanuel still hadn't married me. Like a fool, I sat waiting, but he just kept giving me one excuse after the other.

"George, my fake father, had long ago thrown me out, and Ricky had gotten us a place to live. He was a hard worker and finally got a job as an armored car driver. When Ricky asked me to marry him, I said yes. But that was only to force Emmanuel's hand and make him realize he loved me. Instead, Emmanuel encouraged me to marry Ricky, saying no one would find out about us as long as Ricky was there. As soon as he got his inheritance from his parents, I could divorce Ricky and marry him. I know"—she shook her head from side to side as if she didn't know how she could have been so foolish—"how stupid was I?

"Ricky and I weren't married for long before I began sneaking Emmanuel inside our home and bed. One day Emmanuel and I were making love when Ricky came home early. When he burst through the door, all I could think of was that he would kick me out, and I'd be homeless, without anywhere to go. I knew George wouldn't let me come back home. I don't know what made me say it. I really didn't have time to think, but I screamed rape. I mean, I really cried rape! It was a guttural moan mixed with a high-pitched scream.

"My reaction must have startled Emmanuel because he never thought to defend himself. He didn't protest or contest what I'd said. He just got dressed quickly and ran out of our apartment. Ricky ran after him and slaughtered him like an animal in the streets. He murdered him in broad daylight with a dozen witnesses. I was in shock. It all happened in the blink of an eye. Ricky was arrested on the spot, and he should have been arrested in my young mind. He'd just killed a man. My man.

"Once the town got wind of what happened, they flooded the sheriff's department with calls. The stranger who raped Marie Perry wasn't a stranger at all. His family went there, saying there wasn't any way Emmanuel could have raped me. They knew all along about our affair and our love child. Ricky was released from jail because his firearm was legal. He was under the impression that he'd shot and murdered an intruder, but I was arrested. They said when I screamed rape, I was negligent. It was no different than screaming 'fire!' in a crowded theater. The day the judge allowed me out of the county jail to await my trial, I ran with only the clothes on my back and headed this way. The trial was held *in absentia*, which means in my absence, and I was convicted of involuntary manslaughter."

I was stunned. Gracie had been through so much. It was an awkward moment, and I didn't know what to say. But I had to say something. I kept pushing and wanting to know about her past; now, I knew everything.

"Whatever happened to your daughter?" I finally asked.

"After the incident, Ricky, whose name was on her birth certificate as her biological father, took her out of her temporary foster home and raised her as his child. She ended up working for Doctor Anthony Cross."

The color drained from my face—the resemblance.

"Anika's your daughter."

Gracie dropped her head again in shame. "I've never been a mother to her. She's so much better than me. All I've ever done was hurt her, as my father hurt me."

She began sobbing her little heart out. She held on to me so tightly that I felt all her emotions. Her revelation drummed in my cloudy head. *Anika* was her daughter....

"I've never told anyone what I've told you," she honestly said.

"Don't worry, I'll help you make this right," I told her. There wasn't any way I'd allow her to spend the rest of her life in jail.

"There's more," she said reluctantly.

"Go ahead."

"They've found me."

"Who? Who's found you?"

"The police. When Dakota assaulted me, the police lifted my fingerprints off the knife. Now they're looking for a Marie Perry, wanted felon. Anthony, I have to go. I need to run and get away from here."

"Babe, you can't run. You have to stay and face it, or else you'll be running for the rest of your life."

"My life will be over if I don't run!" she screamed defiantly.

"We can make this right," I soothed, "I'll be here for you. We'll get a lawyer and make them see that you didn't plan on his murder. You had no way of knowing."

"That sounds great in theory, but the law doesn't always work like that. I've already been sentenced to seven to fifteen. My only hope is an appeal and request for a new trial. Even with that, I'm running the chance of getting convicted on a higher charge. What if a jury came back and found me guilty of negligent homicide!

Huh? I could do the rest of my life in jail without the possibility of parole."

She collapsed on the bed hysterically.

After Gracie had purged her heart out, she was drained. She drifted back to sleep, allowing me quiet time to figure out how I could help her get her life back. She needed me now more than ever, but I didn't know if I could be there. Finally, it was sinking in. Maybe Gracie wasn't the one for me. She's been living the last twenty years as a lie. She had all this scandal surrounding her name, and I didn't know if I was up to taking on her problems. I have my own. Not to mention that my best friend, Chris, had committed the ultimate betrayal. What was to say Gracie wouldn't hurt me as well?

CHAPTER
40

GRACIE LANE

I WOKE UP IN ANTHONY'S APARTMENT to several voice messages on my cell. I began listening, and my heart sank. Ed left a message that he had been arrested for fighting with my lover, the doctor, and he wanted me to come to bail him out. Several hours later, the following message was from Ed, saying he was released on his own recognizance and wanted a divorce.

I began getting dressed frantically when Anthony walked in.

"Where are you going?"

"Ed was arrested last night. Did you know that?"

"Arrested for what?"

"He said for fighting with you. You had to have known!" I yelled.

"I didn't know any such thing! Ask him. I wasn't there when he got arrested. He's probably lying."

I looked directly into Anthony's eyes.

"Ed doesn't lie."

I made my way to the front door, and Anthony was right behind me.

"Wait a minute. Let me get dressed and go with you."

"You can't. I have to deal with this on my own. I promise I'll call you later."

I left Anthony's apartment with a sense of guilt. What the fuck was I doing? Ed directly asking me for a divorce had shaken me up a bit. I was so confused. I felt like rubber being pulled in ten different directions. I had two men in love with me, all vying for my attention and undivided commitment. It was like smoking a cigarette to the butt and deciding to get one last drag or throw it out because it had served its purpose.

I entered my home to find Ed flying around the house in a frenzy. His eyes were red and puffy, and it appeared he'd been crying. Ed was packing some items into a suitcase. He ignored me as I came in. He was upset, which made me upset. After watching him gather things and wiping tears away, I finally broke the silence.

"What are you doing?"

"What does it look like?" he hastily snapped.

"It looks like you're packing your things."

"Nope! I'm packing *your* things."

"What's the matter with you? I'm not going anywhere! I got your message about divorce, and we need to sit and talk like adults."

"You're getting out of my sight, or I promise I will make you very sorry!" he screamed. Ed was furious, and I realized my approach was inappropriate. I needed to calm down and level with him.

"Ed, explain why you're packing my things for me to leave. I told you that I'm not having an affair with my doctor. Don't let him come between us."

"I told you I'd divorce you if you were unfaithful. You gambled with my love, and you'll have to live with the consequences. You mean nothing to me. You're just another whore. You don't deserve my last name."

"I've never slept with him. I swear on my mother's grave! All this is a misunderstanding. He said he tried to tell you that, but you wouldn't listen."

"How dare you stand in my face and quote what another man told you! You're cherishing his words like they came straight from the Bible. I'm your HUSBAND! Why do you keep forgetting that?"

"Ed, I'm here, aren't I? How could you accuse me of forgetting about you?"

"How could you leave me in jail and not even come to support me in court?" He shook his head in disbelief.

"I stayed at the Marriott. I needed time alone to think about our marriage and how much you mean to me," I said calmly.

"Don't lie to me. You were with him, weren't you?" Ed asked.

"I answered that already. Now stop acting crazy."

"Crazy! Why are you doing this to me? Me? Do you hear how you sound right now? You're cold . . . and distant. You just want me to roll over and accept you for who you are. Turn the other cheek and let you and your male mistress carry on. You selfish bitch!"

Startled by his outburst, I couldn't move. Ed had to grab me by my elbow and toss me and my suitcase out the front door. The neighbors got a front-row view as I began pounding and banging on the front door, screaming and crying hysterically. My dirty laundry was on display—literally and figuratively.

I ran to the front desk angrily, got the master key, and returned to confront my husband. Nobody kicks me out of my motherfucking house! The nerve of him. I came back ready to battle. He was upstairs when I confronted him.

"Who the fuck do you think you are? If it's over, then it's over! But you're getting out—not me!"

He looked defeated. He was still crying.

"Okay, Gracie, you're right. I'll leave. And I'm sorry...that I ever met you."

CHAPTER

41

ANTHONY CROSS

THAT NIGHT, WHEN GRACIE CAME BACK to me, I was euphoric. I wanted to keep her safe, protect her, and give her the love she never got from any man. The following day, she contacted a high-powered lawyer. She took us on an obscene shopping spree on her American Express Black Card. She had tossed Ed out, and she admitted that she was tired of crying and equally tired of running, scared. I told her that we were starting over. When I pulled out the charm bracelet I had purchased weeks back, her eyes welled up with tears.

"This symbolizes my love for you."

I guess the new piece of jewelry had sparked something in her, or maybe it was the looming fear of a lengthy prison term, but Gracie was determined to spend a lot of the money she had sitting in her bank accounts.

She'd purchased us both matching fur coats. I watched as she pranced around in a chinchilla fur designed by Zac Posen. She walked around my apartment in full diva status. As her chinchilla swept the ground and her stilettos from Jimmy Choo click-clacked against my parquet floors, I realized how happy I was. In light of her situation, it felt good to believe in and pledge your support to someone you loved, and I thought she could be the one. I didn't want or desire to call another woman, let alone sleep with anyone else. I told her I wanted her to divorce her husband and marry me—in the face of danger—and I meant every word.

She took me on a major shopping spree to celebrate our new beginning. I had two tailored trench coats from Karl Lagerfeld being delivered to me in the next four weeks, and I couldn't wait to get them. I also racked up numerous items from the Ed Hardy store. She bought herself a natural Russian sable belted swing coat, a Burberry overcoat, and matching shoes. We also stopped at Tiffany's. She bought herself a diamond bracelet set in platinum and a matching heart pendant necklace. And I picked up a pair of diamond cufflinks set in platinum. But what I loved most was when we went to Tourneau, and she replaced my stolen, stainless-steel Rolex watch with a platinum version. The watch looked good on my wrist. I felt like a million bucks. She also bought us matching Harry Winston diamond rings set in platinum. We both had them fitted for our pinky fingers. Then we went to Barney's New York and Bergdorf Goodman, and she bought an entire wardrobe.

Our day couldn't have been better until I got a call from my doorman.

"Doctor Cross, any moment, you'll be getting a knock on your door for your lady friend. There's no way out. They should be there—the police."

My heart dropped. I looked at Gracie; she had a massive smile as she modeled her new clothing for me.

She detected something in my face.

"What's wrong?" she panicked. "Who was that?"

Before I could answer, the police burst in and grabbed Gracie. They left with her kicking and screaming. I stood there helpless, watching the events unfold before me.

CHAPTER

42

ANTHONY CROSS
THE FINAL CHAPTER

WHEN GRACIE WAS PROCESSED AND extradited back to New Jersey, I decided to visit her. I kept thinking about how she handled being locked up on my ride there.

The lawyer Gracie retained had put a motion into the court. She requested to be released from the case after the State had seized Gracie's bank accounts. The DA's office had gotten a court order asking that they exhume her second husband, Phillip's body. Presumably, to run more tests to ensure he died of natural causes and wasn't murdered. They were trying to label her a serial killer, a manipulative woman, a menace. Gracie—or shall I say Marie Perry's story went national. The news media had a field day. They had side-by-side pictures of her in her early twenties with images of her new face—post-plastic surgery. They claimed that she'd gotten cosmetic surgery to escape paying her debt to society and elude the law. Her brothers/cousins, Andre and Benjamin, came out of the woodwork along with Ed's sister, Tamara. All sold their stories to tabloids showing Gracie in an awful light.

Unless Gracie told me otherwise, I'd believe whatever truth she gave me. My funds were a bit low, but I was looking to liquidate all my assets, sell my apartment, and get her a high-profile lawyer to appeal her case, such as Mark Geragos or Barry Scheck.

Whatever time she got, I would ride it out with her. If I didn't, then who would? Surely not her miserable brothers/cousins, and most certainly not her husband. The freak had turned her in! How could he look at himself in the mirror? She didn't deserve that as punishment for having an affair.

As Gracie came scampering into the visiting room, I could tell she'd been crying. Her eyes were bloodshot and puffy. Her hair was pulled back into a tight ponytail, and the orange prison jumpsuit seemed to swallow her shapely figure. Even though she looked withered and worn, her eyes had a glint of determination as if to say, *"Don't feel sorry for me. I'll be all right."*

I stood to embrace her, and she sat down, leaving my arms extended. She dropped her head into her hands and began to sob.

"What are you doing here?" she asked.

"What do you mean? I came to give you my support," I said. "Why? Don't you want me here?"

"Anthony, you shouldn't have come. I don't want anything getting back to Ed. I need him right now."

"Ed? You need *Ed* right now? He turned you in for reward money!"

"No! He didn't!"

"There was a bounty over your head, and he took it!" I exploded and disrupted the visiting room. After getting a glare from one of the COs, I lowered my voice. "Why are you punishing yourself? You don't need him—I'm here for you."

"Here for me?" Gracie laughed mockingly. "Are you going to make me an offer I can't refuse? Huh? What can you do for me that my husband can't? Are you going to open these iron bars and let me walk away into the sunset?"

"Why are you doing this? Why are you pushing me away? I'm finally committing myself to you—a relationship—and you don't want me. I love you, Gracie…you don't have to be afraid to love me back."

"Anthony, I'm in a six-by-six-foot cell. That, coupled with your being here, is insufferable."

Was this the woman that I'd fallen in love with?

She continued. "I've already spoken to a lawyer that Ed hired. He said that I have a good case on appeal and may be able to get a judge to set bail. If that happens, I can regain my freedom until my next trial. Hopefully, this time I'll have a better ending."

"Are you kidding me? Drop that lawyer. You can't trust someone like Ed. He's a time bomb just waiting to explode. Don't you think he wants revenge for what you've put him through? All of your lies."

"Anthony, I know you may have ill feelings toward my husband and may be feeling slightly slighted, but he's doing what's in my best interest."

"I may be feeling slightly slighted?" My voice rose into a little girl's pitch. "He's sending YOU to the can, so you should reevaluate that statement."

As I sat listening to her, I wondered how she could still defend that man and not hold Ed responsible for her having to sit in somebody's dirty jail in a tacky, orange jumpsuit. Maybe she was punishing herself for her past choices. I decided to try another approach.

"Gracie, baby, listen, you don't have to feel guilty anymore about us. You don't have to feel that this is just punishment for having an affair."

"Please don't do this; make it about you and me because it isn't. A man is dead. My husband had nothing to do with what happened twenty years ago. He's honest, and he's doing what's right."

I listened to how she spoke of her husband—so fondly, passionately, and tenderly. Had she always spoken of him this way, and if so, how could I have missed it?

"Even now, you choose him over me? After all, he's done to you? How could you stay with him?"

"Because he's my husband," she replied simply.

"Really?" I slowly retorted. "Are you in love with your *husband*?"

She lowered her gaze to the table, exhaled, and then looked me directly in the eyes. Thousands of questions went through my head in the seconds it took her to answer. My heart dropped, and my stomach fluttered. Jeez, for the first time in my life, someone broke up with me. I didn't like it. I didn't like it one bit.

"I'd be lying if I said no. More specifically, yes."

There it was. As simple as elementary school. The one question I never asked throughout our whole relationship was the one thing that could have saved me from all this pain I was currently feeling.

"What about us? I thought that we were going to get married. I thought that you loved me."

"Either I deceived you, or you made an inaccurate assumption, but I never said love or suggested marriage. We were just having a good time. You knew I was married when you met me. I never lied...you knew."

I *knew* I was defeated. I *knew* I had to throw in the towel. I *knew* I had been played. I couldn't grovel and beg for her for one minute more. I was a man, and I just realized she'd been playing me like a bitch. I decided to take a good look at the woman I'd fallen in love with and drink in her looks for the last time. I would never see her again. I stared deeply into her eyes, and she seemed to age instantly. Now she looked every bit of her forty years. Telltale signs peeked out at me—microscopic gray hairs, tiny crow's feet, wrinkled and veined hands.

Holding back my pain, I kissed her on her creased forehead.

"Take care of yourself, kid," I told her.

"You do the same."

I looked back over my shoulders with one last burning question. "Did you do it?"

"I already told you what happened. I didn't have any idea that he would be murdered."

"Not Emmanuel. I'm talking about Phillip, your second husband. Did you kill him?"

"You've been reading too many tabloids."

Was that an answer to my question?

I walked out of jail with mixed emotions. The visit had besmirched any fond memories of our affair. I wondered if Gracie felt at least half of what turmoil she'd caused. I'd reached my emotional peak. I thought that we had more than loveless sex. I was a wounded man with an ego. The pain hurt deeply as I tried to understand my past actions. Was I really in love with Gracie? Or was it the chase and challenge of pursuing another man's wife? I didn't know. I might not ever know.

I hopped into my ride and did the only thing I knew how.

"Hey, Anika, what's up, baby?"

"What do you want?"

"You…I want you…."

ABOUT THE AUTHOR

Crystal Lacey Winslow has been featured on BET Nightly News, Vibe Magazine, Black Enterprise, The Source, Upscale Magazine, Black Hairstyles, The Daily News, and Black Issue Review. Additionally, she's been on various radio shows such as The Wendy Williams Experience and 98.7 Kiss Wakeup Club.